Restoration
Lady

By
Sue Allan

domtom publishing ltd

ISBN 978-1-906070-07-6

First published 2008 by domtom publishing ltd

Acknowledgements

The author would like to acknowledge:
her collaborator and researcher,
Roger Thomas Vorhauer together with
Russell Hocking for his contribution to editing.

Cover photograph by Roger Thomas Vorhauer.

Printed and bound in the UK by
DPS Partnership Ltd
www.dpsltd.net

Prologue

London 1664

The bearers stop. I am grounded at my destination. Through the fine mesh screen of my window, I watch the rabble stream in the street suddenly stop mid flow and then hastily begin to pool into a curious mob. One, swiftly followed by another, have now recognised the crimson crest painted upon my black-lacquered sedan chair door. A rising murmur of 'Look!' and 'It's her!' reaches even my age-dulled ears as a wave of excitement quickly ripples out. I can sense that all eyes are now upon me and I know what it is they want. They want to see *it*. They crave even the tiniest glimpse to sate their thirsting curiosity about me. And I? I want to see first if they are deserving enough.

I draw up my black lace shawl high about my shoulders. Then, taking in a deep breath, I steel myself as my footman opens up the door. I thrust out my arm and as my silver-topped, ebony walking cane makes contact with the cobbles below, an eerie hush suddenly descends. The air is charged with anticipation. Like waiting for a roll of thunder after lightening has streaked across a lead grey sky.

Then, gingerly stepping down I slowly emerge from my sedan cocoon like a butterfly, dressed in a riot of coloured silks and ribbons. For a moment, I straighten up a little to gently shake out the creases in my skirts. Then, head held high, I stand as tall and upright as I am able and boldly look back into the staring faces. My deliberate smile is confident as I then give a rather understated wave of of my jem-studded free hand. This is like setting a flame to a fuse. The silence suddenly explodes into cries of admiration. The throng sing out out my name as an ocean of hands reach out towards me in greeting. Some throw compliments my way. Others throw flowers. Not one berates or insults me so, therefore, I am decided. They *are* deserving and I *shall* reward *them*.

1

As I make to walk on, I casually, yet quite calculatingly, let my shawl slip down, just a little, from my chalk white shoulders. It is precisely enough to reveal the ample cleavage caressed snuggly into my low cut bodice. At this, the collective gasp from the crowd is clearly audible. For a few fleeting moments, the mark burnt indelibly into the top of my left breast is clearly visible to all. For *their* delectation and titillation, I have bared my flesh for today's insatiable appetite for notoriety to feast upon.

Having done so, I quickly draw up my shawl once more and make my way inside the grandest building of all the city. May the Lord forgive me, but I have come to quite savour this little piece of theatre. An innocent enough indulgence after so much public humiliation in the past?

Doors open up to me now that are barred to most others. Yet, not so long ago doors slammed in my face as I was left ragged and penniless in the street. Curious, one might think, that after all of the scandal and gossip that I have inspired since the death of my husband, Thomas, that I should now enjoy such favor. Yet then again, our Sovereign King and I share an unspoken understanding. For both he and I too lost almost everything that we had and loved or held dear at the hands of the Parliamentarians and that bloody Civil War...

Chapter One

Bessie's husband, Thomas, had barely survived the injuries he had received at the Battle of Naseby. Their son, James, also on the field that day, never returned home. After this devastating defeat for the King looked imminent and the tattered Royalist cause all but lost.

In 1646, Prince Rupert surrendered at Oxford to Parliament's General Thomas Fairfax and was subsequently expelled from England. The following January, King Charles fled to Scotland but was caught and handed over to Parliament.

Spring 1647

I could not move. Instead, I stood rooted to the ground like a trembling willow sapling shaken by a cruel wind. With a silent scream wedged in my throat like a lump of oak, I watched on. I watched on, alone and beyond all help as the wretched scene played out before my bewildered eyes. I watched as my husband's life was snuffed out in my plain sight.

I had awoken that morning to find Thomas cursing at his crippled arm as he grappled to get his breeches on quickly.

'There's some sort of commotion going on down there,' he explained nodding his head towards the yard below. 'It's Ned's young lad and several Parliamentarians. I had best get down, Bess, and see what is going on!'

As he hurried away, I slid out of bed and across to the window to see for myself. Surely enough, three mounted Roundheads had got our young farmhand, Titus, hemmed in by their horses. They were clearly intimidating him. Though I could not hear them exactly, there seemed to be hot words passing betwixt them along with a lot of jostling as the lad tried to get out of the way of the horses. The erratic behaviour of one, in particular, began to fill me with alarm. I am no stranger to horses and could tell at a glance that this brown mare was highly strung. Nervously, she pranced from hoof to hoof and her loud, high pitched whinnying warned that she was in some distress from the noisy fracas all about her. As the row intensified, she kept trying to rear up to throw her rider off. I could see the officer yanking fiercely on the reign, his face clenching as he gripped his knees in tighter to grab the poor beast in an effort to stay on. Then, I too became frightened. Frightened that Titus was about to be trampled.

Still watching intently, I backed away from the window a little and into the privacy of the shadow-line where I let my black-work embroidered night-shift fall to my feet before quickly stepping out of it. Hastily, I started pulling on my day dress and though still only half-laced, I ran down the stairs to follow my husband outside.

Thomas was standing his ground, firm yet beyond the cage of horse-flesh. Now I could hear. I could hear Thomas, still calm and composed yet desperately trying to reason with the Roundhead officer who in turn continued to snarl back angrily. Accusations flew that Titus had attacked one of his men during a brawl in the town the night before. The soldier in question had later died of his injuries. All the while the nervy mare continued to shift.

The scene was fast turning nasty. Titus shouted back, just as angrily, vehemently denying that he had anything to do with the killing and steadfastly refusing to go with his accusers, as they were by now insisting. Then the three soldiers closed in on the lad and tried to herd him away with their horses, kicking out at him and scoring his bare arms with their spurs. Suddenly, Titus could take no more. He pulled out a hoof pick from nowhere and plunged it into the thigh of his nearest aggressor. The Roundhead fell from his horse, screaming in agony, as his comrade quickly dismounted to go to his aid. In the confusion, Titus made to run off. As he did, the still mounted officer took up his readied flintlock musket, and aimed to shoot Titus in the back as he fled. As he was about to fire though, his skittish mount reared up. Thomas instinctively grabbed the horse's reign with his one good arm but the mare had already thrown her rider off balance. Screaming loudly, this horse then half-reared yet again, circling back towards Thomas in the process. With Thomas still holding fast to the reign, the officer was now turned about face towards him.

I thought it settled. I thought that the officer had gained control once more. Then it happened. The musket discharged. In the process, the lead ball blew away half of my husband's head in a bloody shower of red. Still standing, still tightly gripping onto the reigns, I saw Thomas judder, just for a moment, before he let go and slumped lifeless to the ground in a pool of blood. My knees buckled and I felt sick as I half-fell, trembling, against the wall in shock as the horror of what had just happened began to sink in.

Just then, Ned came running in from the field and began screaming and cursing at the officer who in turn simply ignored the old man as if he was not even there. Instead, and without even glancing down at Thomas lying at his feet, the Roundhead reached into his inside pocket, fetched out a white kerchief and began to wipe away my husband's blood from his face. Maybe, if this officer had known that Ned was Titus' father, then he might have dispatched the old man too. However, this fine Parliamentarian now had more pressing things to attend to, like helping his injured cohort to remount before all three then quickly headed off in hot pursuit of the disappearing lad.

As they rode away, Ned lurched across to me and tried his best to persuade me to go back indoors.

'Don't you fret[1] now! I will tend to the Master, Lady Elizabeth...' he said with his words catching on his quivering lips.'No wife should have to see her husband so...'

I meekly complied. As he took up my trembling hand in his I let myself be led away like a sleepwalking child from a nightmare. The shock of it all had been far too much for me to resist.

As I looked out once more from my bedroom

window, several farmhands stretchered Thomas' corpse out of sight while one young lad had thoughtfully fetched a spade and was using dust to cover up the tell-tale scarlet pooled on the ground. I watched until he was done then I turned slowly and walked back across the room to our bed. With the indentation of Thomas' barely chilled contours, still lingering upon the mattress and pillows, I threw myself down upon them and wept, inconsolably.

Let me tell you what it is like to be so suddenly widowed .'Tis like the sun going down upon you on a summer's day at noon. 'Tis like being cast into an utter darkness with all the warmth that you have ever known, immediately turned cold. 'Tis a deep, black, darkness where even your closest kin can only partially penetrate to reach inside to try to pull you out. Yet, even they do not know how to begin to bring you back into the light for they can never comprehend the absoluteness of your despair. For you, life is turned off like a carefully tended seedling cut down by a sudden sharp frost. A life yet of promise that will now never be. For you, there has been no warning sign. No chance to lay to rest outstanding differences. No final, mutual goodbye.

The first nights are the worst. The missing him. For this time you know that he is never coming back. Yet, the real torment is that for others beyond your grief, life goes on just as before. Soon you find yourself eyeing remaining couples with a jealousy you had never imagined harbouring against anyone before. Watching them, bathing in the light of their own suns, as inwardly you rage in your empty twilight against the inequity of it all. Why you? Why has your man been taken and not theirs? Yet, at the same time, you know deep down in your heart that you would not wish this pain of yours visited upon another human soul at any price. None the less, still you envy.

After my husband had been killed, I wanted to curl up beside him in his grave. I felt as if the life had already been smothered out of me, so why not let the earth pile in upon me too. At least this dreadful, all-enveloping pain would then be at an end.

When Thomas' funeral was over, I walked back home alone, in silence, along the lane past a cheery bank of bright yellow leopard's bane and back to Blackthorn Farm. I immediately took to my bed. Had it not been for Hope, my adopted daughter, and my young grandson, Tom, I might have given up on life, there and then, completely.

However, after numberless blank days, it was their gentle yet persistent coaxing that began to help me see that my self imposed withdrawal from the world was nought but plain selfishness. Why was I inflicting yet more pain upon *them* with my pining just at the time when they too were hurting and had need of me more than ever before?

'I know you are right,' I submitted to Hope. 'You are right. I must try to put away my grief and we must get on with our lives. For yours and young Tom's sake if for nothing else. I am so sorry. For I have only lost my husband while you have now lost your father and your husband too...'

We cried, finding comfort in each others' arms over our joint loss. Then, when she came to ask what we should do without James and Thomas, I assured her that, some way, we would find the strength to carry on. Consequently, I rose up, donned my mourning clothes and went out to face the world once more.

Immediately, I began to take over the running of our farm and to oversee the welfare of our modest estate and its workers. For Hope and I were not the only widows there. Some of our farmhands had also gone off to fight in the Civil War and, like my son James, never returned home again. Unlike most other landowners, my husband,Thomas, had allowed their women folk to stay on in their tied cottages in return for whatever labour they and their children might be able to supply, on the understanding that once the oldest remaining male child reached adulthood he would be allowed to take over their late father's position of work. 'Twas a kindness to them that I also fully intended to honour. By rights, I should also have declared that my husband's only son was also dead but I did not trust this interim Parliamentarian authority. It was fast proving itself petty and vindictively spiteful towards any Royalist sympathiser now brought before it. Especially now that it had the King captured and that he was being held under close arrest. These authorities might use the excuse to march into Blackthorn Farm and demand control of the estate until young Tom was come of age. Until then, Hope and I would have little say about how our own farm was run or how our workers were to be treated. Until Tom reached manhood we would be as but tenants ourselves, albeit adequately provided for. No, I had decided that I would not stand for that. Not until King Charles was released and restored to absolute power would I admit to James' demise. Instead, I would put about the tale that James was alive and well and in the New World overseeing his late father's business interests there. No one else in Stowe, bar our own man Ned, knew that James had joined up to the Royalist cause while away at University. Nor that he died at the very same battle in which my late husband had been so terribly wounded, yet survived. For all any one knew, James had completed his studies at Oxford and had gone overseas to Virginia, just as I had said. Or so I had naively assumed.

Meanwhile, I carried on in ignorance trying hard to piece my shattered life back together,while something quite unexpected began to grow inside me. It was a new found knowledge of myself. It was the rediscovery of the lost inner me that had grown so strong in the face of past adversity in the New World and yet I had let slip away as I had crossed back over the threshold of the Atlantic and into the more coddled life of a country lady. Thomas had made all of the decisions during our married life here, while I had trusted and obeyed him like any other good and dutiful wife. Even when he went away to war, I mainly did as his factotum, Ned, suggested and with little hesitation. I had unwittingly handed over control of my life then, but now I was preparing to snatch it back. At last, I avowed from then on to be my own person.

*   *   *

Lady Bridget and I talked as we walked the long corridor at Gainsborough Hall and watched sparkling rain drops drizzle down the diamond leaded lights from the April shower beyond. We had news of each other throughout the war but had not the occasion to meet up again, in person, until that day when I visited her.

As I had made my way up the wide spiral staircase to meet her, I could not help but notice how deathly quiet this great house had become. Far more quiet than I had ever encountered it before. There were few traders in evidence, as I walked through the Great Hall, waiting to pay their dues and tolls to the bored looking clerk sat at his station. I saw few household staff either about their duties in either the house or the grounds, which in all only added to the air that hinted of the Hall's recent fall from grace.

'How is young William?' I asked.

I had not seen the Hickman's son since the outset of the war.

'Growing into his father's burden,' Bridget replied coldly.

She looked tired beyond her ought and that rose flushed complexion for which I had always complemented her, was now grey, sallow and flat. In three short years she had aged so much. Then again, I suppose, so had I.

'He is like a colt, Elizabeth!' she sighed as she continued. 'Like a carefree, young colt being broken in for the plough. For that is what this Gainsborough manor has been like for my husband. Like a great weight to be dragged about behind him and before long William will be expected to then take it up upon himself. Some day and too soon, I fear, Willoughby will drop dead in his tracks! This estate will be the death of him! It has broken him down!'

I was shocked to hear her express such strong feelings of hatred towards the Hall and its lands.

Willoughby's father, Sir William, had built up the town and the estate from its bankrupt purchase into a thriving and lucrative enterprise that, even just five years since, had been the envy of many a Lincolnshire Lord.

'Where is Willoughby ?' I ventured. 'May I see him?'

'I am sorry,' Lady Bridget sighed. 'He is away in London, right now, making further representation to the Members of Parliament against the outrageous fines they have imposed upon him for his delinquency in not supporting their cause in the War. At first they chose not to hear his pleas that he in fact took no side, favouring none above the the other and instead treating all who came wounded to the Hall equally as Our Lord God himself commands. Yet, Parliament is still stubbornly swayed that all who did not declare for them were, by default, against them.'

I knew full well that Parliament had been making such claims against known Royalist supporters, by way of confiscation of lands or fortune, but never of those who had *not* raised arms *against* Parliament and had instead, declared themselves neutral. It was a stance that, for men who exalted themselves as 'seekers' and true disciples of Christ, as rather perverse. Though by the very nature of it, Thomas' involvement in espionage was not widely known, he had however been duly noted as having supported the King. As a result, the estate of Snype Hall, which had been granted to Thomas by King James, was taken away by Parliament in forfeit of this. All that remained in my family hands by then was Thomas' late father's estate of Blackthorn Farm, though that was more than enough for us to live in ease.

'More than nine-hundred pounds they first proposed to fine my husband!' Lady Bridget wailed. 'Almost a fifth of our estate's worth at the outset of the conflict yet it is not worth anything like sum that since. No account has been made of the huge losses we have faced at both Parliament's and Royalist hands. How our tenants were ravaged as well as our land? Each side, in turn, marched in and stole or destroyed our stores and food until they were all but exhausted and we could barely feed ourselves. Our crops could not be planted or properly tended because of the fighting and loss of our labourers to the armies. The town was almost destroyed and with it our revenues and tolls have all but disappeared. Yet Willoughby is still expected to discharge his obligations towards the townsfolk as the Lord of their Manor! Our family is all but ruined yet what does Parliament then do but to seize our best lands in lieu of the fine which we might only had hoped to pay by the use of. I tell you no word of a lie, Elizabeth. Willoughby's hair turned grey overnight, and though he has since persuaded Parliament to return some of property and reduce the fine, it is still an almost intolerable burden on him. I truly fear for my husband's health. And for myself. For I am not suited to widow's weeds yet!'

'And who amongst us is?' I replied.
Bridget suddenly looked aghast.

'I am so sorry, Elizabeth! That was unforgivable thoughtlessness on my part.'

'It is alright. I know that you meant nothing by it,' I assured her as we continued
to pace in awkward silence.

Soon the rain stopped and sunshine poured in from the lush gardens beyond.

'It looks beautiful weather now, Bridget!' I tried to ease back into conversation.

'Would you care to take the air with me outside?'she responded.
Readily, I agreed.

We began to descend the back staircase to make our way down towards the garden room. Coming close by the dining room door, Bridget paused to reflect.

'It hardly seems possible, does it, that more than six years have passed by since last we sat here around that table together talking about the possibility of war? Now it has come and gone and we are all rent asunder. Do you remember our kinsman, Francis Parham? How he put forward so adamantly in favour of Parliament? And your Thomas, likewise as adamant, for the King? Whereby my dear Willoughby declared that he would take no side at all!'

'I remember it well! Especially Parham's forceful views,' I had replied.

'Our cards were all set plain upon the table. Yet, there was no malice betwixt us then nor even now and yet for others, malice has been at root of this bloody war and I suspect also in its peace!'

'And my Lord Parham? I have not heard of him of late?' I said, moving on.

'He is well, by all accounts and still looking for the best butter for his bread!' Lady Bridget exclaimed. 'I hear that he is at odds with Cromwell and the New Model Army and so is now about currying favour with the growing Presbyterian faction in Parliament and has his sights set on becoming the Speaker of the House itself, no less!'

'First he defies the King when he is called to arms and sides instead with the Parliamentarian Army. Yet, now you say that he now courts the dissenting voice in Parliament? 'Tis all in all, a most dangerous game of chance Parham plays and which ever one, betwixt the King and Cromwell ultimately wins out in all of this, he may well come out the loser for he hath offended both in equal measure!'

'Maybe so. However, perhaps I should be more grateful in my opinion. For it is probably he whom we should thank and our family ties of blood for the Roundheads not destroying this house when they certainly had the power to do so.'

'So,' I dared ask, 'do you and Willoughby think that there is still a chance for the King and Parliament to be reconciled?'

Lady Bridget regarded me with a look of incredulity upon her frowned face.

'Of course!' she exclaimed. 'The King and Parliament now *have* to negotiate peace! There may be compromise to be had on both sides yet but in the end,

King and Parliament *must* be reconciled. Why? Do you think they shall not?'

As we walked through the garden room and outside amongst the overgrown boarders, I tried hard to share her optimism.

*   *   *

'Twas shortly afterwards this visit, that I found myself back in Stowe one morning and standing in the Minster of Saint Mary contemplating the brass plaque placed upon the wall in commemoration of my friend, Amy Burgh, her soldier son, John. He had been killed, many years before, in battle on the French Isle of Rhe. Few bodies then were ever retrieved for burial. It put me in mind of my own son, James.

In life, Amy was often to be found seated in a pew close by that spot, deep in silent remembrance. Now, beneath the flag stones, she lay with her husband rotting together in their tomb below, begetting nothing more than dust. Not for me, I thought, this sterile stone. When I die I wanted to be clothed in the soft, rich earth knowing that spring would come and fine shoots of green grass would feed from me. That through my death, something fresh would make its way back into the world, anew.

I closed my eyes in quiet remembrance, yet even after but these few, short months, I could not recall my own husband's face. All I had inside my head was the bloody vision of his death seeded in my mind.

Burying Thomas was the hardest thing I had ever had to do. For with him, it was as if I had interred a part of me too that would never again see the light of day. For a long time after though, I could not say exactly what that part was. Yet now, looking back, I see that it was my heart and with it my capacity to ever love another man again. Nor, I feared, to put my trust in one either.

As for James, I was determined not to live as if dead inside for him, but rather to invest my unused love now in his precious child instead. As long as Tom lived and breathed, a part of James would still be with

13

me and that thought, I treasured.

I walked back up the lane to Blackthorn farm past a freshly sewn field and watched two young boys who were busy scaring crows. How soon it would be, I remembered thinking, before the crops, once more, were standing there shoulder high and ready for harvest. How quickly the cycle of life turns on with, or with out my menfolk?

May was upon us and I had idled too long, so I had decided that I was now ready to make good use of the fine afternoon by planting up my New World kitchen garden. I had learnt to sew a 'three sisters bed' in Plymouth, in New England, under the supervision of our native friend, Squanto. And when I later left Jamestown and the New World for good, I had made certain to take a pouch full of the seeds needed so I might carry on this tradition back home in England. So, at Blackthorn Farm in my own little patch, I had grown the three sisters for over twenty years .Carefully saving the seed from one harvest to over winter and sew for the next. However, coming from the New World, these plants needed the warmth of early summer before they could successfully germinate.

I walked into the dairy, where I had stored my seeds from the previous year inside some sacking. The dairy was safer to keep these than any of the outbuildings which were prone to infestation by field mice. I fetched them into the kitchen and then sat at the table and carefully unwrapped the cloth bundle.

First, I took up the dried cob of last year's Indian corn and ran my finger tips along its rows of bright multi coloured kernels. They were hard and shiny like tiny polished mosaic tiles set beneath a wide rustle of pale papery leaves. Carefully, I prised out the seed from the cob with my finger nails until I had a neat little pile on the table. It was like pulling milk teeth from a brittle gum. Then I scooped them all up into my pocket which I had already laid out in readiness. Next, from out of a fold of paper, I took out a large pinch of crisp, tear-like seeds and placed them too inside my pocket. Like oaks from tiny acorns, these small, slight seeds would give rise to great bush like plants and fruit.

The first seed that I planted was the Indian Corn, directly into my freshly worked patch and set in a block. For this plant thrives better sewn this way rather than in a straight row. In Plimouth, where the soil was thin and poor, I would have planted it in a tiny mound set above rotting fish trimmings to nourish the hungry plant as it grew it. Here though, our rich, brown Lincolnshire earth needed little more than some well rotted cow manure, worked in once a year, to sustain it.

Next, I planted white beans around the corn to wend their way up the sturdy quick growing sister plants for support. Yet not only for support, for the naturals of the New World had long since discovered some magic connection between these two plants which meant that, for some unfathomable reason, that the corn actually grew better for planting together with beans in this way than it did apart. Mayhap, like us, they enjoyed company in their lives? The beans would be ready to harvest long before the tall corn plants had matured and ripened their cobs fit for picking and were eaten, either fresh or left on their vines to dry ready for storing for winter use.

Finally, while these two crops were growing, a few of the precious papery, tear-shaped squash seeds I had then set upon their sides to germinate between these groupings, would then grow on into succulent-stemmed seedlings. These would then bush up rapidly with their huge leaves spreading out across the bare earth, smothering the weeds and shielding the roots of the other plants from the drying effect of the sun. Meanwhile, their huge, fat round fruit would then swell from out of nothing to provide a source of sustenance that could happily be stored for months and used to make a hearty soup. With these three sisters as a basic staple, a native family in the New World could expect to be supported throughout the long winter months. Three crops growing in perfect harmony. Each one benefiting its neighbours by its very existence and helping all to progress in turn. If only mankind could grow together thus!

Throughout the rest of May, I knew that there was ever to be the chance of a late frost. Frost is fatal to the tender young corn and squash. So, each evening as sun began to set, I would be ready to watch the sky for a warning. If it was clear and still and felt set to turn chill, I would be able to quickly run out to the stables and fetch an armful of hay to cover over the bed of seedlings. I would plump it up full of air and tuck it in place securely with willow branches quickly snapped from the tree close by. Then I would be certain that my precious little seedlings would be safe and warm until the coming morning sun bathed them once more in light. Once June had burst, I could then rest assured that all would be well and the plants would grow on at an incredible pace. How I enjoyed watching them grow!

Once I had finished my sewings that late afternoon, I went over to the well and drew a pale of water. I set it down and straightened up, distracted for a moment by a fleeting twinge in my sorry back. I stooped back down to pick it up, only to find its ripples settled out and the reflection upon it set perfect and still. A beautiful bucket full of bright sky, so blue that it suddenly reminded of the summer sea at Plimouth, a sight I so loved in a past life.

Then, as I made to grab the handle, I suddenly caught sight of my own reflection staring up and was quite taken aback by the image I saw. The grey hair, the sunken cheeks and heavy jowl – when had I got to be so old and so haggard? 'Twas then that I began to realise just how much the loss of my husband and son had taken from me of late.

'Mother! Mother!' Hope cried out with some urgency from the kitchen door. 'Mother! There are men coming down our lane! They look like soldiers!'
I dropped the bucket and ran towards her.

'Go inside, Hope!' I shouted back. 'Stay out of sight with young Tom while I see what they are a-wanting!'

As I neared the farmhouse, a group of about half a dozen Roundheads clustered in about my doorway. As I approached, they immediately barred my way. One amongst them stood out alone. He was a solemn looking man dressed in black, who put me in mind of a rook[2]. It was he who then stepped forward and asked,

'Lady Elizabeth?'

'Yes!' I replied. 'Why do you want to know, Sir?'

'Lady Elizabeth,' he continued briskly, 'you are under arrest...'

Chapter Two

The soldiers gathered in about me listening to their 'chief rook'. In waiting too, no doubt, lest this harmless woman should make her move.

'What is this nonsense, Sir?' I snapped. 'I have done nothing contrary to the law and I certainly shall not come with you!'

'You *will* come with me, Lady Elizabeth!' he insisted. 'You are to come with me to answer charges relating to 'irregularities' regarding your personal status.'

'My personal status? Irregularities? Pray, who is making mischief against me?'

'I am not certain that you fully appreciate the gravity of this matter!'

'Indeed I do!' I replied defiantly. 'Tis grave circumstance indeed for a defenceless woman to be dragged away from her home by a host of armed men! You say I am summoned to stand trial for certain 'irregularities'.What irregularities I have asked you, and to whom am I being taken to answer. You will not tell me. So, no! I will not come meekly away with you until you answer my question.'

'Enough of this! Take her!'
With that I was grabbed at either side as two burly soldiers began to manhandle me away up the pathway.

'Mother! Mother!' Hope came running from the house screaming.'Let her go!'
She was quickly intercepted and her flaying arms, trying vainly to strike out at my assailants, were quickly forced down by her side by a soldier. He held her there, she watching in tears, as they led me away down the lane and out of sight.
They did not take me far though. Soon I was being ushered through the familiar gateway of the churchyard and into the nave of the Minster itself. There I was roughly cast through the doorway with the crow quickly stepping in behind me and locking the door shut behind us.

'Sit!' He ordered.

I stood defiant.

'Very well then,' he sighed. 'Perhaps you will show a little more respect for my master.' With that, he disappeared behind the screens, I assumed to fetch his superior.

I could not fathom what it could be for which I was being asked to answer. I had done no wrong, so assumed it must be some dreadful mistake. A misunderstanding of sorts. Then it suddenly struck me, could this be something to do with Thomas' death? I quickly dismissed that thought, for Thomas was the victim and therefore, where was the reason to treat me so roughly?

I stood waiting for quite some time with my eyes wandering as wildly as my thoughts. Then they fell upon the the stone mount of the font with its ornate carvings. No doubt during the construction of this ancient minster, the olden carpenters and stone masons must have believed that they were adding God into the detail which our present and extreme Puritan ministers now condemned unto the devil. Then, for the first time, my eyes met the wicked gaze of a dragon sneaked about its base. I had never noticed the beast lurking there before.

Suddenly, there was the sound of footsteps, a steady deliberate pace approaching from out of the gloomy main body of the church beyond. Then he appeared, dressed every inch in the manner of an upright figure of a Puritan minister. As he did, I felt my spirit slither down into the pit of my stomach like a cold portion of day old eels. It had been many years since my sorry eyes had last seen that pox-etched face yet, I knew him in an instant. The line of his spidery hair had obviously long since receded leaving the large mole, stranded between his sunken eyes like a lost brown island, even more the Lord of his sullen features.

I had first the displeasure of meeting Mister Rech in Jamestown and soon discovered him to be the sort of man adept at ingratiating himself upon those in society from whom he might foster advantage. I watched him worm his way into the favour of the minister at Jamestown. At first, by offering up his favour to aid the poor overstretched man by taking over his burden of paperwork for the settlement and record keeping of the countless deaths incurred there. Eventually, Rech became utterly indispensable. Yet this was not out of any pure act of kind-heartedness on his part. No, for Rech was a man ever seeking opportunities to glean what official, unofficial or more particularly 'sensitive' information which he could then profitably employ later with his more usual stock in trade – blackmail.

The last time I had seen Rech was one stormy night, there in Stowe on the doorstep of Blackthorn Farm, some fifteen years before. He had stood in our hallway arguing violently with my husband until Thomas forcibly ejected him back out to the blackness to return to whichever stone he had last crawled out from under. I had not laid eyes on him since. What Rech and my Thomas were in such disagreement about, I had never fully understood. Suffice to say, it had something to do with my husband's covert activities in the colony for King James and Thomas was reluctant to discus those in detail. I clearly understood though that Rech had made threats to Thomas, including to expose Hope as having been illegally smuggled into the country and then passed off as a 'twin' to our own baby, James.

Barely acknowledging me, Rech took up his place behind a low lectern set before a handful of carved oak pews. On that, he laid out a raft of papers he had been carrying under his arm. He then glared at me like some ugly stone-faced gargoyle about to preach a sermon. Though gestured that I should sit, I declined, much I think, to his annoyance. For I was not about to show this man any feign homage.

'What do you want with me, Mister Rech, and by who's authority have you had me dragged here?' I demanded calmly.

'By God's ordination and Parliament's will, Lady Elizabeth,' he replied with his practised reptilian stare.

'As you see from my attire, I have for years, as we used to say 'taken orders'. In fact, that is not strictly true, for in my unique position as both 'Seeker of God's Truth' and magistrate, I now both give and maintain order!'

'So it is you who have brought these ludicrous charges against me?'

'Ludicrous? I would not call blatant disregard for God's law 'ludicrous'.'

'God's Law. What law have I broken, Rech? What are these 'irregularities' of which your accomplice in this malicious mischief spoke. And if I am deemed guilty of any crime then, I demand to be taken before the Lea Court at Gainsborough,' I protested, although I already expected this request to be given short thrift.

'That rabble of Royalist lick-boot? I bet you do!' he retorted, locking his fingers together like some spindly mantis in prayer. 'However, they do not have the superior jurisdiction that I enjoy in bringing to trial wicked deviants of Church Law.'

'Deviant? I, Sir?' I shouted. 'How am I a deviant?'

'I think the lady doth protest too much!' he scoffed. 'As I recall, you were quite the devotee of Shakespeare. Too bad that talentless devil's word monger is not alive today or he might have snapped up your sorry tale to weave into one of his heinous whorehouse plays! Probably even to exalt your wickedness into some sort of saving grace along the way.'

'I still do not know what it is of which you think me guilty!'

'I do not think, my lady. I know you to be guilty of being a dirty wanton and a harlot! Yet,' he sneered, 'I do believe I can make you come around to my way of thinking – that it would be best for all concerned if you were to own up to that of your own accord.'

'To stand up and meekly plead guilty to your outrageous charges?'

'Yes. That is exactly what I want you to do, Lady Elizabeth.'

'You're mad! Why should I want to do that?'

'Because if you do not, then I have the power invested in me to remove from your care an unlawful alien in this kingdom whom you have been harbouring.'

'Alien? Am I to take it from this that you are referring to my daughter?' I said, remembering his previous threat to Thomas.

'Daughter? Surely she is no daughter of yours! Any fool with eyes can look upon her and see at a glance that she did not spring from you. From Jamestown, my mind has been almost certain that this wench you then claimed to be your 'daughter' is no such thing. Moreover, now that I have come here myself, I find those suspicions confirmed. For since your coming to Stowe, I see that you have changed your story again for the benefit of your new neighbours and put it about that your 'daughter' is a foundling of the Spanish persuasion! What if I now put to them another 'truth'? Perhaps, that whilst in Virginia, you lay uncleanly with a man of the Powhatan race? Even though I doubt that a bastard begotten between you would have turned out quite so dusky!'

'How dare you insult me!' I flew at him.

'I insult you? Before I am through, all about this village will think that it is you who do insult enough in their sight and in that of God! For what do you think they will now believe when faced with the realisation that your 'truth' about this child had been nought but lies? There is a great deal of difference betwixt the notion of you lying with a heathen savage or with a Christian Englishman, in or out of wedlock? Carnal knowledge of a heathen is but fornication and equally abhorrent in the sight of the Lord. But in those of your peers? They will condemn you double! Worse still would be their outrage if they were then thought that you might have then given your first bastard child in wife to your second! I very much doubt if I could restrain them from hanging you both straight way! Yet do not fear, lady! For mine own purposes I would much rather prefer to conclude instead that this female 'Hope' is a full-blooded Powhatan Indian and unlawfully smuggled out of Virginia by your own hand and without the permission of the authorities either here nor there. So therefore, I would naturally presume it as my God given duty to see that this young women is taken out of England and placed upon the first available ship bound for Jamestown. Once there, I shall see to it, personally, that both she and that sub-race child of hers are repatriated back with her own kind!'

'You cannot be serious!' I screamed at him as I broke. 'She knows nothing of the Powhatan natives! She cannot even speak their language. You cannot expect her to go live amongst them anymore than you could any other English woman.'

The very suggestion of Rech's scenario struck terror into my heart. How could Hope and my grandson survive should this dreadful threat ever be executed. I knew all about the Powhatans and their heathen ways. Women of their own tribe were treated base compared to our own 'civilized' codes of conduct. Yet with the Powhatan, it was always about warring and killing of men from enemy tribes and the stealing of their women and children, which they would then present unto their commander.

Women were the mainstay of the natives economy. They tended to the land, grew crops and processed the skins and hides of the animals that they often helped to kill too as active members of many a hunting party.

In short, Powhatan women did most of the work while their menfolk waged war, or hunted and then returned home expecting to be virtually waited upon, hand and foot. Captive women often fared much worse, often being treated the same way in which some European men treat their cattle. The more head of of cattle one owned, the richer one appeared and the higher one's status. So it was with the Powhatan and the other tribes of the naturals of Virgina. Captured women made for ready concubines, for pleasure and to increase the blood stock of the tribe. These women were also items to be traded or handed on to others by show of favour or to settle a debt. If they were captured with children, more the better – for boys could be raised as little better than slaves while young girls were ready to rear on as more concubines or wives. Again, both readily traded in this polygamous society. However, the multiplicative use of women in this way resulted in a high infection rate of the pox and other dreadful sexual diseases. Instead of increasing their population, these amoral practices conversely lowered the natural birthrate and contributed to the early demise of both the women and the men who over indulged themselves in them. A worse than for most fate would await Hope if Rech carried out his threat. For she would not be regarded as a natural no matter what her native colouring said. The Powhatan would undoubtedly perceive her to be not as one of them but instead as one of us. Whoever received Hope would no doubt take quite some delight in raping her – and attempting to breed out her Englishness. As for young Tom, I suspect they would have killed him straight off. I knew that I would rather take up a knife and kill them both now with my own hands, rather than let them suffer a fate like that.

'Ah! But there we have it.' Rech seemed to crow with delight.' She is not an English woman!'

'She is as English as you or I,' I insisted. 'And a good Christian woman too.'

'Then she can serve God's purpose best by going as a missionary amongst them and to convert them also to Christ!'

'I cannot believe what you are saying! You *know* full well, Rech, that her people will not recognise her as a Powhatan! They *will* treat her as English. You would be sending two innocents who have done you no harm to their deaths!'

Rech parted his hands and leaning forward from the lectern looked me squarely in the eyes and replied quite coldly.

'Then help her, dear lady. Admit your guilt to the charges laid and accept your just punishment! Admit, in public, that you are a wanton and a harlot and that you and Sir Thomas were never rightfully married.'

I was shocked by the suggestion. I had no intention either of ever denying my marriage to Thomas. I could not understand either why Rech would want me to do such a thing.

'But you know full well that Thomas and I were rightfully married!'

'I know no such thing. But if you were, then prove it!' he goaded. 'That is, if you can. Where do you say this marriage took place, in any case?'

'In Dartmouth,' I replied forcefully. 'In Dartmouth, in the August of the year of our Lord sixteen-hundred and twenty. It was while the Mayflower was stranded there in harbour and under repair.'

'Then that should not be too difficult to prove then. Should it? Shall I send to Dartmouth for the Parish records?' he asked nastily. 'How long were you there? Long enough for the banns to be legally posted, I presume?'

It was then that I began to blindly think that I knew what tack Rech was about to take. He must have easily grasped the fact that for Thomas and me to have been a party to the Mayflower venture and the Plymouth settlement, I must have been a dissenter of the Church of England at the time.

'No.' I had to admit to the truth. There were no banns read nor any entry made either of our marriage into the parish records either, for we did not marry within the Anglican Church.

'No banns? No church?' Rech leaned back in mock surprise. 'Then pray, what sort of a marriage was this. From your own account, not a legally binding one?'

'It was legal!' I protested. 'It was carried out in accordance with our Separatist doctrine. 'Twas a legally binding contract such as our congregation had used for its marriages in the Netherlands. A marriage contract of the sort that the State has long since recognised as being binding upon those of the Plymouth colony.'

'True, those marriages carried out in the New

World are recognised as binding now. But you were not yet in the New World! Were you?'

'Even so, a record of it was duly made by John Carver and witnessed by Elder Brewster and William Bradford too.'

'Even so. Let's for argument's sake say that this marriage contract was to be found legally binding. Upon whom was it taken out?'

'I do not understand...'

'I take it that Sir Thomas was entered as the groom?'

'Yes! Of course he was!' I said impatiently

'But who married Sir Thomas? Was it you, Lady Elizabeth, or a common Gainsborough maidservant named Dorothy?'

'Twas I – whatever name was used – it was I who married Thomas. For it is true, that in my younger years I was a maid in the service of the Hickmans of Gainsborough Hall. It was they that decreed that a change of name to Dorothy. So that is the name by which I had become known and answered to for more than seventeen years before I married. Sir Thomas and the others had only ever known me by the name of Dorothy so, when I came to be married, William Brewster declared that I should be married as such and that God himself knew me for who I was, no matter what name I or others had chosen to call me.'

I thought I put my case well, yet if so, why did I still have the impression that I was sliding ever deeper into a bear pit?

'Dorothy? Oh yes!' Rech grinned sourly. 'I have checked with my sources in Plimouth, New England. Some still living there keenly recall that a maidservant named Dorothy came over on the Mayflower. They remember her being married to a fellow dissident named Thomas, who had been part of their original congregation in Holland. But they say categorically that he died before the ship left England. He died before the Mayflower had even departed and so his widow, Dorothy, came over alone to the New World. Yet, by all accounts, she did not stay alone for long, because not long after arriving there she married a carpenter called Eaton!'

'And this hearsay?' I countered. 'Is it admissible in a court of law?'

'Hmm! Maybe not,' he said with more than a hint of mischievous menace. 'But then it is indeed fortuitous that this has come to be in my possession!'
With those words and his lips quivering in delight he reached under his papers and withdrew an old battered, brown leather-bound book.

'The handwriting should be of great interest to you,' he purred. 'A woman's fair hand. Yours, if I am not mistaken...'
I had recognised it instantly. This was my journal that had gone missing after my leaving Plimouth. Yet how had it come to land up in Rech's hands?

'Yes, fortuitous indeed! he continued mockingly. 'Yet you look a little pale, mistress. Are you certain you do not want to sit down?'

I stood my ground.

'Stubborn to the end, I see. So be it! For this clearly spells out your end. This little book makes some very interesting reading indeed, damning, in fact. Which is rather ironic, is it not? For I found this journal amongst the evidence presented during the proceedings to wind up the Virginia Company's interests in America. A heart rending account, and it was purported to be of an unknown dead woman of Plimouth clearly citing the neglect of the company for the near extinction of the Mayflower colonists in New England. And yet she was not dead, was she? This Dorothy, because it was you all along!'
My heart sank away as I realised that my own husband,Thomas, must have taken my journal without either my consent or knowledge and used for his own ends.

'Yes. Yes it was I! I freely admit it, but it was not a proper marriage!'
Foolishly, I had opened a breach in my defences wide

for Rech to ride, roughshod through at will. From that moment on, his words hailed down upon me like vengeful sticks and stones.

'Not a proper marriage? Not proper in which respect? Hmm? Tell me, Lady Elizabeth. Not proper in the sense that it was not not legally binding? Not binding because the man you married in England was not dead at all!' he ranted. 'Well, yes, I should have to agree with you. In that respect you would be right. You would *still* be married to the first man while bedding the second! I can see that now. I can also see that this must also be construed as bigamy.'

By then quite florid, Rech paused before revelling in his final onslaught.

'Do you *know* the likely penalty for bigamy in a case like this? And with so much more deception thrown into the bargain? Like your feigning your own death, for example? And you would be prepared to state all of this in public at Gainsborough and then to throw yourself upon the mercy of the Lea Court? Do you really think they will show you any favour then, Royalist, or not? They *will* hang you, you know? You *do* realise that? Don't you?'

I was bloodied from the fray and almost beaten into submission. I could see no way out. What Rech knew was the ruin of me. I was finished. Their was no point in trying to fight now for my reputation. Yet what about for my family? I had to do all that was left in my power to protect Hope and my grandson.

'Do as I ask you.' Rech could smell the kill. 'That is all you have to do to walk away from here with your life. Admit freely to the charge that you were not lawfully married to Sir Thomas, then you and that Powhatan can walk away from here!'

Suddenly, with horror, I realised the point of Rech's persecution of me.

'But if I do,' I replied calmly, 'then I make a bastard out of my son and forfeit all of my grandson's inheritance into the bargain.'

'Oh, I shouldn't worry about that,' Rech said,

knowingly. 'Your son is dead, so I am not certain that being branded a bastard will bother him much now, do you?'

These words cut more deeply than any he had thrust at me so far. If Rech claimed to know this, then it only served to seal my grief.

'As for the child,' my torturer continued to taunt, 'well he will not be the last son born to a bastard, I am certain. And as for his inheritance? I have seen your grandson for myself and he looks quite the sickly runt to me. I very much doubt that he would reach the age of twenty-one to put in a claim for anything. No, if I were you, I would give this up now. Admit the charges and then the three of you quietly walk away and find somewhere else to infest.'

'Why are you doing this to us Rech? What have I ever done to you to deserve such hatred?'

'You? You have done nothing.'

'My husband, then?'

'Your husband did nothing either. He did nothing when I came to Virgina on my stepfather's behalf to invest his vast fortune in the colony. Your husband did nothing to quietly warn me against taking this action, when all along he knew of my purpose for being in the New World. Your husband did nothing, yet all the while knowing that the Virgina Company, through his own covert efforts, was about to collapse. He did nothing to stop my ruination and the loss of my family's estate. You stand there and whine on to me about your grandchild's inheritance. What about my inheritance? Because of your husband I was cut off without a penny. Cast off by my mother and her husband like a flea from a dog. I was left destitute.

'Then I heard of your husband's good fortune. So I walked over two hundred miles to find him and to ask for a position at your estate – but only for him to turn me away. Then, serving as a clerk at the outbreak of the Civil War, I discovered the truth about your husband's presence in Jamestown, and so I set out to accomplish my 'justice'. I have endured so much humiliation and hardship along the way in order to rise to the position I now *enjoy* today.

But that is enough about me. I will leave you now to think your situation over. All you need to do is to stand tomorrow in front of the village and admit to having lived with Sir Thomas for all of your time here out of wedlock. That is all. After that, you will be free to go. Let me know what you decide, and make it soon. Or else your fate will slip out of my hands, and then even I will not be able to save your life!'

*　　　*　　　*

I was led away by soldiers and manhandled through a doorway and into the tower staircase. There they shut me in with but a slop bucket and a stubby short candle to light up the darkness for at least a short a while longer.

I wrapped my inadequate shawl tightly about me and wearily sat upon the cold comfort of the steps and began to contemplate my fate in earnest. When faced with a cliff's edge there seems little difference between falling and jumping from the precipice, for the end result is just as devastating either way. To my mind, I had but two impossible choices. To be condemned as a harlot for living and fornicating with a man out of lawful wedlock on the wicked pretence of being his wife. Or alternatively, I could possibly hang as a bigamist for living and fornicating with a man out of wedlock whilst being legally married to another. Both would utterly destroy my reputation if not ruin my family also. I now fully understood Master Shakespeare when he wrote that there was little choice betwixt rotten apples for I had no choice in my ruination, only in its method.

Either way I knew that Rech had enough 'evidence' contrary to that which I knew to be the truth, quite literally to damn me. Either way, I feared that my grandson Tom was going to forfeit his rightful inheritance, no matter what I did. If I did as Rech urged, by standing up and publicly condemning and humiliating myself with a false confession that I had not been lawfully married to

31

his grandfather, Tom would then have no basis in law claim to the estate. On the other hand, if I dared to defy Rech, then I feared that he would show no hesitation at all in carrying out his threat to have Hope and Tom repatriated to Virginia. Whatever else I lost, I knew that I could not bear to lose what remained of my family. What use was a reputation anyway if it meant that I did not have them?

Entering into marriage had been both the easiest and yet most difficult decision I had ever to make in my life. I had always loved Thomas from the very first moment I had caught his glance at Gainsborough Old Hall. He was so very handsome to mine eyes, yet I dared not even dream that I would one day know of love with him, for I was but a young serving girl and he a gentleman's son. Yet fall in love we did, and then he betrayed me. He went away, suddenly, to Holland and left me behind even though we had been publicly betrothed. I was left behind to face the deep humiliation of it all and to find myself the butt of malicious tittle-tattle from my fellow servants at the Hall. Even then I tried not to believe that Thomas had deserted me, and so I faithfully wore a sprig of willow in my cap waiting on the day when he would return to me. Then one day I blundered in upon my fellow servants in the midst of a frenzy of gossip as they crowed over news that my Thomas had taken a Dutch woman to be his wife. I was utterly destroyed. So much so, that I immediately ran off to the tower and climbed it with every intention of throwing myself to my death from it.

I did not though, and when Thomas eventually returned as a widowed man to me more than a dozen years later, within hours I had let myself be seduced into falling hopelessly in love with him all over again. I was prepared to leave everything I had worked for and achieved in my lonely life to accompany him into the dangerous uncertainty of a life in the New World colonies. I knew that without him I would always be lost and alone. Far easier was it for me to agree to become his wife, than to watch him turn about again and walk out of my life forever. And it was also extremely difficult, as it meant my summoning up the courage to put my hand once more into the fire that had already badly burnt me.

It seemed all the more unfair then that the circumstances that had led to my present dilemma were never of my deliberate making or intention, yet now seemed set to destroy me. When I had left Plymouth, Devon, upon the Mayflower with the others, it was with compelling evidence that my newlywed husband had been brutally murdered by robbers. Even the principle, most trusted and revered of our congregation had come gently to me to break the news of his death. His closest friends had identified his body so that I might be spared the anguish of seeing his bloodied and brutalised corpse lying dead upon cold, stone slab in a dingy cellar in the town.

Life at the outset of that colony had cruelly deprived so many of their loved ones. Children of mothers, and husbands of wifes. Fathers, brothers, sisters, friends, all had been unwillingly sacrificed in the course of our endeavour to found a new Eden. Later, when we scant few who had survived that winter and had gone ashore to settle the land, tragedy led me into a marriage of convenience.

Governor John Carver and his wife, Katherine, had taken me into their household when 'widowhood' had left me deprived of support. I lived with them as Katherine's personal maid out of friendship. Then John died suddenly, just as we thought that death had had its full measure of us and sated its wicked appetite. Then Katherine, too, succumb to overwhelming grief. Suddenly I was left in a desperate situation.

Without a home or the support of a family, marriage to Francis Eaton hardly warranted deliberation at all. He had desperate need of a woman to care for his child and I had an equally desperate need of a roof above my head. Marriage to Francis Eaton seemed an honorable option.

When I remarried, Francis had only been newly

widowed himself. His wife, Sarah, had died upon the Mayflower shortly after our arrival. In fact, I had helped nurse her in her final hours and prepared her body for burial at sea. It had been I who had tried to ease the burden of her grieving husband by taking my turn in helping to care for their infant son, so tiny and now so vulnerable with the untimely loss of his mother. By that time in Plimouth, his young son was sick and in need of a nurse and so I gave of myself willingly to save the infant's life. Yet in in doing so I might have left myself open to dishonour – by sleeping under the same room as this now single man. I did not love Francis, nor he me. Each of us was still trying to come to terms with the loss of our spouse. Yet he desperately needed someone to care for his son and I needed a home in which to live. So we came to an arrangement for the good of all concerned that might sit well with God and the rest of our company. We would enter into a marriage, in name at least. For us Separatists, marriage is an honourable estate but not necessarily a matter of the Church, nor even religion. Our marriages are more of a 'contract' to do with settling civil matters and to keep us from breaking God's sacred commandments. Therefore, Francis and I entered into marriage on the strict understanding that he, my husband in name, was not to have knowledge of me until, and if, I ever felt that I was ready or willing to do so. I never reached either point, though to be honest, towards the end I was beginning to grow some deep affection towards Francis, and I believe him towards me.

Had I not given myself in marriage to Francis, then I would have doubtless ended up quickly in a marriage to one of the other widowed fellows of the colony. I was but one of only several females of a marriageable condition left alive at the end of that first winter, and therefore my marriage to some man was a foregone conclusion. It was an expectation born out of dire necessity and it didn't matter with whom I entered into marriage. I would not have loved him and so the decision was simple. How could I expect to be hurt again by love if there was to be no love in the first place? Therefore the decision practically made itself for me.

I had very little recollection of when Thomas arrived unexpectedly in New England some two years or more later. He had come in search of me, finding me gravely ill and close to death. Then, on discovering that Thomas was alive and with me being so gravely ill, it was decided in the best interest of all that my accidental bigamy should be kept secret from the rest of the colony and that I should be secretly smuggled away upon Thomas' vessel and that it be put about that I had died.

So, in hindsight, I suspect that the latter is the account of events that would meet any outsider investigating into my past in that colony. They would believe that I was dead and that anyone purporting to be me must be an imposter, unless the truth had got abroad, in which case, in the eyes of the law, I was guilty as charged with bigamy. All the same though, I felt betrayed to think that none still alive there, who had been privy to the truth, had not come forward to speak up for me.

Staring aimlessly off somewhere upwards into the gloom, in a flicker of a candlelight dancing across the rim of the spiralling steps, I suddenly pictured the tower at Gainsborough Hall. I remembered how close I had once come, after climbing that tower, to throwing myself off it to my death. I had just heard then, from servants tittle-tattle, that my fiancée Thomas had deserted me and gone away to Holland. I would have killed myself too, if it had not been for the intervention of my Lady Rose.

How, at her great age, she had found the strength to hurry up those winding steps after me, I did not know. Yet she had, and only just in time to talk me out of suicide. I had heard Lady Rose's words coaxing me into new reasoning just as I was making ready to leap.

She said, 'Against whom I wonder would this be the greater crime? Against God or yourself? Nothing here is broken that the Lord cannot mend.'

I had listened to her then and now, strangely, felt that she was speaking to me again. I remembered the flickering light of Lady Rose's lamp as we sat in the Solar at Gainsborough Hall, reading the Bible aloud together as she patiently taught me to read on dreary winter nights. Often she would be distracted by a passage that raised memories from her own youth. So then she would stop and tell me tales of martyrs who suffered for the Protestant faith. Such suffering she recounted that, with tears, I would ask her how one could find such courage as they had to stand so steadfastly for their convictions. She eyed me that steely stare of hers and replied, 'Child, thou shalt always remember these simple words for they shall serve you well one day, when you may be called upon to suffer under the unrighteous dominion of one who would gladly see you destroyed in a blinking of an eye. To suffer for thine own sake is to work out a pathway alone. Whereas to offer thine self up to suffer for others, is to walk in the footsteps of a hallowed legion. Christ will be with you, as He was, no doubt, with them. For in the love of thine self lies thine own destruction. For if love of thine self lies at the seat of all evil, for then am I not to be found in the middle of sin?'

I could see that there was no way out, unscathed, from this nightmare for me. Yet it was still within my power to deliver my family from further unnecessary physical suffering. Therefore, reluctantly I decided to settle for the lesser charge, even though it meant lying in public and denouncing Thomas as my lawful husband.

'How are we to know what is truth from that which is a lie?' I had asked my Lady.

'Time alone can answer that,' she had replied. 'Truth stays on the lips forever, while lies fade away. Even Saint Peter lied by denouncing Christ three times as the cock crowed. Yet time showed out the truth in his belief in the Lord as his Messiah!'

I knew then that I would lie to save my child. When Rech returned, I would submit to his wicked will and agree to plead guilty at my trial the next day.

The candle waned into nothing and pitched me into black darkness. In the chill I huddled on the bottom stair and pondered over what it could be that had led Rech into becoming such a bitter soul. True, nature had not been kind to him by not blessing him with looks. Yet then neither is a diamond until it is cut and polished to let its brilliance shine. None the less, surely this alone could not be the sum of his obvious 'problem'. Other men rose to defy any deficit in handsome features by cultivating the good graces and talents with which God had blessed them. A pleasant personalty, clever wit, or even just a charming manner and happy disposition, are all amongst the finer qualities on which a less good looking man may still hope to find great favour amongst his fellow man. Or a woman, come to that.

Rech seemed only able to compensate for his lack in other measures with a cold and contrived charm unique to himself, and by his determined effort to render himself 'useful' to the point of indispensability unto whichever unwitting party he chose to cleave. He was like a parasite. He attached himself to other people in order to extract all that he could from them in advancing himself. Then he would drop away again and move onto his next 'host'.

Thomas and I had both witnessed his extraordinary method – both during his stay in Jamestown and aboard the ship that was to carry us all home to England. Rech was a 'user', and the most dangerous of his kind. He seemed benign – until his true malignancy was outed. And because of this, I found it hard to show him any pity for the sorry and lonely state of his personal life which ever doomed to remain so. For here was the needy child of a loveless mother turned in upon himself in the face of bitter rejection. Most of those rejected so early in life strive, instead, to find love and affection elsewhere, and along the way learn to spurn this wretched example set for them. Rech though could not. Instead, following on from his own rejection, he rejected the rest in the world about him until he could find no other comfort than inflicting misery upon others who had succeeded in discovering love. And for Rech's infliction, I was afraid that there would come no easy cure.

Around midnight, the door suddenly opened to a shroud of bright lamp light revealing Rech's gloating features.

'So?' was all he said.

I asked, 'If I admit to these crimes, Sir, and confess my guilt, then my family will forfeit all claim to our estates – but I will remain free to leave Stowe of my own accord?'

Rech smiled.

'Of that, Lady Elizabeth,' he said, handing me a blanket, 'you have my word...'

Chapter Three

Hope is not my daughter, not born of my flesh. As the Lord God above is not my physical father, so it is that Hope is my daughter in the Holy Spirit. Yet, I carry her in my heart as if I had carried her in my womb. I remember the day she slipped into my life as clearly as I do the birth of my son, James. For it was upon the very same day that both happened.

James had come a month or so sooner than I had expected and the birth was mercifully quick and easy and he was a big healthy baby, despite his early appearance. I had delivered James alone, snowed in at our cottage at Jamestown, while my husband was away on a hunting trip with others from our settlement. Quite unexpectedly, our men had chanced upon *them* deep into the forest – a small group of Powhatan naturals, also desperately hunting for food. Amongst them, some women and boys.

Thomas burst through our door in a state of deep distress. His eyes were wild and his commonly steady frame was shaking. Thick blood matted the fur of his cape. It was smeared across his face and on his hands and the cuffs of his jerkin. At first I thought that he had been injured. I tried to comfort and calm him but still he trembled and could not even look me in the eye. I soon discovered the awful truth.

'Another massacre?' I asked him, remembering well the one that had taken scores of English lives barely two years before.

Thomas broke down and told that there had indeed been a massacre. Only this time, it was they who had gone on a bloody rampage. With that, he took something out from under his coat. It was a large, bloodied kerchief contain something limp and still. Thomas had gone off in the hope of returning with desperately needed game, instead he came home to me with the bloody carcass of a newborn child.

All about him had been mayhem and confusion. None of the others noticed Thomas. They were far too busy themselves ransacking the corpses of the naturals in search of trinkets and trophies. No one witnessed a devastated Thomas quickly snatch up the child spilling out from its butchered mother's belly and tying off its cord before bundling it up and stuffing it under his coat. These civilized Jamestown men had behaved like mad animals. They had become as savage themselves then as their despised Powhatan enemy, open to carrying out bloody massacre as the naturals had led by example.

Thomas had laid out the child's body on the bare wooden table. She was as still and cold as ice. The small silent face was contorted with her eyes tightly shut as she had tried to blot out the cruel abomination that had played out just as she made her way into this world. Her tiny fists were clenched as if in outrage.

'She was alive when I snatched her up,' Thomas explained. 'I heard her gasp. I tried to keep her safe but its too late. She's dead.'

'No!' I told him. 'A body's never dead from cold until it is warm and cold.'

I had heard in the past how cold can do strange things to a body, especially to a child's. Sometimes something happens when cold, instead of killing a body instead seems to fix a soul in limbo, trapped betwixt this life and the next. Trapped, and yet with coaxing *sometimes* a miracle can happen to bring that soul back to life.

I took the child up and ran to my fireside chair with it. I laid her out, face down across my lap. The infant girl's skin was fixed and creased like the rind of a smoked ham. As I began to gently massage her tiny limbs and body, I could feel Thomas' anxious breath on my neck as he watched silently from over my shoulder. At first nothing happened, then after a frantic minute or two to our deep relief the child suddenly mewed like a kitten then gasp loudly and began to cry.

Almost at once, a second cry had suddenly began to fill our tiny cottage and took Thomas quite by surprise. He looked at me in sheer bewilderment.

'Go over to the bed, Thomas,' I smiled at him

proudly. 'Go and meet your new son while I attend to this little one.'

Tenderly Thomas picked up James and cradled him lovingly in the nook of his arm as tears of joy began to stream down his face.

'He is so beautiful... so beautiful, my love,' was all he could say.

James was hungry so I beckoned Thomas to pass him to me so that I might begin to feed him. As I did, the tiny Powhatan child became increasingly agitated and began to suck frantically at the cloth of my shirt in search of milk of her own. What could I do? Feed my child while this one starved? I did the only thing that I could. I picked up this natural child and I suckled her. I wet nursed my countryman's now sworn enemy without hesitation. For as my husband said to at the time, does not the Bible command us to love thine enemy as thyself?

We named her Hope. Hope for a future time when Powhatan and Englishmen might live in harmony as I knew that we surely could. Hope that we had not travelled so far down that bloody road of warfare in Virginia that we might still be able to turn back. We were at war though with the Powhatan and knew that our kinsmen would not share our forgiving and sentiments towards the foe. In fact, we were under no illusion that if it were discovered that we were harbouring this child, then she would be forcibly removed from us and probably put out in the forest to die. From the moment Thomas had picked her up, we were committed to keeping her in secret an impossible ask in such a tiny community as Jamestown. So, we planned to pass her off as the twin to our own child and were able to much disguise her complexion with a specially concocted lotion used to ward off the vicious biting insects of the colony. We knew, however, that we could not keep up that pretence indefinitely, and so planned a hasty return to England where we could pass Hope off as a Spanish foundling.

How we agonised over the fate of that child! And

managing to get her to England did not mean that she would survive. Indeed, when Thomas and I had visited Captain John Smith at his London home, the last thing he had said to me on leaving was a warning. He told me not to become too 'attached' to the child – for it was becoming clear that there was something about the English air that doth congest their lungs and do them 'grave harm'. Pocahontas had died after a brief stay in England, and so had one of her retinue who had become a Christian and remained in London at the home of George Thorpe. Smith filled me with dread that the same fate might befall Hope too. Yet, instead of distancing myself from the child, as he suggested, I was determined to love her all the more for what little time I might be destined to be her guardian. Thankfully, time was to prove Smith wrong and Hope grew up to be an extremely robust child and flourished into adulthood.

She and James were like chalk and cheese. Not just by way of skin and hair colouring but in a myriad of ways. Hope was born with a shock of black hair and was always first to reach those important milestones in childhood. She walked in her ninth month without ever having attempted to crawl. Instead she had leant early to pull herself up by the chair leg and to stand, laughing and grinning at all in attendance. She was daring and agile and soon trying to climb, while James was a placid baby happy to shuffle about on his bottom until well over a year old. Hope cut her first tooth and said her first word long before her brother, whom she soon began to call 'Ya-ya'.

Thomas and I were at pains to educate both of our children equally, but this was soon to prove impossible. For while Hope was without a doubt exceedingly bright and quick witted, when it came to reading and writing she struggled to grasp even the bare basics. And though she could eventually read it was always a trial unto her to do so. Meanwhile James leapt so far in advance of his sister that by the time they were both six, Thomas and I were forced into teaching them separately, lest James suffered and became frustrated by his sister's woefully slow progress.

Mathematics proved the same. Hope could count with relative ease. With a glance she could estimate, with uncanny accuracy, how many sheep were grazing in a pasture at any given time. Yet, multiplication and division were all concepts far beyond her grasp. He memory for facts though, was quite phenomenal as was her skill for picking up all tasks practical.

As a result, while James studied higher things in the company of his father, Hope remained with me as we went about our daily chores on the farm. We grew close, as a mother and daughter ought. Then we grew far beyond that, she became my helpmate and friend. And then when James went away to university and Thomas to war, we became closer still, more like sisters, and I confided more deeply in her then than in any other living soul. During that time, I told her everything. Even about Plimouth and how it was that I came to marry Francis Eaton. Hope understood completely. Therefore it must have come as quite a shock to her to hear me stand up during my trial and deny her beloved father as my true spouse.

*   *   *

When they came for me I could hardly rise to my feet. My bones were so terribly stiff and cold from the night in my makeshift prison. But somehow I managed to meekly shuffle after my captors out into the sunlit body of the church, like an old ewe being led into the slaughter house. Inside the temporary court room, made up in the nave, were dozen upon dozen of faces familiar to me. One or two met my gaze with a reassuring smile, whilst most chose to look away in awkwardness – bewildered as to why I was being brought to count in the first place. For all of my years of living in that village, I could not recall one word of ill will passing between any of those assembled there and me. Many had been friends of Thomas and his late parents, or had dealings with my husband on a weekly if not daily basis. They all at least knew me by name, yet not one person called out to me with a word of support. They just crammed tightly together, cheek by jowl, like a playhouse rabble waiting for the performance to begin. It was obvious to me by then that Rech's men had already been about the village reciting a prologue of wicked gossip.

Then my worst imagined moment came from out of the sleepless night before.

Hope was led in with young Tom in her arms to bear witness to the blackening of my name. Her eyes were red and swollen with tears, and yet she immediately smiled to greet me. I had no idea then if she had even an inkling of what was about to unfold, but I suspected she too had spent the night before as much in the dark as I had.

I was made to stand before the high church pulpit as Rech mounted the steps and started to make his deliberations from on high. Precise and correct, like the true seeker he purported to be, he spoke long and stern about the righteous and their search for truth. And then he began with his allegations as to the legitimacy of my marriage to Thomas.

Being hauled before the villagers among whom I had lived for more than twenty years was humiliation beyond words. For they were in shock of the revelation that one of high social standing amongst them was about to be publicly marked out as a liar. Former friends listened in disbelief as Rech made a meal of laying out the charges against me.

'So, Mistress Elizabeth, tell this court if you will... He paused for dramatic effect. 'How do you plead to the charge that you were not, and never have been, lawfully married to Sir Thomas according to the Church custom of this realm?'

'I plead guilty, Sir' I calmly and clearly replied.

The incredulous gasps of outrage as I then stood up and pleaded guilty will stay with me for the rest of my life. I was so sorry that my daughter and grandson had to witness my downfall too. Yet more haunting than any of this was the look upon meeting Hope's gaze as she sprang to her feet and with quivering lips mouthed but one word: 'Why?'

After the commotion had died down a little, I was fully expecting to be released from custody, to quietly gather up my belongings and walk away into exile. How stupid could I have been – to have thought that I could trust Rech to keep to his end of the bargain. Instead of being ready to let me be, I was soon to find that Rech had not yet had his full measure of twisted retribution.

'Take this criminal out to the whipping post!' he barked to the waiting guards.

The words struck my ears like a sound beating. The room suddenly burst into noisy uproar as I was suddenly grappled roughly and dragged outside, across the churchyard and to the green beyond.

I heard Hope screaming, 'No! No! No! Leave my mother alone!' But it was to no avail.

The crowd quickly followed, crushing in about me as my back was slammed against the hard wooden post and my wrists forced up into its manacles until I was snared, like a defenceless rabbit in a trap. All the while Rech strutted like a black cockerel amongst his hens, crowing with his own importance.

My heart raced as I waited for my punishment to be carried out – for I was certain that Rech was determined to have me publicly whipped. Yet, if so, why was I trussed up and facing forward?

Rech suddenly threw his hands aloft and ordered that there be silence, so his words might be heard above the clamour. Then he rambled on for some time about the wages of sin, and how evil must be purged from our midst in order that justice should prevail. But my mind was was fixed somewhere else entirely, for I had spotted something from out of the corner of my eye, something that then filled me with terror. Two soldiers were carrying a metal brazier from the Smithy's forge. It was filled with glowing coals, and in it was wedged the long slender handle of a branding iron.

'Prepare the prisoner!' Rech ordered. He had obviously already fully instructed his men as to how I was to be 'prepared' for my torment. For without hesitation, one of the men stepped forward and ripped open the front of my bodice with a ready blade, exposing my lax, bare breasts to everyone. With my arms outstretched and held fast by chains, I had no way of covering up my modesty. Instead, I was left like meat on a hook come market day, hung out for all to view. I did not know where to look in my shame, so my eyes fell upon that loathsome man instead. Rech stood with his arms crossed and with his beady stare fixed victoriously upon my distress. If he had but a speck of remorse for what he was about to put me through, he did not show it.

'Proceed with the punishment!' Rech demanded excitedly.

With that, Master Hill, our doleful looking blacksmith dressed in his tan coloured cow-hide aprons, stepped forward. He had heavy wet rags wrapped about his hand as he lifted the red hot iron from out of its sheath of coals and slowly bore it towards me. The wet cloth made it hiss loudly, like an angry snake, and it sent a plume of steam rising from where he gripped it. I saw at once the glowing 'H' of the head of the brand, and I could I feel heat permeating the still chill morning air. Hill hesitated momentarily when he was but inches away from me, and then looked towards Rech with forlorn hope that the order might be rescinded.

But instead Rech screeched, 'Get on with it, man!'

A handful of hardened Puritan zealots amongst the crowd shouted in support of my punishment, while Master Hill then looked back towards me.

'I am so sorry, my lady,' he said softly.

Then he thrust the head of the brand hard against my left breast. Strangely, I seemed to hear my own screaming as if from a distance.

But it is not the excruciating, fiery pain that I still remember with intensity. For in truth, that left relatively little impression upon me. No, it was the look of utter satisfaction – a perverse joy – in Rech's eyes, along with the smell of my own searing flesh, that comes back to haunt and to taunt me. Even after all these years. Had my Thomas been there, he would have been beside himself with rage. He would have torn Rech limb from limb with his bare hands. He would not have been able to bear it, to see me suffer in his stead for whatever he had done in the past. I knew this. More to the point, so did Rech. This wasn't about me or taking away my grandson's land. This was pure spiteful revenge against my dead husband, now beyond his reach. It was about making a point to me and to him, it was about retribution reaching far beyond my husband's grave. I believe it was this knowledge that served to heighten Rech's climactic pleasure up to the point of sheer ecstasy in seeing me tortured in this way.

I then fainted, for when I next came to my senses I had fallen. Fallen as far as one can whilst still chained by the hands to a whipping post. I had slumped onto my knees and in the process almost wrenched my arms from out of their sockets. I am told, for I did not see, that the Smithy was so disgusted by the task he had just been forced to undertake that he threw down the still hot branding iron barely missing Rech's feet. Hill had then seized up the wooden cooling pale intended for the iron, and immediately poured its cool water slowly over my already blistering skin. He must have known full well from his own painful past experience that this action would help ease the burn and hopefully limit the result of my future scarring. It was an act of kindness from this strongest of men.

Barely had I come to my senses only to find Rech still not yet satisfied in his appetite for revenge.

'Now slit her nose open!' Rech yelled like a demented harpy proffering up his own small paring knife to a bailiff nearby. The blacksmith stood astride me and defiantly yelled back.

'No! This is enough! More than enough! Leave her be!'

Rech glared only to find the bailiff also unwilling to carry this out. Angrily, he gestured to one of the soldiers.

'I am here to protect you, Sir, and to uphold the law. Not to do your dirty work!' he protested.

'Then I will cut the Royalist bitch myself!' he

screamed, lunging towards me with the knife.

With that, a near riot broke out, as outraged royalists amongst the villagers, unmoved to aid me up until then, stepped forward to bar Rech's advance and to shield me. At the same time the blacksmith broke open my bonds to set me free. Hope barged her way through the crowd and desperately tried to help me. Confused and upset, Tom clung crying loudly at her side as I tried, unsteadily, to rise to my feet.

Fearing then that the majority of the crowd was fast turning against him, Rech declined to press on with this additional cruelty. Instead he screamed out a torrent of abuse and denounced me as a common whore.

'Whip this woman and her insolent pup out of the village!' he ordered the soldiers.' And should she dare to make any attempt to return, then let her be held in contempt and then 1 *shall* split open their noses, on sight! Including the child's!

This time they did as Rech bad and dragged me to my feet. Those good and godly Puritan citizens amongst the rush then raised up their gads[3] and began to whip me out of the village like a diseased dog. And when Hope tired to help me up after I stumbled, they started whipping her too. Even as she cowered low in a desperate attempt to protect her young son from their wayward blows, they continued their onslaught without mercy. As they did, one or two other men, along with the blacksmith ran and caught them up and tried to intervene. A fist fight broke out with the mounted soldiers, who had been trying to break apart the two waring factions, being dragged down off their horses and set upon as we continued to be driven up along the lane and out of the parish. Shock made me quiver as I weaved this way and that, not truly knowing where I was going – only that I had to get away to safety.

When suddenly we found ourselves free of the mayhem, we staggered and stumbled into the nearby woods where, as I did my best to re-cover the violated parts of my body with my torn and soaked bodice, I fell exhausted to the ground and passed out again.

When I regained conciousness I was desperately thirsty and very ill at ease. But there would be no immediate peace or comfort, for Hope was standing over me and seemed also to have turned against me.

'How could you do that?' she cried 'How could you denounce my father like that?'

'I had to...' I mumbled thickly through my bleeding mouth. I suddenly realised that, in my agony, I had bitten deep into my tongue. The blood had begun to clot around the swelling and had crusted on my lips. 'I had to do it,' I continued.

'Why? Why?' she kept demanding.

'I had to do it for you... and for Tom. I also had to do it for myself. *You* are all I have left in this world.' I tried to explain. 'Your father is dead. So is James. Rech threatened to send you away... back to the Powhatans in Virginia. I could not let him do that. I could not bear it if I lost you too!' I broke down and wept, punctuating my wails with sobs that seemed to resonate through the rustling trees.

'Oh, Mother!' was Hope's reply, as she fell to the ground beside me. After she gathered Tom up close, we collapsed onto each other and cried until we could cry no more.

Much later, as I stirred and emerged from a near stupor, I found myself moving awkwardly, catching the roughness of the cut cloth against my breast. It smarted terribly. And my thirst was raging.

'Let's look at your wound,' Hope said.
Reluctantly I re-opened up my torn bodice to reveal the ravaged skin – red, blistered, and oozing.

'Ugh!' Hope winced. 'We need to lance those blisters and put on a poultice to ward off infection.

Fortunately, I had schooled her well in the use of herbal remedies. For as I cradled Tom in my arms, Hope set off in search of a certain combination of leaves growing wild. On returning, she took them into her mouth and chewed them, then spat them out into her hands, and moulded them together into a pat which she adhered to the now pricked blisters. Then she bound it close to my skin with strips of torn petticoat. It felt so wonderfully cooling against the painful inflammation.

By now it was afternoon and Tom was hungry, bless him, and badgering for food. Yet we had nothing to give him, so all Hope could do was to rock him until he had cried himself to sleep in her arms. Then, after we'd drunk deeply from a stream, we too lay amongst the bluebells to rest and to gather up our thoughts into some plan of action.

I was so relieved to have got away from Rech and Stowe with my family intact and yet I knew that *somehow* we would have to go back there. What else could we do? We had absolutely nothing but the clothes upon our backs. No food for Tom. No money and nothing of value to see us upon our way to somewhere else. There was the strongbox though, still buried out in the yard at Blackthorn Farm and still safe from pillaging hands. My pearls were in it and silver too, along with the deeds of our property. I had to go back. I had to try to retrieve it.

'You shan't go alone!' was Hope's immediate response to the suggestion.'You heard what Rech said he would do to you?'

'And that is why I must go alone. He said he would split your and Tom's noses too. Besides which, Hope, he would have to catch me first. And I am determined not to give him that satisfaction!'

'Then he would have to catch the both of us...'

Hope would not be dissuaded and so it was that, as the sun began to set, we made our way along the back lane towards our farmstead once more. Slinking along in the shadow of the hedgerows like sly vixens towards the chicken run.

Creeping through the horse field and up to the front yard wall, we were mightily dismayed to spot two soldiers camped out front for the night and noisily tucking into their supper. I knew then that there was not chance now of retrieving my strong box buried in the garden beyond.

'What do we do now?' Hope whispered. 'They've even boarded up the doors!'

'Wait,' I said. 'I have an idea. What about the dairy? I know the window there is small and set high...'

'Yes, and I wager that I could get through it.' With that, we made our way around to the back of the farmhouse. We wrapped young Tom in his mother's shawl and, flattening the tall cow parsley, made a little nest for him to snuggle down in.

'Shush!' Hope bad him gently, 'Stay here, Tom! Mammy and Gran'mam have to go an errand to get you some cheese for your supper but you must stay as quiet and still as a little bunny in hiding from Mister Fox. You understand, my lovely?'

Tom nodded wearily and curled himself up into a silent, tight ball. When we were as certain as we could be that the child was safely settled, we slid silently in and out of the shadows and up to the wall of our house.

'Are you ready?' I whispered anxiously. Hope nodded confidently that she was.

'Just in and out as quickly as you can!' I warned her. 'Grab whatever food comes easily to hand and that is all. Please, Hope! Do not take any chances!' Again she nodded, then made her move.

Hope had been right, for after standing upon my crouched back she managed to slip, head first through the opening, like a greased rat and onto the stone counter below. It was as pitch black inside, and later Hope had admitted that had she not known that place like the back of her hand she would have been as if blind. But she did know it and so easily found my wicker basket and carefully filled it with cheeses, though she found no ham where she had fully expected to do so. No doubt that had been commandeered by whoever had nailed up the boards.

I waited anxiously beneath the window for Hope to return, and found myself unwilling to imagine what could be taking her so long. I had no way of knowing that Hope had blatantly disobeyed me and had somehow managed to find the courage to creep through the kitchen and past the bare windows with the soldiers sat almost directly outside. She had then made her way quickly upstairs to my room. After an age she eventually reappeared. Her head and shoulders wriggled through first with the now heavy basket dangling down from her finger tips for me to catch a hold of. I did so, quickly putting it on the ground before looking up again. Hope was proffering something hard and wrapped in cheesecloth. It was my Geneva Bible and my journal. Only then did I realise why she had taken so long.

Then Hope slithered out of the window, this time feet first, and lowered herself from the frame before gently letting herself drop the last two feet or so to the ground as lightly as a cat. Then we leaned in tightly against the contours of the wall, quietly listening for footsteps in case we had been heard by the watch. There was nothing. So confident that we had not yet been discovered, we headed back towards the horse field and to the spot where we had left Tom. To our great consternation, he was not there.

Then, suddenly, we heard a child crying somewhere near the front of the house and then the sound of the soldiers voices.

'Mam... Mam-may!' he was wailing. He had probably come too and could not remember why he was outside and alone in the darkness instead of inside the house and tucked up in his bed.

We were terrified. If the soldiers heard him, then we were all done for!

'Oh Lord!' Hope tried to hush her angst.

'We have got to try to get to him before they do!'

The consequences of our failing to do so were just too awful to contemplate. Hearts racing, we crept along the far side of the wall until we could see the guards by the light of their lamp. To our horror, one already had my grandson by the arm.

'Who are you lad?' he was saying. 'And what are you doing out here all alone?'

Tom just kept crying.

'Oh no! Hope gasped in despair. 'Whatever shall we do?' If they find out who he really is, they will split his nose and do who knows what with him. 'A thousand horrific thoughts seemed to race through our minds at once.

'I shall have to give myself up to them and beg for their mercy on the child,' I said.

There was nothing else that I could do. I took in one last deep breath and prepared to walk out from our hiding place and to turn myself in. But just at that moment, quite unexpectedly, a voice called out from the blackness – as a man briskly strode towards the soldiers.

'Praise God!' I half gasped and half whispered to Hope, recognising the man's lilting tones. 'It's Ned!'

'Ah, there you are lad!' Ned exclaimed, advancing upon the child. 'Come to your old Gran'pappy Ned!'

With that, Tom wriggled his tiny hand from out of the soldiers grasp and up to Ned and jumped into his open arms.

'He's your's then?' the soldier quizzed the old man.

'Ah, he is that, the little rascal!' Ned replied. 'Near frightened his old Gran'pap to death, he did. My daughter would skin me alive if'n she knew that I had let 'im escape!' Ned cradled the boy tight to his chest. 'Thankee kindly, sirs,' Ned smiled with genuine gratitude upon his leathery face. 'Thankee for finding the little lad for me.' With that he turned to walk away, back up along the lane.

'Stop!' one of the soldiers barked abruptly.

Ned froze in his tracks. I turned to Hope and she to me, both in dread fear of anything that could unfold next.

'Take a care, owld man!' the soldier scolded rather than warned. 'Or next time you mayn't be so lucky. Next time you might instead find him in't morning face down, dead in a ditch!' The tone of his words would

53

have been better used for a disobedient child than as a warning to a troubled grandfather.

Ned took the rebuke with all the shame and humility it would take to satisfy the Roundhead, also nodding his head and bowing slightly in suitably contrite and servile agreement, before making off once more with the boy.

We too crept away and soon caught up with Ned further along the way.

'God bless, you Ned!' I said as I hugged him, 'You saved us all!'

'Happen. This time!' he said quietly. 'But I did not save you earlier, did I Lady Elizabeth?' Then he sighed with regret as he added, 'I should have been able to have done something!'

'Do not blame yourself, Ned.' I replied. 'Twas none of your doing, and there would have been no good to be had if you had been taken as well. Who would have saved us just now?'

'Maybe so, but I still feel reet badly about it.'

'What were you doing up at the house?' Hope asked.

'Looking for the two of yown, of course!' he replied. 'I knew you couldn't have gotten far and not with Lady Elizabeth like this.'

He had keenly noted from my stance that I was in some discomfort.

'I am alright, Ned.' I reassured him. 'The brand smarts for certain, but thanks to the blacksmith's quick action and a poultice of herbs Hope was quick to apply, it is not as bad as could be feared. Though I will end up with a nasty scar, I am certain. But I am also sure that the worse will soon heal, if only I can keep the wound clean.'

'Where will you go, my lady?'

'Do not worry for us, Ned. I intend to make our way to Gainsborough Hall. I am certain our friends Lord and Lady Willoughby, will help us. After that? I really have no idea.'

'Well, you durnst be thinking of walking there tonight in this dark, my lady,' Ned pleaded. 'And 'tis not safe for you to be caught abroad. Come instead with me. You can bide at my cottage tonight and I will help you get away from the village afore daybreak.'

Exhausted, we gladly followed his lead scarce thinking of the consequence that our doing so might have for our dear fellow. Ned's wife, however, proved not so compassionate towards our plight. As she set out a mattress upon the downstairs floor, and out of her husband's hearing, she did vent her anger upon me.

'See this? 'Tis Titus' bed.' she snapped. 'Tis my dead son's place you are now a taking and I for one hopes that it gives you no rest!'

'I am so sorry,' I tried to tell her, yet she would hear no words of condolence from me.

'My son lies dead in unconsecrated ground a cause of yown! And now you would risk having my husband punished severe for harbouring you here. Shame on you, lady! 'Tis shame on you and all of your family to risk my husband so! He is an old man. Has he not suffered enough for you yet? Here,' she said, tossing me and old bodice. 'Take this for your modesty's sake and if you have a scrap of decency left in your body, you will not be here when my husband awakes!'

With that she took her candle and followed Ned up to bed.

Her words seemed to burn deeper than the brand iron, though causing a different kind of pain.

So once Tom and Hope had eaten and slept soundly for a few hours at least, I got them up and we were on our way out of the village before even a cockerel had yawned. That was the last time I saw our man, Ned, and our friendship that had spanned more than twenty years was now spent.

Chapter Four

Gainsborough was no longer the proud town that I had once known. And less so now that I was travelling through it by foot instead of riding the outskirts by carriage or horse. Much had, and still was, laid waste by cannon and fire of the Civil War. Where once ordered streets thrived, crammed full of a vast array of tradesmen, a dirty shanty town had grown from its ruination, squirming with desperate and hungering people. The only trade that seemed unaffected by the deprivation was that of the ever busy cluster of ale houses still busily plying their dubious trade up and down the Trent side of town.

Even with my being in a sorry state and clothes dirty and rent, three spindly beggar boys ran out from Swan Lane and sidled up to scrounge whatever they could from us. We dare not uncover our basket and give away the sight of the cheeses inside or I am certain we would have been swiftly robbed. Instead, Hope and I had to shoo them away with our hands and say firmly that we had nothing of value to share, and so pressed on through the chaos towards Gainsborough Hall.

I made way to that ancient manor house with the hope of finding sanctuary. After all, I was no stranger there. I had served the Hickman family long and dutifully in my youth. I had even helped raise Sir Willoughby from his childhood. However, I was soon to find how quickly such ties and duties upheld are forgotten or cast aside when no longer convenient to acknowledge.

As we approached the front door, we were curtly intercepted by some senior member of the household staff. Before I could even explain who I was, we were shooed away towards the direction of the kitchen door. Twas an easy enough mistake to make, I thought to myself at the time, to in error take us for vagrants in our present sorry state. So we did as ordered and made our way instead to the servants' entrance. But there we were stopped once again.

'Sorry ladies... there are no more scraps left today. Try your luck again tomorrow' the curt steward told us.

'Wait!' I said holding on to the door as he tried to close it in our faces. 'I am not here to beg food! I wish to speak with Lady Bridget.'

'You do, do you?' he said with a patronising air. 'I see. And what would you wish to convey to my lady?'

'That is of a private and delicate nature...' I replied.

'Very well then. Let it remain private then,' he said, shutting the door once more.

'Wait!... Please!' I blurted. 'Please tell your lady that her friend, Lady Elizabeth of Stowe, urgently seeks her assistance.'

'Very well,' he said reluctantly with a sigh. 'Wait here while I convey that message.'

He shut the door and went away leaving us to await his unhurried return.

'It will be alright, Hope,' I tried to reassure her. But Hope looked far from it.

We waited and waited until the steward finally returned. He opened up the door with a wry grin on his face.

'May we come in now?' I asked.

'No, you may not,' he replied.

'Did you not take my message to her ladyship?'

'Yes, I did. Moreover, she instructed me to ask you to tell your mistress, Lady Elizabeth, that she is not welcome here. Sir Willoughby lies ill in his bed and my lady insists that she does not want him worried further by the likes of *her*. She has heard what has befallen your mistress and says that she cannot help... Good day!'

With that he slammed the heavy door in my face and I felt curtailed by shame...

'No mind, mother,' said Hope. It was now her turn to reassure me. 'We do not need the help of friends such as these.'

'We have only some cheese to eat, and no money to buy anything else.' I said, as we walked away with heavy hearts.

'We do.' Hope smiled.'I have this...' And with that she held out a shiny silver shilling coin she had from inside her pocket.

'What is this?' I asked.

'My lucky piece.' Hope smiled, and with that flipped the coin spinning upwards into the air and then called out 'heads' as she watched it fall to the ground. 'Heads' it was. Hope quickly picked it up.

'This is how I have made up my mind when posed with a decision that I was not sure how else to make,' she explained. So I've let my lucky piece decide for me.'

I was amazed. For one, that she did such a thing, and for another, because I had no idea that she had.

'Where on earth did you get that coin from, and how long have you been letting fickle fate make your choices for you?'

'I do not know exactly,' she replied. 'I have had this since I was a little girl. Father gave it to me when we all came here to the Gainsborough market one Eastertide. It was to buy ribbons for my hair. He pressed this very coin into my hand and told me to buy something pretty for myself. But when I opened my hand and saw the beautiful image of the Virgin Queen shining up from my palm, I could not part with it. And later, when Father asked me what I had bought with it and I replied 'nothing', he told that I should keep it.

We used the coin to buy three penny loaves for our travels, and for a mug of milk for Tom as we stopped to eat and discuss what scant options were now left open to us. We could not go back to Stowe, and Gainsborough held very little by way of us finding help now that my destructive 'reputation' had preceded me. No. I had to think of somewhere else to go. Somewhere far away enough not to have heard about my branding yet within walking distance. Above all else, it would have to be somewhere where our true identities would remain unknown while we nevertheless 'fitted in' with the community.

'I have it!' I exclaimed. 'I know where we can go. We can go home to my mother's.'

'But I thought that you said that your mother was dead?' said Hope.

'Yes, she is. But when she was alive your father gave me the money to allow me buy her cottage so she might have at least that as security in her old age. She is gone now, but the cottage is still there – and so we have the right to live in it. That is, if we say that James is still alive and in the New World. We could easily explain that he sent us back for the sake of our health and that of the child. That we are newly returned from Virginia and will live in the cottage until James has finished making his fortune and returns. Thus we can also explain away our present lowly state and lack of money. We could find work in the village and live off the fine vegetable gardens that come with the cottage.'

'A cottage? Oh! That sounds perfect...' Hope sighed with relief. 'How far is it?'

'Not far. Half a day's walk when I was sixteen.'

'Then we should easily make it by nightfall?'

'Yes, I believe we should.'

Lighter now in spirit and heart, we made our way out of the town and began the slow climb out of the Trent Valley and up along the Rasen Road. Two hours in and the broad bands of fluffy white clouds – that reminded me of elderflowers – all at once gave way to ragged sheets as black as the devil's nutting bag.

'Oh my! But look how beautiful the sky looks!' Hope exclaimed, pointing upwards towards brilliant beams of bright light, shafting down from behind the worrisome grey.

'Aye, 'tis the moon is milking the sun,' I said. 'And marking out a spot for the rain to fall.'

A cooling breeze sprang up from nowhere and the temperature rapidly dropped to chill. And then driving rain fell as heavily as hob-nails, turning the already rutted road slippery with pools of mud and water. To continue on our way, Hope and I hauled up our skirts and tied them up at our sides, as our hems soon became sodden and began to drag.

This was the same road, with many a winding turn, upon which I had made my way to Gainsborough Hall all those many years ago – when I was just a young woman in flight from the clutches of my evil step-father. Back then I was of an age when a walk such as this was as nothing and easily taken within my stride. Now though, trudging through the rain, both mentally and bodily exhausted from my ordeal, and with a tired young child, I knew that there was no way that we would reach my village before nightfall. We were wet and bedraggled, and with the light already beginning to fail as quickly as our strength, we desperately searched for a farm or a cottage where we might beg shelter for the night. But we could find none. Instead, we huddled together like lost sheep in the lee of a dry-stone wall. There, we ate bread and cheese and planned to attempt resting until morning.

Although the night turned a little chill, beneath the shelter of that wall and cradled in the arms of mother earth, we were not really cold. Propping myself up with my spine hard against the silvery stones for support, I grappled with my thoughts. While Hope and Tom slumbered restlessly in each others arms, way off in the fields the familiar yip-yap of foxes broke into the silence. And somewhere much closer, an owl began to whoo-hoo.

I watched the sky begin to clear and the crisp moon rise to shimmer up betwixt the blossomed bough of a hawthorn amid a bright blue hallow of light. Stars scattered off across the sky beyond the dark wolds and twinkling into infinity. Despite our circumstances, I could not help myself but to be dazzled by the infinite beauty of it all.

Then my mind returned to the previous day and the ravishing cruelness of my accuser. Also of those whom I had long considered friends, and yet who unlike friends had stood aside and watched me suffer such cruel indignities. While others, like the blacksmith with whom I had only shared passing pleasantries, had risked harm to themselves to come to my aid. To me that desertion by my friends was a blow smarter than any lash could inflict and more scarring than any blistering brand iron. Yet, I found comfort in the knowledge that the same had happened to many a past Separatist dissidents and even our blessed Christ himself.

'Twas then I heard it. I heard a blackbird sing. That first bird to defy the darkness that besets it upon all sides. He, that alone rises from out of the blackness to sing out, to shatter the stillness of the long lingering night to herald the yet to come dawn. How does he know, I have oftimes wondered. How doth that one solitary bird, alone on its perch in the darkness *know* that the time is come to defy the dark and instead begin to sing? To dare to awaken the world to a new possibility? How alone he sounds and yet how strongly he doth sing out? Is he not afeared that his enemies, crouched hidden in the shadows, hear him too and now know of his place and position? That the fox or the cat, now alerted will try to take him out? No, he sings out regardless of risk to himself for he knows his purpose. He knows that *he* is the one. He is the chosen one to sing in the new day. He knows that he may, at the outset, stand alone yet also that after, from out of that same oppression that tried to hold him silent, the song of another shall shortly join with him, followed by another, until a whole chorus, each of his own accord and melody shall join into one harmonious choir that hath the power and strength to awaken the whole world and set it rejoicing in new light.

If only I could have known then, that I should have held fast the knowledge that day must surely follow on after even the blackest night. That the wrong that wretched men do shall not be allowed to prevail over right. That a Christian's suffering shall never be for nought and that ultimately each good man shall do as he ought. That the wheel must turn and wrong put to right and that the beasts that choose to dwell amongst the shadows shall perish and die come the light. If only I had realised and held fast to that faith then mayhap my pathway through the coming hell's of my life might have been made all the easier for travelling...

*   *   *

Hope stretched and as she rubbed the sleepy dust from out of her eyes, yawned as wide as a cellar trap door.

'Be sure to cover your mouth when you yawn like that,' I gently scolded my child in jest. 'Else the devil will come up and for each tooth that he can count, he shall steal away a year from your life!'

'Oh, Mother! I have not heard that since I was a girl and Grandma were alive!' she laughed back. 'But I am too old now for old wives tales!'

'But ne'er too old to be setting a good example to the child!' I replied watching the unguarded gape of my young grandson waking beside her.

'Tom!' Hope warned him sharply.
With that the boy giggled wildly and quickly clasped his hand over his mouth but with a wide grin still yawning beneath. My, how we laughed!

We broke fast quickly and set off once more on our journey. The morning light smiled warmly upon us , quickly burning off a rising mist from out of the fields and beckoned us on into the bright prospect of a fine hot day.

'The village? Is it far now?' Hope asked as we started eastward upon our way. I looked about ,trying to get my bearings. So long – so long since I had last walked this road yet memories of it were not all completely faded.

'I think there is a well not much farther on. I remember stopping there once on my way to Gainsborough Hall. If so, then we cannot be far from Caenby and my village is but a short stride from there.'

I had been right. Soon we crossed over the old Roman road and from there on began passing through the familiar landscape of my youth. My heart quickened with anticipation as I later spied the grey stone tower of my old parish church rising up amongst the subsiding tree line. Once at its lichen covered churchyard walls, we stopped for a while to catch our breath after the long uphill climb along the top road. After so long a walk and being led tightly, Tom, despite his tiredness, was grateful for a few minutes play chasing butterflies through a rash of bright yellow buttercups. Meanwhile, my daughter and I meandered through the verdant churchyard until I came to that beloved spot where I had not been for so very long.

'This is where my father lies,' I said as I gently beckoned Hope to the unmarked grave.

'And your mother?' she asked.

'I do not know, Hope. I shall have to ask, once we are settled. Someone should be able to tell me for certain where she lies. But I expect that she is buried somewhere here about, along with Judd, as the row is newly continued and the ground still not yet fully settled.'

'So this Judd? He was her second husband?'

'No, Hope. Her third. My father died when I was still quite young and she married a man named... Nathan.' I could hardly bring myself to say his name.

'And what happened to him?' she asked.

'He... He was a bad man who then died badly,' was all I could summon up to say.

'And Judd?'

'He was an old friend of my real father...'

We gathered up our basket once more and headed downhill along the little lane and towards the beck. It ran high and wide after the recent rain, gurgling and swirling beneath our feet as we clattered across the rickety bridge to the orchard side. My old home was close by. The cottage that I had shared with my mother and father and later with *him*. I could not bear to look at it, nor even to point it out to Hope. The father I loved had raised me there but then Nathan had come and defiled my once happy home and filled it with dreadfully bad memories.

Instead, I made straight away up the other winding lane, past Long Acre field and towards Judd's old homestead at the far end of the village. This was his tied cottage that he had shared with my widowed mother, the little building which I had later persuaded Thomas to purchase. I knew the cottage well, though I had not seen it since I first left the village as a young woman.

Long after my evil stepfather Nathan had died, I had heard by chance that my mother had remarried, and I had greatly approved of the match. However, it was not until years later, when I first returned from the New World, that I came back to the village to try to remake my long shattered relationship with her. I had then come so close, to the village churchyard in fact, and with all good intention of seeing her, only to find that it was not in my craven heart to go through with it. Instead, after meeting by chance with my old friend, Humility, whose in-laws owned much of the land there abouts, I had managed to purchase the cottage so that in old age, the pair might at least have a secure roof over their heads.

Humility was a good woman who well understood the reason for my family rift, and so willingly informed my mother of the sale yet also agreed to keep up the false pretense that I was still far off in Virgina. Thus, I had carried out that which I had perceived to be my duty to my remaining parent, yet without the pain of an uneasy reunion. 'Twas something that I would grow to regret.

As we arrived at our longed for destination, my spirits suddenly crashed. Lord, what wicked tricks our memories use to colour our expectations! For in my thoughts I was taking my family back to some last vestige of my childhood, frozen in time as last I saw it. What cruelty!

The small holding of land, that went with the cottage, was surrounded by a thickly layered hedge which had helped keep the sheep out and off Judd's carefully tended vegetables. His patch of land was the envy of many in the village, along with the amount of good things that Judd was able to grow for himself and, deservingly so, on account of the sheer hard work he expended upon it. For after a hard day's labour in the fields, Judd would come home and take but a mouthful of supper before setting about tending his own land until the last of the light had faded and gone. Then, come dawn, he would be out there again feeding his foul and watering his seedlings before setting off to work. Not at all like my stepfather Nathan,who did not a hand's turn aiding my mother and me as we struggled upon our cottage plot. Consequently, his slothfulness led us to hunger the winter long.

However, instead of the vision of homeliness that I held inside my head from long ago, the reality was this - that which man doth not attend nature shall swiftly reclaim. Instead of neatly tended hedges and a well ordered plot, we were greeted by a thicket of unwieldy thorns and briar enclosing a sea of impenetrable waist-high grasses and weeds. Inwardly I cried. I cried with utter despair at our plight. What was I to do? How were we meant to live off this?

Yet, for the sake of Hope and my grandchild, I was unable to break down and weep aloud. Instead, I tried to make light of our situation and picked my way through the yard to the abandoned tool shed, where finding an old rusty sickle, I fetched it out and set about hacking out a pathway up to the cottage itself.

'When e'er a virgin piece of land here abouts is first broke in by the plough, do you know, young Bessie, what its first harvest be?' I remember my father once asking.

Puzzled I was, and did not know the answer. So I replied that I thought that it must be wheat or barley – because they were the most crop I saw in the fields.

'No lass, it's stone!' he laughed. 'As soon as you breach the top o' the soil, up it comes by the cartload!'

In fact there was so much limestone brought up this way that, when my father was a boy, the farmhands used to make a heap of it at the side of the field, free for the taking. Mind you, not that limestone ever lies idle for long, because it can be put to so many good uses.

Limestone is used all around my homeland of Lincolnshire. From stacking up to form dry walls for keeping in stock to using it to create pathways and boarders. Mostly though, it is a true gift for those who cannot afford the luxury of brick and is the main staple for building houses and simple cottages, like the one in which I grew up, with great thick double walls of mortared stones then in filled with rubble and dirt in betwixt.

My childhood home had been a humble stone-built cottage, very much like that I was trying hard to reach. It was just as well that it was built of stone, for had it been made of mud and stud, or of timber, wattle and daub, like most in Gainsborough, then it would have rotted back into the ground for standing so long empty and idle. But apart from being dirty and dusty, and the odd place where the thatch looked rotten, this simple building seemed perfectly sound and mayhap well able to last for even a further fifty years or beyond.

Once I had cut down a passage through to the house, I pushed hard to open the door but it would not budge. It was warped shut and so Hope and I had to persuade it to give with our shoulders pressed hard against it. Once inside the air was stale and a haze of thick dust, kicked up by our forced entry danced in the shaft of bright sunlight now creeping in across the threshold and peering into the darkened recesses. The low beamed ceiling was strung with dirty cobwebs as big as my hand. On seeing those, Tom suddenly clung to his mother at the doorway and refused, steadfastly, to set foot inside.

'Take me home, Mam-may!' he began to wail. 'Mam-may! I want to go home!'

Hope, by then close to tears herself, was telling Tom to hush, for all was going to be alright and that she and Gran'mam would soon sweep them all away and make this cottage cosy and clean. Yet, as Hope threw open the shuttered windows, I looked about me not knowing where or how to begin to turn this hovel into a home.

An old besom[4] stood propped beside the door so I took it and began sweeping out the ground floor room. While I did so, I sent Tom off with his mother to collect some wood for a fire. It would take the child's mind off his fear of the spiders that might be lurking within, and would also provide me with precious time to try to make the old place look a little more inviting to his tender eyes.

As I began in earnest to work my way through the cottage trying to clean, a strange sadness overcame me as I looked about more closely at the scattering of belongings still lying where they were last left by the former occupants. A lone chair stood out from the table, the partner to it being tightly drawn up neatly underneath and out of use. One bowl, one spoon, one beaker, still set out on the table top in anticipation, perhaps, of one last meal that was never to be. A black pot, now bloomed with orange flowers of rust stood empty over a long dead fire of fine grey ash. A rush light, set in a holder on the mantle above, still waited to light someone's way up to bed. As I stood in wordless regret, I began to wonder, who was it who had last sat waiting alone in this cottage. Waiting for the final dark to fall or the day that was not to come? Was it my mother, widowed once more and in solitary sadness without gentle Judd. Or, was it he, grieving over the loss of her? I felt a lump in my throat and great sorrow, for I knew then that I should have come back here long ago. I should not have been a coward, but come home and made my peace with my mother while I still could. I should have brought her only grandson to make her acquaintance and maybe offered some shred of comfort in her dying days, instead of pretending that I was still an ocean away in the New World. Had she called to me in wishful sighs in those last hours on earth? Regretted our parting on such bad terms? How could I, after becoming a mother, in turn have not then a care for she who had given me life? Why had I instead given in and served only my own selfishness?

Chapter Five

Thunder growled across the night sky like the low snarl of the devil's cat as lightening cracked open the black of night with flashes of brilliance. All about and above the sky beast prowled. Sometimes with a low purr in the distance, at others with a deep rumble that sent shudders trembling down the spine of the old roof of this house. I could feel the tension of the storm growing. A stray dog across the way barked out in terror as the flashes of lighting grew steadily more. I looked across the room. Thankfully Hope was deep asleep from exhaustion with little Tom equally soundly a-slumber in her curve. That first night, up in the one tiny bedroom, the atmosphere was barely breathable in the growing, oppressive heat as we lay baking like loaves in an oven. The shutters on both sides of the cottage were wide open to the sky yet the room remained airless in the stifling stillness. It put me in mind of that August I had spent in Jamestown. I had not thought about the heat and humidity there in years. The recollection of that made this unusually hot weather that we were experiencing now, somehow cool a little. Lincolnshire could never compare with the hell-hot summer that I suffered through in Virginia.

Suddenly, I felt the stirring of breeze flutter through the rough sack-cloth curtain as thunder shuddered ever closer. All at once, the air freshened and I could hear the pad of heavy rain drops start falling against the roof. Swiftly, they quickened into a steady and welcomed patter as thunder crashed more loudly now and lightening lashed out angrily at the night. Within moments, the patter gave way to a loud, frenzied drumming as galloping hooves of rain clipped across the roof and went gushing down in a torrent from the eves like a waterfall, thudding onto the parched ground outside.

I could not hope now to find sleep again. All I did was to lie with the slip-slopping of thoughts in my head feeling as demented as the poor tortured creature now scratching furiously at the door downstairs to get in. It was probably not any person's dog, just a stray that I had fed a few mouldy scraps of cheese rind the previous evening, food that even I could not bring myself to eat. I could hear it yapping and terrified, yet I was resolved against my better nature that wanted to get up and to let it in. That would be folly, I coldly reasoned. If I were to trip on the ladder coming down and break my neck, what use would I be to my daughter and precious grandchild then? No, I told myself, the dog would have to fend for itself just as we would have to. For once in my life I was determined to put my own needs and those of mine above anything else. Yet, its continued cries haunted me. For were we not all but frightened creatures howling in the dark?

It was then that the cursed slow drip... drip... of water worked its way through the rotting thatch just inches from my head. As I slid an old chamber pot under it, I cursed my dead husband. I cursed him that we had been forced to come to this. By now the steady stream of rain outside was splattering in through the window too. I rose and reached out to try to pull the shutters back in and shut, but was taken aback by the furious rain slapping in against my face. It felt strangely exhilarating as I breathed in the now cool-charged air and felt the tingling thrill of cold fingers of wet begin to caress my body. I suddenly felt good. Even fearless. Just as I had in my younger years. It was that moment that made up my mind. I had decided. I had decided then that we were going to survive all of this. I was adamant that we would come through... no matter what may stand in our way. I was not going to give into life so easily again. I would fight back at whatever life threw at me from then on. I'd fight back with every sinew in my body whatever came our way.

'That's my girl!' I could almost hear my father's words speaking out loud above the rain. 'You are a fighter, my lass. A born fighter. You show 'em what you are made of!'

My father was dead. Long dead but it never stopped

him from coming to me from across death's veil to bring comfort in my times of need. Not like my husband, Thomas. He was dead too but he never came to comfort me. He had deserted me. He had left me to fend for myself like that poor bitch out in the storm. The anger inside me towards Thomas was still raw. Something strange had happened to me since Stowe. Instead of the deep grief I had suffered after his death, something else inside me had began to propagate. Something nasty and previously hidden had begun worming its way out like a maggot from a seemingly sound apple. It was resentment and anger. I had began, instead of continuing to mourn for my late husband, to resent him instead. Not just for dying when he had, but for keeping so many things secret from me over the years. Like the full extent of his spying activities on behalf of the old King James while we were in Virginia, and the gravity of which I had not appreciated at the time. Nor had I grasped the true role of his espionage for James' son and successor, King Charles, and for the Royalist Army during the Civil War. To be an honest soldier is one thing, but to be a spy? Spying, by its very nature, demands deceit. So it was that my anger grew as I began to wonder what other deceits Thomas might have played upon me. Then I thought about my trial and Rech holding my journal in his grubby hands. If it had found its way to London, as Rech had claimed, by Thomas' doing then it must have been Thomas who had taken it from my possession in the first place as we sailed upon the Delver to Jamestown. I had asked for it then... when it appeared to be missing. Thomas had claimed not to have seen it. He had lied. He had lied straight-faced to me while all along he had it in his possession. He must have intended to use it for the King's own purpose and to further his career even as I lay ill and possibly dying in delirium. How could he have been so callous? Having just been reunited with his lost wife in one moment, how could he then lie and steal from her the next? What else might he have kept from me? However I realised then, as I have had to accept since, that I might never fully find out. If only Thomas could have come to me then. I would have slapped him hard on the face... if only I could remember his face. Instead ,whenever I tried to picture him, the only image that would come into my mind was of the red mist exploding from out of the back of his head as he was shot dead.

I have said before that to lose a husband is hard enough, but to lose a child is quite another heartache. For then, a part of your own body is truly dead. A part of your flesh, your blood, your very substance, has been rent from out of you. And yet, you are supposed to go on... I had witnessed Thomas die, sat in vigil by his body all night, and in the morning watched his coffin being lowered into the ground and covered. But James? How I was tortured by the fact that I did not know how he had died or come to that, even when or where. I kept thinking, if only I had been with with him as he died, held him close in my arms, one last time, and whispered him my love to see him on his way. At least maybe then I would have had some sort of peace of mind. Without a body to grieve over or a graveside to visit, how can one let go?

When I had last seen my son, I had fully expected him to return home again. Had I known then what was going to happen, I would have clung to him and begged him to stay with us at Stowe, at least until that wretched war was over. If he had, then I could have had so many more years with him. He and Hope and I could have shared so much happiness in watching young Tom growing up.

He had always been such a studious lad, and had already entered into his final year at Oxford when the King and his army made camp there for the winter. Although my husband had been a staunch Royalist, up until then our son had always refused to support either side. 'Twas only when I had sent our man Ned down to Oxford to collect James come the following spring that I was to learn the awful truth – that he had followed on after his father in order to catch up with the Royalist Army that had already headed off towards that fateful battle at Naseby. Perhaps, if James had not chanced to meet with his father at Oxford, then he may not have taken that eleventh-hour decision to join the Royalist cause. Maybe he would still be alive. Maybe Thomas would have played out his final days in peace instead of being tormented as he blamed himself for the loss of our only son. If only I knew what had passed between them – as Thomas persuaded our son to his side – maybe my husband and I would have parted on happier terms.

Within months of the battle of Naseby I had come to accept that James had died there. If he had been alive and well, then surely he would have made contact with us in some way. Hope, however, grimly clung on to her faith that James would return to her. She even took to wearing a sprig of willow set fresh in her cap each day just as I had done that very first time Thomas had gone away from me to Holland. For James was not only the nearest thing she had known to a brother, but he had also been her husband and lover and the father of my only grandchild. Selfishly, perhaps I often failed to acknowledge the full depth of her own loss as I wallowed in mine.

*   *   *

We had arrived too late in the season to hope to have sewn much of a crop on our holding. However, I know not whether by luck or by provenance, when I took off my pockets to be washed, I found a few seeds caught up in the seams from when I had sewn my 'three sisters' bed back in my garden at Stowe. I smiled, for there was just enough to start over with a similar garden here and still just enough time to do it.

At the back of the cottage lay a small south facing strip that would normally get too hot in the height of summer to grow much but would be perfect for my New World planting. So Hope and I set to quickly breaking up the earth to make a small bed – about six feet long and four of five feet wide. We dug it over as deeply as we could and mixed in whatever old muck we could find rotted down on the floor of the old empty chicken house.

I knew I had not enough wayward seeds in my pocket to grow a large crop this year, yet it was a start. I could grow enough to provide us with at least a little something this season. But more importantly, with care, I would be able to produce more than enough seed to sew a much greater quantity the following year.

Our meagre store of cheese and bread was soon used, and so Hope bought some flour with the rest of her money and then went about the village finding odd work to do in order to earn some more. It must have been hard for her after the relative life of ease into which she had grown, but to her enduring credit she never complained, even though her tasks were often menial and dirty.

As for clearing the rest of our smallholding, that would prove to be work of Herculean dimension. While Hope worked abroad, I toiled like a creature possessed through those impossibly long days of June. I worked from afore five in the morning and the coming of broad daylight on until after sundown, when the cast of deep shadow crept over the plot. On a rain-free day, some sixteen hours of back-breaking toil I would work, stooped low and long to pull up the ever creeping runners of nettles and bind weed. Or else I would be bent over and stabbing around in the earth as I brought up the long thick tap-roots of docks that had grown as bushy as cabbages and infested the whole of our patch. Yet, once this tangled mat of wayward nature's growth had begun to yield to the scythe, beneath it lay such rich dark soil as would give way to my spade like pudding to a spoon. Here and there, I still came across the odd seln[5]-sewn carrots, small reminders of the days when Judd Lowe kept these vegetable beds in immaculate order. I pulled those up and gave them to Tom to collect for the pot along with any other edible root or leaf I could find. Even nettles made a nourishing steep to revive and refresh.

Then, with a day done and weary, I would trudge indoors with my back and joints so sore that I could scarce straighten up. At last, grateful for some respite,

I would drop like a stone, exhausted, into my bed. My hips and knees feeling as if they were on fire and the knuckles of my fingers smarting and tingling from the countless stings of nettles. I would lie wanting nothing else than to be able to sleep forever. But all too soon I would awake again to the raucous chirrup of fledglings nestled in the eves of our roof as their parents set to work at first light to gather food for their brood.

Despite these being the longest days of the year, there was so little time in which to tame the land and grow on or gather in as much wild foodstuff as I could before winter set in. I knew then that, no matter how early I arose and set to work or how late into the night I eventually left off, there was no earthly way in which we were going to be able to find enough food that summer to sustain us through the coming hard winter. But I kept my own council about the urgency with which I carried out these tasks, because I did not want to worry Hope. She was busy doing her best for young Tom and naively believing that I, her sole remaining parent, had the solutions to satisfying our needs at my fingertips. Like those fledgling birds trusting blindly in their parents to provide for their survival, Hope had always put her trust in me. And I? I would wake restlessly early each day with worry heavy upon my mind – trying desperately to contrive new ideas, and to work out the best methods for saving and conserving what little we had, and to procure new and free food sources.

Hope helped out by my side as much as she could, but this was limited by her own day of labour – by necessity much about her duty to her child. He was still so very young and had much need of his mother. Besides which, although I knew what I was about when it came to tending our land, Hope had so much to learn. Therefore mostly the task fell to me.

In my youth, I was certain that I could do all that was needed within a week or so. Yet, in my mid-life, my strength was not as it had used to be. So even after three weeks in the cottage, only about half the patch was cleared and dug over. July is no time to be sewing main crops. All I could achieve would be a head start on the following spring, when it would be time. Meanwhile, who could predict what state of body we would be in by then? I told Hope that my doing all that work was so that we would raise a better and earlier crop in the next season. But what I really wanted to say to her was that I best did as much as I could on our land now because we knew not what the winter might bring. Come spring time we could be all be laid low by fever, or if the winter was harsh, then mayhap we would we too weak through hunger to work the land at all. If we could not grow a crop then, we might as well give up and die.

'What we need now is a strong young gardener to finish off the rest!' Hope said in jest. But suddenly I realised in the moment when her words left her lips that we might get one at no financial cost...

I went to the nearest farm and asked the 'pig man' there if he had a runt that he needed caring for. As good fortune would have it, he was able to say that he had one and offered to sell it to me. However, I had no way of affording it. So, instead, we struck up a deal. I was to take the withering creature with me and put in my time and effort into raising it up into a great, fat boar. In return, come slaughter time, the pig man promised me a share of the meat.

To begin with I had to laboriously hand feed the piglet – with a swill made of cooked roots and leaves – and kept it warm by our fireside. Quickly it grew, so that within weeks I could pen the hungry creature in upon the un-worked part of our garden. There it turned over the earth with its snout as it searched out all of the tasty docks, weeds and brambles to eat, and so soon fattened up nicely on the proceeds. I could then expend my efforts upon tending my precious three sister's bed and make the most of the wild foods in the hedges and in the woods.

The Indian corn in my three sister's bed had grown tall by August, and we also had a fine crop of beans. Hope excitedly showed Tom how much we were growing with wide-eyed optimism whereas I instead looked on... I saw not a vast quantity of what we were growing but – with increasing anxiety – the shortage we were bound to face over the coming winter. I saw not thirty or forty fat cobs of corn but how many meals we might realistically expect to make of them.

From the first real bite of winter that would surely come by around *All Hallows* and until the passing of *Lady Day* and the coming of spring, I would need to find at least one-hundred-and-fifty main meals, which perhaps would turn out to be the *only* meal of each day that we could expect. I would need at least three hundred heads of corn if we were to have even starvation rations.

The same went for every other commodity that we had at our disposal. Most of what we could expect to find wild aplenty come autumn would not long store. How was I to confide in my daughter all of my feelings of desperation at our plight while she sat dandling her precious child from her lap and laughing in the warm summer sun? All the while I knew that she was still deeply grieving for her father, husband, and the comfortable life so recently torn from us. How could I then take what little warmth remained in her life away with my stark thoughts just now, when the last of the summer was all she and the child had left? What profit could be had by casting her soul too early into the shadow of the misery of winter of want on such a summer's day as that? No, she needed this time, this fool's season to sustain her and Tom's spirits for as long as possible. However, I did take pains to impress upon her how mindful we should be about making waste, and how we should show caution in dwindling away our storable assets too soon. I also mentioned how we should concentrate upon the importance of seeing to it that she and Tom made good use of every bit of available seasonal food that we could find. I explained that we should be like the wildlife all about us, frantically feeding amongst the hedgerows and gorging ourselves while we could on what would otherwise wither and go to waste. We too needed to fatten up our bodies against the winter ahead.

Come harvest time, all three of us set off to the fields to help bring in the crops. Hope and I took turns of carrying Tom upon our backs as we hacked our way through the golden stand of corn with our scythes, reaping alongside the other men, women and children of the village. Together we sang Lincolnshire songs walking after the heavily laden carts towards the master's barns, and afterwards to collect our ration of bread and cheese and some pennies in return. Come harvest home we joined in with the others, weaving corn dollies and dancing at the village supper, making merry awhile before the chill set into our days and bones and began to confine us to our cottages during the ever shortening days.

By this time, Hope was beginning to realize our true situation.

'Do not fret. I was brought up on this land,' I tried to reassure her. 'If anyone can get us through this winter, I am certain it is I. I may have been a maidservant for many a year and thereafter a gentleman's wife but I tell you, you never forget your roots! Which is just as well? For in times of need you can always go back to your roots in order to survive.'

'Survive? Will it come down to a matter of survival?' she asked.

'Yes Hope,' I replied as my motherly smile gave way with a sigh to frankness. 'I very much fear that it may.'

Chapter Six

With the harvest safely gathered in, there would be little work for Hope and me from now until spring. With not much else than a store of some three sacks of flour and one smaller filled with a mixture of turnips and carrots, I wondered how we were going to feed ourselves until then.

'My people die from sickness – seldom from hunger', Squanto had once said to me, as we stooped together planting Indian corn at the Plymouth settlement. 'Your people?' he chuckled with more than a note of superiority in his tone. 'You Englishmen, you would starve to death through ignorance! You have no vision. You cannot see the food set all about you!'

Those wise words hit me now like a Powhatan arrow. Squanto had been right, of course he had. It was not we settlers' lack of provisions from our homeland that caused our hunger initially, but our lack of knowledge of the abundance of natural food that lay all about us ready for the taking. And that was it! That was the key to our present predicament. Hope and I must gather in as much wild food as could in order to survive.

We had already scoured the September hedgerows for blackberries and ate them to our hearts' delight, until our stomachs were sick and the devil had spat on those that remained and turned them rotten. We had also gathered in baskets full of bright red rose hips which I had set, along with assorted bunches of herbs, to dry hung about the hearth.

Then, walking out one morning , we met a swine herd in the lane driving his pigs down towards the woods. Young Tom had laughed with such glee to see the pigs trotting along with their curly tails held high in the air, excitedly squealing and grunting their way along our lane.

'Where are the piggies going, Gran'mam?' he had asked.

'Acorns!' I remember suddenly exclaiming aloud. 'Quickly Hope! We must run home and get all of the sacks we can from the outbuilding!'

'What for?' she asked looking rather bemused.

'For the acorns, of course! Those pigs are ready for their final fattening up. The herder is going to set them loose to forage amongst the woods for acorns. We must get the sacks and go gather up as many as we can before they eat them all!'

'Acorns?' her eyes flashed as if I had taken leave of my senses. 'But what are we going to do with acorns?'

'Eat them Hope! We are going to eat them!'

'Eat them? But they're awful!'

'Not if we prepare them properly. Trust me. When I lived in the New World, we often had to supplement our flour stocks with ground acorns. I know of a well tried way to take away all of that bitter taste and I will show you how.'

The next few days we spent scavenging in the woods, just a few yards ahead of the pigs as they snuffled amongst the undergrowth. In that time, we were determined to gather in as many sacks of acorns as we were able. At first Tom eagerly helped, joining in with this strange new game – thrashing through the woodland floor with the pigs. They were quite sweet natured creatures, despite their great girth and furious snorting which was occasionally intermixed with bouts of excited squealing and boisterous nudging, a gentle sort of in fighting amongst the herd to assert their pecking order. These swine would root around in the fallen leaves in a frenzy of feeding, and then lay flat out on their sides and flatulent with their huge bellies bulging while snoring so loudly as to bring on a fit of the giggles amongst we hapless humans looking on.

Collecting acorns for our food stocks was laborious and tedious work, with our having to stoop low to gather them up. Naturally, our young boy soon grew bored with it. So, to lighten all of our spirits, we sang songs to Tom and made a game of it all – just for him. Then, once done, we struggled along with the sacks thrown across our aching backs, trudging our weary way homeward, utterly exhausted.

Preparing the acorns was an even more arduous job, but one befitting the dank wet days that soon followed when not much else could be profited from going outside. First the acorns had to be shelled. It was a fiddly, time consuming task although easily done with the aid of a good flat stone and another with which to crack them open. Then, when we had the first batch shelled, we gathered the acorn meats and slid them into a pot of boiling water set above a lively fire. As they boiled away, the water soon discoloured to a murky dark brown as the tannin began to leached away into it. After about a quarter of an hour, with sleeves rolled up, Hope got down the slotted iron ladle from its hook above the mantle and started to fish out the par cooked pieces – to carefully transfer them to another pot of already boiling water.

'The water must be boiling, Hope' I was at pains to point out. 'For if these meats are now taken and and put in too cool a water, the remaining bitterness shall be locked inside instead of continuing to diminish.'

'It is alright, mother,' she chided .'You told me already! And my pot *is* boiling away!'

Satisfied, I meanwhile quickly took up the brackish liquor from this first boiling and poured it into a readied barrel, for this too would be pressed to good use in time. This tannin water has about it a great antiseptic quality when used on wounds and is a marvel for laundering clothes clean and fresh smelling, though it tends to turn our whites oft to beige.

I refiled the pot and set it once more to boil, ready for the process to be repeated. In all, we did this three times until the cooking liquor remained almost clear. Then we drained the meats and set them on a tray to dry by the fire, making them easier to store before grinding them down into a very corse flour for our needs. It was an uplifting experience to see our sacks for bread increase after mixing in our acorn meal with the remaining wheat flour.

*   *   *

The nights drew in so quickly as autumn dwindled into winter. Soon it was dark by four of the clock and not fully light again until almost eight in the morning. For the want of candles we were forced to go into our beds early, for there was little enough light by the fire alone to do any chores in the evening, let alone to sit and sew nor to even read our Bible together.

'If only we had some meat fat!' I often bemoaned to Hope as we lay abed in the dark, waiting for sleep to come and claim us. 'With but a little melted tallow we could make some more rush lights by which to see.'
We had no tallow because we had no meat, and without any more money they were both destined to remain equally in short supply.

Despite common knowledge that I was born and raised in this village, I had been away from it for so long that I and mine, I am certain, we were being treated no differently than 'incomers', and therefore least favoured than most amongst my neighbours. In the forty years or more since I had gone away, all of the old ones that had known my parents,or had been born and raised there in my own time even, were mostly now passed over. Then I had arrived back, unannounced and with speech and manners accrued way above my expected station, 'twas no wonder that the other villagers treated me with some suspicion and mayhap even contempt. Perhaps some even thought that I had deserved being brought down a peg or two for daring to assume airs and graces for which I had not been born. Besides which, none could possibly have known that I had also been, until lately, a titled lady in my own right. All for the better, especially as I had to be careful then to maintain the identity of a widow to a lowly Virginian colonist, only recently returned while her son remained to work off the family debt. If they had suspected me of being a lady, then they might have heard about the downfall of one of Stowe and guess my true identity. So it was that I played down my gentility as much as I could in their company and advised Hope to do much the same.

I would not say that, at first, our fellow villagers

went as far as cheating us, but more that they sorely under served us in our early dealings. Take the pig man for one. After months of us fattening up his boar runt for him, he then met our diligent care of the beast with but two racks of ribs, two trotters, some more-fat-than-belly meat, and offal. That was not at all in the spirit of our initial bargain. I had justly supposed for much more. That I might have had some decent meat to smoke and to tide us through more of the winter. However, being the nature of it, most of that we were given had to be consumed almost as soon as we had received it, though I did smoke some of the belly. We also chopped some of it together with the offal which we did make into haslet[6] to last a little longer. Yet even the caul in which to boil these, we had to shame out of the wretched fellow.

'At least you have got plenty of tallow now,' Hope tried to cheer.

Yes, at least we had tallow to make into rush lights to brighten up the long drawn out drear of those endless winter nights. Yet spring was still so far off in the future and I feared that our food stocks were dwindling too fast.

Soup made with pig nuts, wild roots and nettles, consumed with cakes of acorn bread or roasted hazelnuts patties, though monotonous, at least sustained our bodies from starving. But such did not prevent our thoughts from wandering back to heartier meals from the not too distant past. This diet was harder on Hope than on me, or even on young Tom come to that. For I had known hunger so often in my past, but Hope had never hungered. I had always been able to provide for her. She, at first, heaved at even the thought of some of the things that we later came to eat, where as Tom was too young to know any different and would eat almost anything set before him without question.

Gathering fuel was also a constant challenge after we had used up all that had come to hand around the homestead. We had no store of seasoned logs and green wood was almost useless for fires. So instead we were forced to go out and to gather dead wood wherever it might lie. In the woods, amongst the hedgerows, equipped with no more than keen eyes and a small hand axe, we sought out suitable branches and gathered them up into a great willow pannier that Hope and I took in turns to carry upon our backs and home again. Each day we could, when the weather was fair, we went out foraging thus for any fuel or food that came our way. But as winter wore on we could do this less and less, while the need for both grew ever more crucial as bad weather began to set in. Without a strong man to fend for our family, life was becoming one desperate challenge after another.

Despite my best efforts to scavenge food from the wild, maintaining ourselves for many weeks upon a diet of little more than plant stuff and roots, we grew pale and thinner as the winter pressed on and a strange listlessness set in. I knew what we needed. As desperately as warmth, we needed more meat. Yet we had none and no prospect of getting any.

'Man needs flesh or the blood grows weak,' Squanto had also said after planting up our beds. 'The three sisters are good to us but a body cannot stay strong through them alone. That is why we hunt.'

With the pig meat long gone, I knew it was true. I could feel my own blood growing weak. I knew that we needed meat. But where was I to find it?

I remembered Mad Jack, seated with his three-legged dog beside the gates of Jamestown telling tales of past woe. He had arrived with the third supply back in the late summer of sixteen-hundred-and-nine. Eight ships had come in out of a fleet of nine, bringing new colonists and supplies. The flag ship, the Sea Venture, was missing at the time, believed lost in a great storm off the Summer Isles. I had already known of this from my time in Plimouth. For my friend, Stephen Hopkins, had been aboard the Sea Venture and marooned with the crew for almost a year. Yet he had not told me what had happened to the colony before he could rejoin it.

Jamestown had stood at some two-hundred-and-fifty or more strong at that time. Yet with this third supply the number of colonists had suddenly doubled. It had been hard enough for the town to feed itself up until then, but all the more so since the last few months, because the spring and summer that year had been so extraordinarily hot and with little rain to speak of. It had been so dry that season that even the natives' crops had failed to thrive. So, come autumn, the forest scrub all about quickly became hunted out. And as supplies both stored and natural dwindled to nothing, starvation arose to engulf Powhatan and English alike.

During the course of that winter to follow, desperate men took desperate measures to survive. The few horses were quickly slaughtered for meat. Then dogs and even rats were killed for their flesh... though there were not enough of these to satisfy demand. God forgive, after that some even turned to eating the corpses of their fellow dead in order to survive. Though Mad Jack had lived through this wretched time, he almost reveled in telling my husband and me of the grisly details of one man caught with the corpse of his wife – smoked like a ham and hidden up in their chimney. He had been quietly feasting upon slices of her body. The man was then executed for what he had done. By the following spring, of the five to six-hundred colonists of the autumn before, only around sixty souls had survived to speak of the horrors.

Mad Jack tales stayed with me. Having been in close company with hunger so often in my life, I had been naturally disgusted by such extremes. But at the same time, I understood the desperation that must have driven the man who had been executed to such deeds. For I then found myself teetering on the brink of similar desperation to survive. Now we were becoming so wanting for meat that I nightly prayed that the stray dog from earlier would wander by our cottage so that I might quietly slit its throat and dress its scrawny carcass for our table. Or mayhap I could lie in wait for a rat – and then club it to death for the pot. Our situation had fast exceeded the point of desperation.

'Twas not pride that had stopped me from

begging at my neighbours' doors but want, even amongst themselves. The whole village was short of food that winter and cut off from the town for many weeks at a time by snow. The harvest had been poor and so there was little spare for barter, let alone for charity. For we were, in truth, two widows and a fatherless child without any kin for support. It made us all the more vulnerable at a time when everyone was vulnerable. Yet, even so, I recall winter often being like this in our village when I was growing up. While those at the big house had cattle, pigs and fowl to help see them through the winter, we peasants who worked their farms depended greatly upon what we could grow on our tiny plots to help supplement the meagre reward of our great labour upon their behalf. At Christmastide the village feasted and expected our masters to gift us meat, which they did as their duty. Yet, with duty done from January until the springtime blossomed, we were expected to fend for ourselves. Most years, many on the land died from a myriad of illness that could most likely have been overcome if not for underlying starvation. This was just another year.

*   *   *

With cold fingers and stiff limbs, that is how I remember waking that particular morning. I was freezing cold. So very cold! And my body would not obey me when I pleaded with it to arise. It was as if I had been drugged, yet I knew that somehow I must arise. I had to rise or die. But the cold held me under my inadequate covers in its vice-like grip, whispering quietly to me stay in bed... 'For what warmth has the world out there to offer? Stay... stay here. Bide 'neath the blanket and then surrender yourself into that long, grateful, peaceful sleep.'

Starvation by its very nature is a long drawn out suffering – but one that can be reversed in a very short time of plenty. Cold, though, is a more immediate killer. It can creep up on a body. I had learnt that from my time in Virginia. I had heard of fit young men being lost in a whiteout, and then sitting down in the snow and simply giving in to death – though they had been but a few hundred yards from safety. Some, having barely survived such a fate described how, with cold, the increasing desire to fall asleep and give in to death was so bewitching as to be almost irresistible.

Barely with the strength to turn my head, I looked across the room and saw Hope huddled on her mattress with young Tom pressed close in to her. Her face was deathly pale yet with a faint haze of her breath still visible in the bitter atmosphere of our dire condition. I knew then that I had to get up. I had to get up and light a fire or we would all freeze to death.

I struggled down the steps to our one room below and went to the wood basket. It was almost empty. I quickly lit a fire with what I had and, knowing that it would not last long, made ready to go out alone to scavenge for more. Then, with not much more than a beaker full of hot water infused with rose hips inside me, and rags tied about my feet and legs for added warmth, I hauled the empty wood pannier upon my back, picked up my walking staff and made off to search for fuel.

In the shivering sun, the sky shimmered like polished pewter, and within moments came snow, slipping through the bare black branches of the sycamores and dusting the earth below like flour upon the table top of those glorious bake-days of the now distant past. How I longed for even a little of that wasted flour! Oh, to scoop it up and bake into a batch of biscuits for Tom!

With each new day that winter, I had already walked further and further afield – from hedgerow to spinney, from spinney to copse – hunting for twigs and branches to fuel our fire. That morning though, I knew much more depended upon my efforts than ever before. I knew that so long as I could find enough to keep my family warm, I could keep them alive just a little longer. I could have done with help but also realised that young Tom was too weak to walk any distance and could neither be left alone in the cold nor alone with a lighted fire. Far better, I reasoned that he stay inside the cottage with his mother so that they might conserve what little strength they had.

I ate whatever I could find on my way and I can tell you that was precious little. For the frost had long since cut down and blackened even the nettles and any other lush green growth. I chewed the odd shrivelled hawthorn berry that I spied lingering in the hedgerows to get what little goodness I might before spitting out the bitter pips. Was I reduced to this? Competing with the birds for a last few rotten berries? I even gathered a few in my apron pocket, storing them along with fresh pine needles to take home to infuse with hot water for the others. The brew would help warm hungry innards and dull the pain of an empty stomach.

I came across a little wooded area well on the way to Norton, the next village from where we lived. It seemed to offer promising pickings, so I ventured off the rutted lane and made my way in searching through the ivy tangle trunks of the otherwise bare oaks, elms and ashes for dead wood that I could easily harvest. There was little of such wood to be had, but plenty of elder that even I could easily snap into kindling. I hesitated before touching it at first, for they do say about those parts that the devil is in elder wood. I was desperate though! So I cast aside the superstition, set my pannier down upon the ground, and gratefully proceeded to gather in as much as I could. It was then, while stooping, that I suddenly spied a fat rabbit crouched high up on a ridge amongst the heavily frosted tufts of grass just poking through from a carpet of frosted, brown leaves. Its back was toward me and it appeared unaware of my presence. So as its quick, white breath, panted quietly out into the still and cold air, I slowly began to creep towards it. Though I never really expected that I might actually catch the creature, desperation saw me forward.

Incredibly, I was so very close... I suddenly sprang upon it! And then I was astonished to discover that the rabbit was already trapped fast in a snare. Quickly, I grabbed its neck and snapped it, then struggled to wrestle its entrapped body free. Yet barely had I when a voice boomed up at me from down in a hollow on the other side.

'I do so hopes that you are not thinking of stealing that thar rabbet from my trap?'
A rough-and-ready looking man, dressed in a sheepskin jerkin glared up at me. As he stood poised lightly upon a crutch, I could not help but notice that from below his right knee the rest of his limb was missing. I also quickly sensed that this fellow harboured not real anger towards me, but rather more a reluctance to be bothered by the nuisance that I could become if I turned and ran away. Nonetheless, this unexpected confrontation rendered me into feeling like a common thief caught red-handed mid-crime.

'No sir,' I replied with a start. Though in all truth it had been my intention to take it. To make the point, I immediately held up the creature by its hind leg and proffered it to the fast approaching fellow. He snatched it from me and holding it high himself, inspected it closely.

'Tis a fine one this, alright! he remarked with great satisfaction. And no doubt, after quickly gauging the level of loss in my eyes, he added, 'Nice and meaty too! Pity. You look like you could have used a rabbit, mind. Could you?' he asked, letting the creature hang, enticingly from his hand.

'Yes sir, I could,' I answered honestly.

'Then maybe I could trade you for it.'

'I am sorry, but I have nothing to trade,' I told him.

'I dunno about that,' he replied with a broad grin. 'I am certain that you must have something about you that I could use.'

'The wood? But you could easily pick up your own?'

'Not the wood,' he said. 'A woman of your experience and years should *know* what it is that I could use.'
Suddenly I realised. He wanted carnal knowledge of me.

'Are you mad? I must have above twenty years on you?'

'Durzn't bother me,' he said coolly. 'Least it means you won't be catching with a child.'

I should have been horrified by his proposition but in truthfulness, at that moment, I was not. I could still feel the weight of that rabbit meat in my hand and the thought of taking it home with me was overpowering.

'What of your wife?' I asked, not wishing to add adultery into the equation.

He grinned, and pointing down at his missing limb said: 'There may be no shortage of women 'ere abouts but them that be single and are wanting of a man, wants a whole one! Besides, I just about keeps myseln these days since...'

He did not need to finish. I already knew by 'since' that he must have meant the loss of his leg to the war yet he showed no sign of self pity over it. On the contrary, he seemed a most pleasant and cheerful fellow.

'Well?' he persisted. What is it going to be? Yes or no?'

I could see in his eye and hear from the tremble in his voice that this man bore a great need and with a lusty desire that craved to be sated in order to be at peace with himself. For myself, desires of the body lay cold and sheathed in the earth. Love or lust beckoned me not, nor would I ever let it again. My only desire for flesh now lay in this man's hands. Without hesitation I nodded to him that I agreed. With that he laid out the rabbit carcass upon the ground and beckoned me to come down to join him in the hollow.   As I did, he reached out his strong arm to help guide me down to where he stood beside a slender sycamore tree.

'There,' he urged gently, already loosening his breeches, 'turn about if you please and grab a hold of that tree. It the only way I shall manage these days.'

I did as he bade. I bent forward and embraced the smooth young trunk like a lover in my arms, then leaned in with my shoulder to press hard up against it for support. He was quickly in position behind me, pulling up my skirts and clinging to me for support as he briskly made mount and went about his pleasure.

'I am not hurting you, am I?' he gasped between breath.

'No', I replied.'You are not.'

In fact, I felt nothing. It was as if he were not even there nor I come to that. I felt nothing physically and even less emotionally. Not shame. Not regret nor even after, remorse. I was detached from it all. If I felt anything, then what I felt was relief. Relief that I was going home with some meat for the pot. Though, in the long years that have since passed by I have deeply repented of this act and fallen upon my knees and begged the Lord's forgiveness for my trespass, if I could be transported back to that time to relive those moments ten times, then ten times I would have given my body over to that poacher in return for that meat to save my family.

Within a few minutes it was over. He was pulling together his breeches and I straightening out my skirts and quickly picking up the rabbit in case he should think of breaking his word.

'Thank you.' He smiled and with that, reached inside his great pouch and pulled out a huge hunk of bread. 'Here! Have this as well. Its not much but you are so thin, woman!'

I snatched it from him gratefully and stuffed it in my apron before making my way up out of the hollow to where my back basket of wood lay. As I tied the rabbit to my side he called up to me once more.

'I'm here abouts often should, you know. Should you ever have a mind to come trading again...'

I nodded, quickly loaded up the wood on my back and walked away along the lane back to my village. I did not care about what I had just done. All I could think about was that I was going home with meat.

I will never forget the look on Hope's gaunt face as I walked indoors with the rabbit in my hand. Sat beside the faded fire, her greyness just burst into a great bright smile such relief.

'Look, Tom!' she shook the poor lad awake in her lap. 'Look Tom what Gran'mam has brought home with her!' His old man's eyes that were set sunken within the dark rings of his child face suddenly widened with excitement as I lay the carcass down upon the kitchen table.

'Do you know what that is?' Hope asked him.

'A bunny-rabbit?'

'Yes!' I replied. 'Gran'mam is going to make a big pot of rabbit stew!'

He raced over and ran his tiny hand across the silk soft fur.

'Rabbit stew? Will we eat its hair too?' he asked.

Hope and I laughed out loud for the first time since I couldn't remember when.

'No, silly!' I reassured him. 'Gran'mam will take the fur off first and turn him into meat. You can sit and watch, if you like, just like I used to watch my father skin rabbits for the pot.'

I was surprised at how intently young Tom watched my every move as I took up my knife and began to prepare the rabbit. He showed no sign of squeamishness as I had expected from one so young. I showed him the excised skin and explained how I was going to tan it for him to keep.

Meanwhile, Hope fetched some water for the pot and prepared the handful of shrivelled roots we had expected only to be in our soup for supper. I dreaded the prospect of lying to her about how I came to be in possession of that first rabbit but, curiously, she never asked and I never offered up an explanation. I do not know if she suspected, for if she did, then she did not say anything.

Soon my task was done. The meat was jointed and shortly bubbling away over the fire. Words cannot convey how indescribably wonderful that aroma of its cooking was. We were so hungry! And it tasted so good when at last it came to the table. We ate and chatted and laughed and for the first time in months as we savoured the meat before cracking open the bones with our teeth and sucking them dry of every last bit of goodness. Then, after we licked our bowls and fingers clean, we went to our beds that night full and content, and knowing that there was plenty of stew left in that pot to last for several more days. That one rabbit brought us back from the brink. When the pot was finally empty and mopped out clean with hungry crusts of stale bread, I knew what I must do again and gave it not a second thought...

Chapter Seven

I returned to the woods, where true to his word, I found the poacher near by once more. I put down my wood basket and we soon settled down to conduct our 'business' arrangement. Afterwards, we sat a while and, with he being in a chatty mood this bright clear afternoon, we began an unexpected exchange.

'So where is your husband?' he asked quite bluntly. 'Why isn't he feeding you, woman?'

'He is dead,' I replied quietly. 'And now I am a widow.'

'Hard to provide for your family when you find yourself dead,' he sighed. 'Many's the widow of fallen comrades of mine who will vouch for that, sure enough!'

'You were a soldier then?' I had not known for certain but supposed that to be the case.

'Yes... Your husband too?'

'Yes...' I added hesitantly before proffering, 'of the Royalist cause.'

'So was I!' He threw back his head with a comfortable laugh .'A musketeer with the King's own! Though matchlocks aren't none too accurate in most hands, I can proudly boast that given my time to take my shot, I could easy kill a man at two hundred yards! Only problem with them though is the time it takes to reload, and the need for a reliable match. Those Ironsides were relentless. We were used to them charging on through our rallies, firing with their short-barrelled muskets and carbines, then wheeling away and then charging at us again with cutlass and sword. I always kept my nerve and stood firm, mind! That is, until we were overrun at Naseby .'Twas the one time that my serpent[7] came down and failed to light the pan. I went to fire and – nothing! As a result, I got my leg sliced through,' he said, gesturing towards the missing limb.

I winced. For I recalled the dreadful gaping wound that my Thomas had been dealt by an enemy cavalry man.

'So,' I asked as sensitively as one can in such circumstance, 'was the leg then cut clean through?' I do not know why I asked for details .For no sooner had I said that I regretted my intrusion for fear of raking through painful coals for the fellow. I need not have worried though for, to the contrary, I began to sense that this lonely fellow had in him a great need to talk with somebody about it. So,why not me?

'No,' he replied matter of factly. 'Twas but a flesh wound first, and with a little cursing and some good strong thread and a needle, I could have quickly sorted it out quite nicely. But instead? Instead I was taken prisoner and kept like an animal with the others, so the wound festered...

'But I'll tell you something. We had those bastards beat so many times before, yet we let their wounded walk away from the field .Left them well alone we did, and to their own devices! Those that could not leave, we left unmolested. Aye, and their womenfolk too, who came on after to attend to their dead and dying. As far as we were concerned we were done. We had shown them who was the better and stronger side and in their defeat, and those not fit enough to ride on to fight against us another day no longer mattered. They no longer posed any threat to our men, so we turned our backs on them and rode away.

'But at Naseby? Naseby was different. It was a dirty, shameless affair on their part. This time it were we who got the pounding. They won and those of ours left, that could, retreated with the King. Yet, there were countless scores like me. Too injured to get up and fight yet not badly hurt enough to lie down and die. But as we lay on the ground and waited for their army to clear, we were not overly bothered. We knew that Cromwell's men would soon go after our lads and leave us be. The bulk of the Parliamentarians busied themselves rounding up our surrendering army, more than four thousand of our most seasoned men were taken prisoner. Some of the other Roundheads were quick to spot and capture the King's baggage train containing his complete stock of guns and ammunition – and so went off after that. Then it started. A whole pack of stray bastards had been left behind with officers on horseback to supervise. They started by making a sweep of the field, going amongst the wounded and telling them to get up and line up along the roadside. Then to our disbelieving eyes, they starting killing those that couldn't. Only with the order from the gentleman officer to 'spare the powder for later' they instead stabbed or clubbed at us instead. 'Twas not done out of any kindness or as a mercy, or by way of putting those beyond help out of their misery. No! For with a little help, many of those men could have been nursed whole again by their own. 'Twas instead naught but wicked murder.

'Of course, when we seen what was happening, those that had their wits still about them, made every effort to make shift for the road. Though I had lost a lot of blood and was in great pain, I soon tore off my shirt and bound up my leg and hobbled away as directed. They marched us off, along the road to town to carry their wounded with us, with the last screams of our own comrades still ringing in our ears. I do believe that had we walking wounded no fit usefulness left in us, then they would have dispatched us too.

'About halfway into town, we come across a cart, upturned in a ditch by the side of the road, with all its contents tumbled out. Then another and another. All tossed aside amongst the sedge like rags, we saw the bodies of women folk. They were the wives of some of our soldiers. Lying dead, they were, with their noses split open like common whores. Those bastards had taken their vengeance out on our helpless women.

As I dragged myself on past that wretched scene, I vowed then that if we lost the War as well as that battle, I would never live amongst Parliament's men nor be subject to their will, no matter what hardship befell me. And so now I don't. Instead I live here...' Then he threw open his arms full stretch and continued: 'This is my home! This is my kingdom, and in it I answer to no man. No Puritan pastor calls me to account of a

Sunday, and if I feel like singing – I do. I will not comply to their laws, and neither shall I be held accountable by them, nor by any man lest he be the rightful King of England.'

I could feel the bitterness in his voice and the image he painted so vividly with his words brought me straight to tears. And I thought of James.

'Come now, Mistress,' he said as he wiped my face with his hand. 'Pay me no heed. 'Tis but soldiers words. See, I told you afore! I am not fit for a good woman's company.

'You are fit enough,' I assured him, 'and should not waste your life out here! You owe to those that died on that field to live out the life of which they were deprived...'

'I am sorry...' He must have sensed more. 'Your husband?' he asked. 'Was he...'

'Yes. He was at Naseby. And Donnington Castle, where he wrote to me of his horse being lame and so, and with him being a good shot, that he had bedded in with the musketeers under cover in the moat.'

'But I was there at Donnington too!' he exclaimed. 'Surely I would have known your man. Yet, I do not recall no-one bedding in with us musketeers. No one, that is, apart from Sir Thomas...'
He caught me wiping another tear with the corner of my apron.

'Oh God!' he exclaimed again. 'Please don't be a telling me that you are Sir Thomas' wife! God, what have I done?' he cried out, remembering that he had already had the advantage of me.

'I am,' I replied.
He fell to his knee and openly wept before.

'I am so sorry...' he pleaded 'If I had known that I would never have put you through such a humiliation. Please! I beg your forgiveness, my lady!'

I gave it willingly. For how was he to have known. We were but two strangers meeting in a wood in desperate times far removed from those that we knew.

I helped him up to stand and, after a moment

or two, he was able to talk more about my husband, telling me what a brave man he had been and how many Royalist lives he must have helped save through his secret missions.

'Did Sir Thomas die at Naseby, my lady?' he ventured.

'No.' I replied 'But we believe our only son did. My husband was gravely wounded at Naseby and left upon that field for dead. But our man Ned, coming on from Oxford and having got word of the battle, found him the following day and brought him home to me. He was barely alive and never fully recovered.'

'Died of his wounds then?'

'No. He was shot to death by soldiers some time later, outside our farmhouse.'

'Deliberately?'

'I do not know... though they would no doubt say it was not.'

'So there was no trial?'

'No. No trial.' I sighed with contempt. 'Roundheads came looking for one of our young farm lads. They said that he had been involved in some fight where another Roundhead had supposedly died. Yet, no one afterwards could say where this fight had been or if anyone had heard of a Parliamentarian soldier dying in such circumstances anywhere near to our village.'

'And Sir Thomas? I suppose he naturally spoke up for the lad?'

'Yes, of course he did. Titus would never have harmed a fly! Let alone kill another human being. He was a gentle and sensitive boy.'

'And no doubt then, Sir Thomas played straight into their hands.'

I did not understand but I could feel my stomach beginning to tighten with his every word.

'Only, I have heard of other Royalist gentlemen, invalided out of the cause, who have met with such accidents after a run in with Roundheads. Usually with an officer, accompanied by one or two others, calling on the unwary victim on just such a pretence.

A misunderstanding... a heated exchange and then – boom. Rumour has it that they are a revenge squad. Assassins, if you like. Sent out specifically to track down and mop up any one who might have proved useful before and could do so again should the King ever be free to rally more men, as he has now done after his escape. Your husband's death was more likely to have been an execution rather than an accident.'

I could not believe what I was hearing.

'And the boy, Titus?'

'They probably murdered him too.'

I was shocked, yet it all began to make some macabre sort of sense. Yet, I had met Oliver Cromwell myself, face to face during the retreat from Gainsborough. It did not strike me true that he would have taken such heinous steps.

'Surely Cromwell would never sanction such action?' I argued. He claims to be a man of God'

'So do they all, but it did not stop them from mutilating those women? Still, maybe you are right. He may have no knowledge of it at all. It could easily be someone lower down the chain of command. But what does it matter. If it has happened, it has happened. Unlawful? Against God? What is done is done. And to that end, again I am also truly sorry for what I have done to you. Truly sorry for I would not have held you to our bargain had I known then that you were Sir Thomas' wife...'

'It is alright. You weren't to have known... and it is done.'

'Yet, why are you here, my lady? Why are you brought so low as to be scavenging in these woods for food?'

'Sir Thomas' lands at Stowe...' I did not quite know how to tell him. 'We were deprived of them by a magistrate named Rech, of whom my husband had fallen foul many years before. Rech saw to it that my reputation was destroyed, and then he cast my family out of our home. I grew up in this village and owned a poor cottage that the authorities did not know about, and so I am here with my widowed daughter and grandchild and living as best as we may...'

'Please, then,' he said gently, 'meet me again whenever you may. I am often here abouts and I will gladly help you out with more game, or logs or however I can. If ever I can help you, I will.'

'Then teach me how to better feed myself,' I said to him. 'Show me how to set my own snares, for example,' I suggested with a wry smile of my own. 'Then I will never have need to bargain for food with any man again.'

'That my lady,' he smiled, 'I shall gladly do...'

*   *   *

So, my husband was most likely murdered. As I later confided to my musketeer friend, I began also to suspect that Rech had somehow been involved in it. Knowing that Thomas' death was probably a deliberate and coldly calculated and executed act somehow helped to heal the rift that, I must confess, I had felt opening between my Lord and myself. For I had lately harboured a gathering dislike for my God, who had taken my husband from mine sight in such a cruel and callous way. Yet, after my talk with the musketeer, I began to see that it was not the 'carelessness' of God that had taken him, but the wickedness of man. The pain I so keenly felt was not inflicted by God but by the evil that men do.

Whilst my faith had in one began to return, my despising of the other grew. Knowing the circumstances of my husband's death did little to close the schism I felt with him. For my anger did not lie in his death or even in the manner of it, but in the lie of a life which he had led. That he had deliberately chosen to exclude me from some part of him that I had never known or now ever could know.

*   *   *

Hope arrived home with the hems of her skirts so sodden and muddy that they slapped about her ankles. It had been a many weather day, so typical of

April. She had left the cottage that morning to make her walk into the fields in bright and glorious sunshine. However, soon this spring idyll had disintegrated into a day full of blustery showers, of hail and rain, then sleet, then bright again at day-close as the sun slunk away leaving a chill breeze biting at her cheeks as homeward she trekked. You can never trust an April sky.

'I have such a head on me,' she groaned, placing two large, fresh, white duck eggs in the dish on the table. Then she slumped beside it in her chair and cradled her head in her hands.

'I am not in a bit surprised after you being out in all that!' I sighed, trying to offer her comfort. 'You rest there a spell while I steep you a mixture of rose hips and willow bark to warm you up and ease your pain.'
I felt truly sorry for the girl. I really did. Thomas and I had raised her in relative luxury, though not to be as soft as some gentlemen's daughters, who never did a hand's turn about the house. That was not our way. So she had of course been used to helping out about Blackthorn Farm, and even more so after so many of our menfolk had gone away to fight in the war. None the less, this new harsh life was harder than she could ever have imagined. Never had she had to endure such relentless labour as now beckoned her on with the start of each day and left her as limp as a discarded drop cloth by its close. Yet she endured all of this, ungrudging, to help eke out a living for all of our sakes.

I was already far too old and stiff to be regularly employed on the land. No farmer would pay out a good day's wage for the likes of me, except of course for a few days come harvest, when every spare hand was eagerly considered. Instead, I took on the full-time task of looking after young Tom. I cared for him while I cooked, cleaned, laid the fire, gathered wood, attended to my snares, and worked our own small plot of land. Hope, meanwhile, laboured all day with planting and weeding. She bore such wretched many-weather days as this had been with a quiet dignity. Yet that day was different, for I could see it in her face and body that it was beginning to take its toll on her.

I made the steep while young Tom eagerly cuddled with his mother. After handing her the beaker of steaming brew, she began spinning out her woes between welcome sips.

'The weather has not been the least of it today,' she sighed. 'For that farmer had promised me a young cockerel for the soup pot in return for two days' stooping in this to sew his carrots. Only when I went to collect it this evening, the wife cheats me by handing me, in a basket, the sorriest hen you ever did see. 'Tis small and scrawny and so old that its chest is bare of feathers! Then she had the cheek to smile at me and say that if I could not make use of it then I could always go hang it from a tree!'

'Where is it?' I asked curiously.

'Out by the door. I felt too foolish to bring it inside after being duped so easily.'

I went and fetched the basket in and gently opened up the lid a crack. From inside two bright beady eyes fixed on mine, staring up from out of a nest of straw. I smiled broadly.

'You have not been duped, Hope,' I told her gently. 'In fact, I think that the farmer's wife was instead out to do you a kindness.'

'How so?'

'This scrawny old hen of yours is a bantam and its gone broody. It may be tiny, but these bantams are famously good at bringing up young. And they are very reliable at staying put on their clutch of eggs until hatching, and unlike those huge white ducks they also rear up on that farm. Those are far less than reliable in hatching out their own eggs, and ever worse when it comes to raising up ducklings. I fully expect what the farmer's wife meant was for you to try setting those duck eggs under the hen, if you didn't want to eat them that is!'

'But the eggs have gone cold, Mother. Surely cold eggs won't hatch now?'

'You are right. Once most birds' eggs have gone

cold they are hard to hatch out. But duck eggs are far more forgiving, so that the mother can wander off for hours at a time. If we set these under this broody and keep her snug and well fed and warm, then there is a good chance that she will do the job nicely.'

I took up the basket and set it quietly in the corner of the cottage nearest to the fire and out of way from the drafty door. Then, I carefully picked up the eggs, one by one, and after gently sprinkling them with warm water, opened up the basket lid a little and set the eggs beneath the bantam. As the back of my hand glanced the naked flesh of the bird it felt hot to the touch.

'There,' I said. 'We will leave her to settle to them tonight and then, come morning, I will open up the lid and set her out some water close by so she might venture out to feed. When she does, I will quietly turn the eggs and sprinkle them with water again.'

'Why, Gran'mam?' Thomas asked?

'Because mammy ducks come back to the nest from the river wet, Tom. If I wet those eggs they will think that it's their mammy duck atop them and they will hatch out properly,' I told him.

'I see, so then we will have duck eggs of our own in time!' Hope exclaimed.

'Yes, but more importantly, ducks are far more meaty than chickens and the young drakes do not fight like they do when growing on young cockerels for the pot. The feathers are more useful too.'

'Then that was a good wage, after all! But...' Hope was flummoxed[8], 'why did she tell me to otherwise hang the hen from a tree?'

'That's what you do,' I explained, 'to chickens that you don't want to stay broody. You hang them up high in a tree in their baskets. They don't care for the draft, you see, so will soon snap themselves out of it after a couple of days and come back into laying eggs again.'

'You are a wonder,' Hope laughed, 'for knowing so much!'

'My father taught me all I know about keeping chickens. Besides, knowledge also comes with old age, Hope. And the Lord knows, I have enough years under my apron!'

'So, Mother? Tell what it is that I can smell cooking?' she asked with a growing smile. 'For I do believe I now have got an appetite for it!'

'It's pheasant, mam-may!' Thomas exclaimed excitedly. 'Gran'mam caught it in a snare near her garden! Didn't you, Gran'mam?'

'In a snare, you say?' Hope smiled. 'You know, I do not recall you ever telling me before about your father teaching you to set snares, Mother.'

'No,' I replied quietly,' busying myself at the bubbling pot. 'You are quite right. I never did...'

*   *   *

It had started on the Friday just as Hope had got home from working up at the farm. The heaven's opened with a mighty clash and rain fell heavily throughout the coming evening.

''Twill do no harm!' Hope said. 'For April's showers bring Mayflowers, and the seeds I have sewn today will have good need of a watering in.'

I should have been out myself that day, sewing our patch with the precious pinches of seed Hope had managed to scrounge or barter from all about the village. I had not though. Tom had been poorly with a childish stomach, something and nothing as it usually proves. Yet I decided to indulge the boy and to let the garden wait for one more day while I nursed him and got on with some indoor chores instead.

Saturday was blustery with the odd scattered shower, so again I bided indoors waiting for clearer skies to plant my seeds.

The Lord's Day was bright with sunshine and wide patches of blue sky with white clouds racing across at speed, drawn on by a still brisk breeze. Even had it not been the Sabbath, the ground would have been far too sodden to be worked. In fact, going up Little Lane to church was precarious enough, because Hope and I

105

were forced to hoist our hems almost all of the way, to avoid the deep water-filled potholes.

'Never mind,' I said over supper. 'With this breeze drying out the ground, I should be able to make a start outside tomorrow morning.'

Scarcely had dawn broken and morning come, than the rain started heavily once more.

'I shall need to bide here a might longer before I dare try setting off for the farm!' Hope frowned, as she peered outside through the half-opened door at the sheets of water running down off from our roof.

Eventually the rain eased a little but the clouds overhead still loomed low and ominous. Undeterred, Hope donned her tattered straw hat over her linen cap and made off towards the farm. Within minutes though, she huffed back through the cottage door while wearing a very worried expression.

'You should see the lane, Mother!' she exclaimed. 'It is flowing like a river coming down from the hill!'

'Let me see,' I said, as I grabbed my shawl and followed after her outside. 'Stay here, Tom!' I shouted back across my shoulder as I pulled the door onto the latch.' Stay here and don't you dare venture out! Gran'mam and Mam will be back very soon.'

Then Hope and I made our way up our path and out into the lane beyond. My daughter had not exaggerated. Water was channelling down our lane from the cleft above and beginning to pool into a great lake just beyond our garden hedgerow. Even the dyke at the far side of the lane was overflowing.

'Oh my! I do not care for the look of that,' I said as I turned to look at Hope. 'The wash-dyke beyond must be overflowing. Mayhap even the Ancholme too, after all of this rain we have been having of late.'

We hurried back towards the house and were just nearing the door when I suddenly felt the need to go check behind the cottage on the sheep field. The land inclined downwards towards us and often water settled there into a dew pond close by. As I did so, I was met by a great swathe of glistening water.

'Lord!' I remember praying out aloud. 'Please do not let it rain anymore!'

My plea went unheard.

'What is it Mother?' Hope asked. She had backtracked after I had failed to follow her in and caught me rounding the corner of the house.

'Out there. Back yonder,' I pointed. 'There is a might of standing water not yards from the cottage!'

'Oh, no! Will we flood?'

'We are a ways from that yet a while. So... hopefully... we shall not. Still,' I added cautiously, 'I think it best that you bide here for the rest of today.'

We made our way back inside to Tom and I made us a warming brew.

Within the hour the sky blackened as if smoked, and then it started to rain with a vengeance. As it did, I kept a watchful eye upon the rivulets of water now creeping in under the hedges and reaching out across the garden, until they began to swiftly merge as one. At that point, I ran upstairs and threw open the back bedroom shutters to get a better vantage point from the window. To my growing despair, the dew pond was now almost lying at our back wall.

'I think now, Hope, that we should take whatever we can and move upstairs.'

Hope did not even stop to reply as she hurriedly began to snatch up our humble possessions and ferried them up the steps. I grabbed my hat and made for the door.

'Where are you going?' Hope asked, obviously worried about me.

'To the woodshed to get in as much dry fuel as I can. If the waters keep coming up it will be all ruined. Then what shall we do?'

What shall we do indeed, I thought quietly to myself. 'Twas all well and good my rescuing wood for the fire, but how was I going to cook if the water came in and flooded the hearth? Come to that, what was I going to cook if I could not get out to the woods to check my snares?

'Let me go,' Hope reasoned. 'I am stronger.'

107

'Indeed you are. But no, Hope, I will go. You stay where you are. You are much more fitted to be climbing up and down those blessed steps than I am.'

I lumbered out and across the muddy yard over to the woodshed, where I frantically began filling the large willow log basket. Suddenly, I was startled as a large figure slopped up behind me. For a second my heart pounded as bad memories flashed into my head. I immediately turned about with my fists already raised to fend off my attacker. He fielded my blow just in time before I knocked him off balance.

'Whoa! 'Tis only me, Lady Elizabeth!'
It was my musketeer from the spinney.

'I am so sorry! But you gave me such a fright! What on earth are you doing *here*?'

'That's the problem. There is no earth in the woods to be on. It's all flooded! Besides, knowing that you were here and without a man, I thought I had best come to see what help I can give you.'
He had such a wonderful smile on his face that from that moment I felt my spirits lift.

'Thank you kindly,' I smiled back. 'It was very good of you to spare us the thought.'

'Here, Lady Elizabeth. Let me do that,' he said handing me over a large sack cloth bundle as he took on picking up logs. 'You take this indoors for me, while I finish up fetching the wood inside.'

'Wait... ' I had a panicked thought. 'My daughter is in there and I have not told her about...'

'You... and me... We are just casual acquaintances. Someone you met in the woods.

'That's right. She does not know...'

'And nor shall she,' he said cutting in gently. 'Not from me, at any rate.'

'Then I shall see you inside,' I sighed with relief. 'Oh... and it is 'Bessie' in front of my daughter... Remember? Not Lady Elizabeth!'

'Very well then, Lady Elizabeth. Mistress Bessie it is...'
I went back inside the cottage.

'Who is that man, Gran'mam?' Nothing escaped Tom's eager young eyes.

'What man?' Hope exclaimed from above, poking her head down through the hatch.

'There was a man outside, Mam-may, with Gran'mam. A man with only one leg!'

'Is he a beggar' Hope clambered down to see for herself.

'No. He is but a hunter. I sometimes chance to meet in the woods.' I replied taking off my dripping hat and hanging it up high on a beam.

'A one-legged poacher more like!' she said trying to spy him through a crack in the door.

'He came by to check that we were all right.'

'That was kind of him,' Hope said rather dismissively. 'Is he going now?'

'No, I think not. He is busy fetching in wood for us. Are you done in here?' I asked, trying to divert her attention.

'Yes, I am. All that can be lifted or will be spoiled is upstairs now. A one-legged poacher,' she mused, 'fetching in our wood?'

Then she noticed the bundle still clasped tightly in my hand.

'What have you got there,Mother?' she said inquisitively.

'I really cannot say... I mean... It is not mine. It is his. So I do not know.'

'Then peek inside,' Hope urged.

'I cannot do that. It would not be right.'

'Then let me.'

I gave in to that look in her eye.

'Do it then, but quickly if you must! It would be awful to offend him after taking such a care over us.'

Hope teased out one corner of the cloth and peered in.

'Why, it looks like a hunk of roast meat!' she exclaimed accusingly. 'Roast venison, if I am not mistaken. He *is* a poacher. Mother! He could be taken to the assizes at Lincoln and hanged if he's caught! We too I wager!'

'Shhhhh!' I warned. 'He is coming!'

'There you are, Mistress Bessie,' he said, dragging the heavy wood basket through the cottage door.

'My, but you are very nimble for a one-legged man!' Hope exclaimed with mischief in her voice.

'Hope! Where are your manners?'

'That's alright, mistress!' he made reply to me. 'No offence taken from the young lady.'

'This is my daughter, Hope.' I made the introduction.

'Pleased to make your acquaintance, Mistress Hope' he said, leaning upon his crutch and bowing politely.

'And I yours, Mister...' she trailed, boldly seeking his name.

'Quick. Captain Quick. That's what they called me in the Army. Been called by that name so long that I can hardly recall my given name any more.'

'Army? Were you a Parliamentarian?' Hope was hasty to ask.

'No, mistress. I was the King's man and proud of it!'

'Then, maybe you knew my husband, James?'

'Sorry, mistress! Quick replied. 'So many faces came and went. Yet I ne'er put a name to but hardly a handful. As I recollect, there was no 'James' amongst those that I could. Sorry mistress...'

'It is of no matter, Sir.' She replied, though naturally she sounded disappointed. Some word of what might have happened to James was all she craved. I too.

'Well, I best be going now...' Quick seemed ill at ease. 'Or is there anything more I can do for you?'

'Not unless you have the gift to hold back water, Captain Quick!' Hope said a little curtly, I thought.'

'But what about you?' I asked. 'If the woods are flooded, then where will you find shelter?'
Quick shrugged.

'Then that is settled,' I said. 'You must bide here with us until the waters settle.'

Hope looked appalled by the prospect, and the Captain immediately realised her feelings.

'I cannot, Mistress Bessie,' he replied graciously. 'That would not be right and proper, what with my being a single man and under the same roof as two vulnerable women. If news like that gets out and your reputations will be ruined.'

I smiled, knowingly. He smiled back, a little embarrassed, mayhap recalling how I no longer had a reputation of which to speak.

'I am certain that we can trust you to be a man of honour, Captain Quick,' I argued, hoping to put him at ease. 'Anyway, who is to know that you are here? I do not see any of the other villagers wetting their boots to come and see how we fare. No. You are welcome to stay here for as long as you need.' I genuinely wanted to repay his kindness.

'Thank you Lady...' Quick cut himself short, yet not short enough from the look that Hope then gave him. I knew immediately that she must have suspected that the Captain had been about to address me as 'Lady Elizabeth'. If she had, then she let it slide. Instead, she smiled like a cat who has just spied a mouse.

'Then we best see what we can find you to eat,' Hope ventured.

'There is no need', he said quickly gesturing towards the bundle still in my hands. 'I thought to bring plenty of food with me . Enough for all of us to share.'

Just then, Tom shouted out excitedly.

'Look Gran'mam!' Watter[9]!'

A large trickle had begun to run into the cottage. Flood water was seeping in through the saturated lime mortar of the walls from the dew pond beyond and up through a crack in the compacted dirt floor beneath our feet.

'Well, it looks as if there will be no keeping it out now,' I commented, resigning myself to the imminent prospect of our entire home being wetted.

'Best you make your way upstairs quickly,' the captain advised. 'I will be back in moment.'

Then he picked up our wooden pale and opened

the door.

'Where are you going?' I asked.

'To fetch water from the well.'

'Water!' Hope exclaimed in disbelief. 'We are flooding indoors and you are going out there to fetch water?'

'Yes, water Mistress Hope,' he replied firmly. 'We could be holed up in here for the Lord knows how long. We will need fresh water to drink. If the flood water rises much higher than this, then it may contaminate the well.'

'You are very astute!' I praised him.

'I learnt that soldiering,' he replied proudly. 'Anticipate! 'Tis not enough to be swift at reacting in a battle. To survive, one needs to be able to anticipate the enemy. Be that in human form or not.' Then he went back into the rain.

He was bright, this Captain John Quick. And I remember thinking to myself then that Mad Jack back in Jamestown might well have approved of this man and his name.

'What about the fire?' Hope asked, trying to recover from feeling foolish.

'Leave it.' I replied stoically. 'It is not as if it is going to be able to burn the house down much longer. Help me to stow this dry wood upstairs though, Hope,' I said as I manhandled it up through the hatch. 'I feel we will have a need of it. There is no telling when we shall be able to find some more that is dry.'

I had just climbed upstairs when the captain returned. He handed me up the bucket of water, and then his crutch, before shimmying up the steps to join us.

From upstairs we could see far beyond the cottage. On all sides, the land lay submerged by a great trembling mantle of water. We were like a tiny thatched island cut off from the rest of the world. I shuffled across the room and to the top of the stairs and looked down from the hatchway. Water was leaching in through the walls at quite a pace and lapping over the threshold of our ill-fitting door. I kept checking, back and forth between window and stairs. Before too long the downstairs floor was swamped by several inches of brackish water.

'It won't rise up and drown us, will it?' asked Hope.
I had thought that she would have had more sense than to frighten Tom like that. He began to cry. He did not like the water.

'No!' I said firmly. 'It's more likely to be little more than a blessed nuisance when it begins to go down again.'

'And when will that be?' she replied.
I had no way of knowing.

'A day or two... who can tell?' the Captain was quick to fill in. 'Depends on how much more of this rain we get. But I cans't say that we are in any danger of drowning. Like your mother says, it is just going to cause a fine mess to clean up, that's all. Lessen...' he had an after thought to share. 'Lessen of course that the water durzent[10] cause the earth beneath us to slip away...'

That was one prospect that I had not considered and upon which I did not want to dwell. Had we not been through enough these past months without the fear of losing even this meagre refuge?

So I suggested that we eat. As we did, I made small talk and tried as best as I could to make light of our troubles, especially so for Tom's sake. Captain Quick was very good with the lad, considering he was a man with no family of his own. And he showed great patience with an extremely sullen Hope too, who made conversation with him impossibly difficult by giving up only clipped and precise answers to all of the questions that he had posed to engage her. I wished that she could have shown him more courtesy, more so considering that we would have gone hungry had it not been Quick's ample supply of cold meat.

Night came and we settled down to the darkness not knowing now what was happening outside. The rain had ceased by late evening, but I knew that the land still had to drain and that rivers could continue to rise for many hours to come. If more rain came, then our situation could only be expected to worsen. We were isolated and alone, and with any way of leaving cut off. All we could do was to sit tight and pray.

Thankfully, at first light we awoke to find the day bright and the water outside rapidly receding towards the lane and draining into the ditches at the edges of the fields. By afternoon, Quick was busy helping us to mop up and setting a fire to help dry out the cottage.

I told the captain that he was welcome to stay on for a day or two more but he declined. Instead, he thanked me for my hospitality, adding that he had best be heading off lest anyone from the village came by. He was wary as to not risk ruining either Hope's or my reputation. Once he had gone, Hope quizzed me hard.

'Mother,' she said, 'you knew this Captain Quick before, didn't you?"

'Yes,' I replied. 'I told you as much before.'

'Yes, but it is so obvious that you know him better than either he or you would admit .You have not told me all, have you, Mother?'

'What do you mean?'

'Was there more to him coming here than merely to help us?'

'In what way?'

'Mother, tell me straight? Have you conspired with him?'

'Conspired?' That was a strange word for her to use if she suspected me of having lain with this man. Suddenly the latch dropped on the clap-post[11]. But I was suddenly at a loss for words as I tried to grasp what Hope meant.

'Yes Mother. Conspired! Had you a mind to matchmake between the Captain and me?'

'Matchmake?' I laughed with relief. 'I most certainly had not thought to matchmake betwixt you and Captain Quick!'

'Then all is well .For I must tell you now that I

love you dearly and will do all in my power to continue to be a dutiful daughter towards you. But please... please understand that I shall never marry again.'

'Why ever not? A young woman like you should consider marrying again.'

'I do not want to,' she replied bruskly.

'But you *need* a new husband, just as young Tom needs a father.'

Then, after thinking for a moment, I added: 'Are you afraid to marry because of what happened to me?'

'No,' Hope replied, trembling as she spoke. 'No, it is not because of what has happened to you. It is because of what has happened to me. There can never be another husband for me. I love James. I shall always love James, and only James until the day I die!'

Captain Quick called at the cottage a few days later to bring me some wood and a rabbit for the pot, and to check upon our well being. Then he rarely called again, visiting only when he supposed us to be in need. And so in the coldest weather and at times when we were indeed in great need, he could be relied upon to suddenly reappear with him some sort of rare commodity – be it food or fuel or some other.

I would always take pains to thank him profusely, yet quietly out of Hope's hearing. Unfailingly, in reply, he would always claim that, 'it was nothing,' or that 'it was for Sir Thomas' sake, or 'it was to make up for his terrible trespass when we did first meet.

I concluded that despite our first encounters, that Captain Quick was a good man at heart. I could see that plainly. 'Twas just more the pity that circumstance had contrived to lead him into a life of poaching and hiding out in the woods like an outlaw when he was so deserving of a much better life.

Chapter Eight

Hope had dragged herself off to the fields at first light but had come home before noon feeling weak and feverish.

'Maggie Fuller is ill too,' Hope said as she clambered up the steps to her bed. 'She took bad, last night so her brother says.'

'Then something nasty must be doing the rounds. Best I go out and gather up some ingredients to make up a batch of remedy, lest Tom and I come down with it too.'

It was just as well that I had, for soon both Tom and I became ill with a raging fever and the flux. Had it not been for my gift with herbs and God's grace we might not have recovered as quickly as we did.

Before the week's end Hope had returned to work, but only to return home early and in some distress.

'It's Maggie,' she said with tears in her eyes. 'Maggie Fuller is dead. She was only standing at my side on Tuesday last, larking about as we weeded High Field, and now she is dead of the flux. She was barely twenty and only just wed.'

'Oh Hope, I am so sorry', I said. 'I know how fixed you and she were as friends.'

'Yes we were, but there is worse. The mistress up at the farm is sick with it too and so is her little lad. The master says that both are so poorly[12] that they might not live. So I told him about us having been ill yet now fully recovered, no doubt thanks to your herbal remedy. He near begged me, Mother, to come fetch you to see if you can help his family.'

'Me? What about sending for the doctor?'

'He has already done so, but he got word back from Rasen that the doctor there is overwhelmed by the sick and mayn't come out this way for a week or longer.'

I had no choice. It was my Christian duty to go and to see what I could do for our neighbours. Yet, the prospect made me feel sick with worry. What if my medicines did not work? Would I somehow be held responsible for their deaths? Nevertheless, I brushed these thoughts aside, grabbed my basket of herbs and steeping mixtures and went off immediately to be nurse to them.

When I got there, both mother and child were being violently sick betwixt rapid bouts of the flux. The stench in their chamber was overpowering. In the crowded hearth the fire was stoked high and the room felt as hot as furnace. All of the widows were shut tight to help keep up the heat and to drive out their fever. When I bade the master to let out the fire and instead to let in some fresh, cool air, he at first refused, saying that the pair were shivering enough already. It took a lot of my persuasion to get him to trust me. But I succeeded eventually, for he was a desperate man and only wanted the best for his loved ones. He realising that, despite his own best efforts, his family had not improved at all. However, I had already at least cured myself and mine by my own methods, he reluctantly gave in.

'They need cooling from within as well as without,' I explained as I showed him how to sponge their hot bodies down with wet rags.

'Try to get them to take sips of some cooled boiled water,' I said. 'At least enough to wet their lips whilst I go downstairs to steep my herbs.'

The poor man looked ill himself, so when I returned I packed him off to his bed with a steep while promising to stay to nurse his family through the night. As it happened, I did so well into the next day also.

To my relief, gradually the family began to improve, though at one point I was most worried for the child who was at the time spewing forth every few moments and could not even down the tiniest sip of water, let alone any of my steep. He had been lying limp in my lap with sunken eyes and barely responsive. Yet, with patience, I managed to get my medicine into him and by morning the violent fits of nausea had stopped along with the flux and stomach cramps, after which he took to sleeping like a baby. Even so, his fever persisted until well into the afternoon before it gradually subsided and allowed him to recover completely. On the third day, both mother and child were able to sit up and take a little frumenty[13]. The master had been taken ill too but recovered quickly, and then being overjoyed to find his family so much improved.

'How can I ever repay you!' he cried. 'Ask me for whatever you want and I shall send it to you.'

'Tis the Lord you should thank, not I,' I replied. 'But if you wish to repay me, I could always use a little milk for my grandson.'

I returned to the cottage so weary that I went straight up the steps to my mattress and fell sound asleep. Later, Tom came up and shook me awake in some excitement shouting for his Gran'mam to come down and see the 'milk' that the farmer had sent.

I felt bemused that he should be so moved by the mere sight of a little milk, none the less I made shift downstairs in pursuit of the lad – finding him over by the open door and pointing outside. I had misheard the child.

'Look Gran'mam!' Tom cried excitedly. 'Milker!' There it stood... tethered in our yard. The most beautiful brown cow I had ever seen! And sure enough, she was in milk. From that time on our lives changed dramatically for the better. For with a cow of our own we had more milk than our needs – and so made cheese and butter, with surplus to sell or to barter.

And so soon we were able to buy and trade for chickens and ducks that provided us with meat and eggs. We had a growing plot full of all manner of vegetables and soon another large bed dug and given over entirely to growing herbs and physics. As I distributed these, gifts of all description soon began to find their way to my cottage from others gratefully healed . From near and far, my reputation as a successful herbalist was fast grew.

*   *   *

Mister Lollop became a member of our family by accident. He was just a fledgling when young Tom found him lying in the soft undergrowth beneath a birch tree. My grandson came running in to me with the poor creature cupped between his tiny hands as if it were made of precious gold.

'Please Gran'mam,' he said, looking up at me with such a mournful look on his face. 'Please make my friend better. Please!'

'Let me see,' I said, peeking in between the cage of tiny fingers.

The bird was barely half grown. Its grey translucent skin, with a network of delicate blue and red blood vessels clearly visible, was covered by dark grey down and stubby little feathers which had already begun to sprout from equally stubby wings. One of these looked slightly deformed. The little bird's great feet looked far too large for his podgy little body and his bright and ridged beak gaped open waiting for food.

'I can't cure what afflicts him, Tom,' I tried to explain as gently as I could. 'You see he has left his nest far too young and needs his mother to help him grow.'

'Then how do we get him back to her?' Tom asked.

'I do not think that we can. Wherever the nest is, it must be way up high in the branches and impossible for us to reach.'

'Then can we keep him? You can be his Gran'mam too, can't you?' Tom pleaded.

I tried to explain to him that it would be kinder all round to put the little lost creature back where he had been found so that at least it might see out its last day with some dignity. The prospect of hand-rearing it to adulthood was bleak. And besides, I could scarcely fit all of my chores into the hours God gave as it was.

Tom's bottom lip began to quiver and with that he burst into a flood of tears. I could not bear it. Not to watch, hard-hearted, at the tears trickling down his innocent face or at that accusing look in his eye that could not comprehend why the Gran'mam he loved so much could dismiss this little bird's life so easily. So, I gave in. I went into the shed and looked out an old wicker basket in need of a handle and lined it with a handful of soft hay.

'Here,' I said. 'Pop him in this and take him into the house with you. 'Tis chill out here now and I cannot be doing with looking after the pair of you should you go catching another cold.'

Tom smiled broadly as he put the bird into the basket and carefully carried it into the cottage. Meanwhile, I finished up outside and soon joined him.

'He is hungry, Gran'mam.' he mithered. 'What are we going to feed him?'

'He shall have to have the same as you and I have. Bread.'

Tom laughed.

'But how can he eat bread? He's got no teeth.'

'Well, now there's a question! I really do not know, Tom. I've only ever raised hen chicks and ducklings before, and they can usually feed themseln[14],'I said laughing back. 'But this little fellow is neither.'

'What sort of bird is he then?'

'I do not rightly know, for I have never seen a youngster like him. He's too ugly for a blackbird. Mayhap he is a starling. Yet, I suppose all young birds would eat the same sort of thing.'

I know, I suddenly thought, we will soak some biscuit crumbs soft in warm water and try him on that. And so with that I set a small portion of rusk[15] in some water from the pot that I was already using to boil some eggs.

'What have you there, Tom?' Hope said as she came home.

'A bird, Mammay! A baby bird! Gran'mam says I can keep it!'

'Mother!' she exclaimed with a light-hearted scold in her eye. 'You would fill the house with waifs and strays!'

I knew that I was being indulgent, but where Tom was concerned I had such a weak spot. He so reminded me of Hope when she was that age too. She could melt anyone's heart. Then too, I dare say, if only she would have but glanced another man's way. I know. She was my dead son's widow as well as my adopted daughter. But James *was* dead now and it seemed so wrong for such a young woman to so readily have resigned herself to widowhood for the rest of her days.

Hope peered inside the basket.

'My but he's a lop-sided little thing! What kind of bird is it?'

'I don't know, Mammay.'

'Then, mayhap, that is no bad thing. 'Twill stop you becoming too attached to it, for I very much doubt that it will see out the night.'

Tom's face dropped sending his lips into a quiver once more.

'Maybe so, but my grandson and I plan to give it all the chance that we can!' I replied firmly, sending a smile back to Tom's face. 'Come on lad! Let's set about giving him some supper while your mother watches over ours.'

With that I fetched the soaked crumb and set about trying to feed the young bird with Tom.

'Here,' I explained. 'If we pick up a pinch like this, just between our thumb and forefinger like this, as I'm doing with mine,' he might just think that this is his mother's beak a coming to feed him.'

Tom looked on intently with his face beaming as I moved my hand in close to the fledgling, and then it began to gulp greedily at the food.

'My! You are a hungry little soul!' I said with relief. 'Right, Tom. Now that I have shown you how, why don't you try? My old grandmother fingers are far too big really. What's needed are your little ones. They will be much better at the job.'

Eagerly, Tom took over from me and fed the bird repeatedly until it could take no more. Its crop was bulging as it then nestled down into the hay to sleep.

Hope was to be proved wrong in time. In fact, even I was surprised at how quickly Tom's foundling grew and thrived on the young boy's constant attention. Soon it was strong enough to perch on Tom's hand to be fed, and showed no fear of him or us at all. Tom in return petted it and stroked its fast growing-in feathers. But as it grew we soon noted that it had a peculiar way of movement. It was such an unusually lopsided creature.

'Is there something wrong with this starling?' Hope sighed out loud. 'Just look at it lolloping about the place!'

'Lollop?' Tom repeated.

'Yes, "lollop", Tom,' I said trying to explain this new word to him. 'See how he moves so funnily from side to side as he hops? That's a lollop.'

'Lollop!' Tom cried excitedly. 'I want to call him Lollop!'

So the bird received a name of its own at last – Mister Lollop.

Before the month was out, Mister Lollop was almost fully fledged and ready to fly. This frail orphan 'starling' had amazed us all by growing into a very large crow. As he had, Mister Lollop had outgrown his basket, preferring to hop up instead and perch on its rim. And when he soon grew too heavy for that, Tom found a portion of birch branch and wedged it into the basket to make a better perch around which the crow could wrap his feet.

After that, Mister Lollop grew swiftly in confidence and learnt to lurch down from the basket and to hop about the cottage at will. I remember thinking then that it would not be long before the ungrateful bird would make its way to the open door and fly away, while taking Tom's heart with it.

Soon the day came when he did just that. It was a beautiful Sunday morning and all about us the air was filled with bird chatter as we busied ourselves in getting ready to walk up the lane to church. Mister Lollop lazily stretched out his wings and then, without warning, hopped down from his perch and across the bare stone floor to the open doorway. Craning out his neck, he tilted his head to one side – as if listening intently to the throng outside revelling in the warm sunshine. And then Tom watched open mouthed in horror as the bird crossed the threshold, hesitated for a moment or two, and then launched himself none too elegantly into the air and onto the ivy covered roof of the shed. From there, in the following moments, Mister Lollop suddenly took off into the trees and disappeared from sight.

Tom cried about his loss all the way up the lane. He was inconsolable

'Do not be sad' I told him. 'Mister Lollop just needed to go find his family.'

'But we are his family,' was all he would say.

Tom made his way back home after church just as sombrely, and nothing his mother or I could say would comfort to him. But then, as we reached our cottage door Tom suddenly called out with joy.

Down swooped Mister Lollop and landed without grace upon Tom's out-stretched arm. The bird, so it seemed, was destined to stay.

Although we paid him no heed, Mister Lollop took most visitors into our cottage by surprise. For crows were shrouded by country lore and myth and seldom seen at such close quarters, and especially not sitting upon a perch by the fireside, and being so at ease with human companionship. Indeed, for a few callers it proved so unnerving as for them to refuse to set foot inside, and to instead take consultation for cures out in the cold. For others, the bird held a deep fascination – because a creature so wary of man had be tamed by a child.

*   *   *

With the King captured and the Royalist cause all but expunged from the country, the long labour of the Puritan movement was coming to its end. The reforming of a nation was close at hand, but like any birth, it was an event awaited with great anticipation mixed in with feelings of even greater anxiety. Would the mother[16] survive? Would the offspring[17] prove free of deformity? Was the given Father[18] truly its sire?

Thus, the bastard Puritan progeny of a far gentler parent was set to burst out into the world, kicking and screaming with the name of God burning on its lips. Wrapped in a lamb's skin it would open up its eyes and bay, like a wolf, for blood...

Deep within, our village sympathies lay mainly with the Royalist faction. Yet an outsider passing through would not suspect this to be so. For all had suddenly taken to wearing sombre Puritan drab. I thought of a flock of sheep stampeding to the far end of
the field in pursuit of the skittish lead ewe. It seemed the safest thing to do in light of the predominantly Puritan authority now in charge of our country's affairs, and their witch-hunt against those they saw as dogs who had run with the King. Most wary of those and quickest to been seen to comply with the new feeling of austerity and godliness were our local yeoman farmers and landowners. In their defence, they plainly had the most to lose. Simple folk followed their masters' example. Though one or two individuals did openly refuse to conform, they soon found themselves wishing they had not.

A new Puritan minister had became encumbered with our church. You might think that I, as a committed dissenter in my youth, would have met this change with happiness. I did not. This preacher proved to be as stern and unyielding a man as you could fear to meet. For fear is what he brought with him. It was not a godly fear – a deep and inspiring respect for the Lord of life and grace, but an unhealthy fear of a vindictive God. He preached about this avenging God of wrath on a Sunday with great zeal – with warnings of certain damnation facing those of us who fell so miserably short of this preachers vision of perfection. For Master Ezra was a 'seeker', a 'precise and correct' minister and a 'true' follower of Christ, and in the worst Puritan tradition.

When Thomas and I had first returned to Stowe,

we had worshiped in public as Anglicans. Just as we had done in Jamestown for the sake of appearances. Though separatists still by conviction, we now found ourselves without the spiritual support of our beloved congregation and its gentle leaders. We had found few other like-minded worshipers among the rising numbers of radical Puritan sympathisers over the passing years.

Despite the mood of the times, St Mary's of Stowe had always clung to the high Anglican tradition. Once this hallowed minster had been the centre of faith in Lindsey before the great cathedral of Lincoln was built. Although usurped, the minster retained its aura of spiritual supremacy above the neighbouring parishes, yet even here we noticed a softening towards the mood for reform slowly leaching inwards.

In the privacy of our own home at blackthorn Farm, we had observed our Separatist principles, and so in some ways distanced ourselves from our neighbours – who often broke the Sabbath and made merry on Christmas day. 'Twas not that we disapproved of merriment, for on the contrary my family and I could make celebration for weddings and such as good as the next. However, Christmas was not, according to our Geneva Bible, a holy day. And nor was it anywhere set that Christ's birth occurred on the December date – which was that for the old pagan winter ritual observed in the dark days before Christianity had reached our shores.

Considering that King James had been so opposed to Separatist and Puritan doctrine alike, when Thomas had returned to find me at Plimouth, I had been somewhat surprised to find him now such a Royalist sympathiser. At first I had wondered if the severe head injury he suffered back in England had somehow changed his way of thinking, much in the same way as some of his memories had been either lost or distorted. Then I began to wonder if he might not have lost faith through the sheer wickedness of things he had endured while in Virginia. Yet he went there, knowingly, in the King's employ and in public, at least, and then lived out his life in denial of his Separatist leanings. But now I see that not to have done so would have been extremely dangerous for him and me at that time. For 'tis easier to stand up to be counted when one is not standing alone.

Then, as we hurtled headlong towards civil war and Thomas came out in favour of the Royalist cause, I had begun to rent inside. For I believed deeply that we should have sided with the Parliamentarians – whose bulk was richly endowed by Puritans, and with whom we should have found a natural affinity. However, Thomas in time convinced me otherwise.

He told me that a man or woman should fight for what they believe to be right. Though we believed beyond doubt that the Church should be reformed and purified, should we allow it to be 'remade' through ungodly ways? What then? Shall the persecuted then persecute? If our sovereign King was put here above us by divine intervention, then who were we mere mortals to try to depose of him? If reform should come, should it not be done by quiet measure? Was it not better to flavour the stew by being one of the ingredients? If our struggle was great and long, was it not intended that way so that our spirits might be tempered?

'Yet you are willing to go to war?' I had asked. 'Will you fight against those with whom we have shared persecution in the past?'

'Aye, Bessie, my love. But not on the attack!' he argued. 'I would raise my arms only to protect the King, and with as little bloodshed as I can get away with! Besides, when this war comes, I do not believe that it will be because of anything to do with tolerance or freedom of religion. It will be about what wars are always about - seizing power and control to force the victors' will upon the vanquished. And for that reason I am conscience-bound to side with the King and the rule of English law. The alternative is anarchy, and with that I believe we may all lose our spiritual freedom, not gain it.'

Thomas was dead. Yet in my head we continued

to argue.

*   *   *

This village church had changed so much of late. The rood I remembered as a child was gone, burnt by Parliamentarian soldiers camped out in the churchyard while in retreat from Gainsborough. Likewise 'idolatrous' stained glass in one of the windows had been put out and anything considered a 'Popish embellishment' also removed. As was anything bright that might otherwise 'distract' us – the congregation of sinners – from our pure worship of God come a Sabbath. Even the walls were whitewashed, turned plain to discourage wandering eyes. Also gone was the silver communion chalice and plate. They had long since 'disappeared', mayhap buried by the last true Anglican incumbent at the start of the Civil War in order to save it or else he had failed to do so and these had been, like so many others, seized by Roundheads and melted down.

I thought back to my days as a Separatist and realised that much of this was that for which we had petitioned, but not in the way in which this new wave of Puritans now revelled. Our services within the secrecy of Gainsborough Hall and later in Plimouth were such uplifting comings together as to bring joy into every heart with each passing word of the sermon. Now, seemingly, there was to be no more joy. Joy was slowly being stifled out of almost every portion of our daily life, and our 'seeker' saw to that. No more singing of hymns in our church, nor the singing of folk songs without. No more maypole dancing to see in the summer, nor the singing of traditional songs on the last of the corn carts at harvest home, nor roast hare, nor fools at Harvest Supper. No more a-playing at skittles on rare holidays beside the village ale house, where the menfolk were also banned from playing cricket, by special command from Cromwell himself. Instead, all bats and balls were ordered to be collected up and burnt by the common hangman.

Above all other traditions held dear by simple

peasants, there was to be no more celebrating Christmas of old - not for anyone. No more 'Lords of Misrule' and their quivering fools, nor gambling, nor gaming and riotous entertaining. And no more fourteen days of Yuletide feasting on pig-cheer[19], which would help provision the poor folk in our villages for struggling through the worst of the winter shortages.

All was now strict observance – closely scrutinised by the preacher – to make certain that the village conformed, so that every soul might be salvaged. In short, life became miserable. Six long days of work and one long day of enforced religious observance throughout. Though attendance at church was no longer strictly compulsory, woe betide him who was noted absent. For the seeker had ways of to 'punish' those in subtly round-about ways that often ended in a spell in the village stocks.

I hated the man. He told our young Tom, young as he was, that he was a wicked child for not learning his Bible verses by rote, and threatened to make him eat mouse pie lest he did not, and so made the poor boy cry. That, I let by.

Then, towards the middle of October, and on the first real bright dry day in weeks, Hope stood chatting in the churchyard after service with Mistress Cook, a young wife much of her own age. I lingered but a few paces on, my mind cast idly upon what, well I cannot now even recall. Tom was skipping along the path, hand in hand with the young Cook girl when suddenly the minister grabbed them both by the scruff of the neck, near lifting their heels clean off from the ground. He strode towards their two young mothers and cast the children down at their feet bothersome puppies and saying that such wayward children should be shown the birch.

Mistress Cook cowered in fear while Hope grasped Tom close to her skirts as he howled in terror. Then I sprang forward and gave the minister a piece of my tongue.

'What waywardness is there?' I demanded. 'They

are but little children at play!'

'It's the Sabbath and they must observe it with sombre propriety. Children must stand corrected lest they become by and by a rod for their parents backs!'

'And you would suck the joy out of every living thing in the name of propriety!'
Many about me stopped and smiled as I delivered my scathing rebuke.

Then Minister Ezra raised his finger and pointed ominously at Tom as he retorted with fury.

'It takes but one bad apple to spoil the rest of the barrel.'

'Mayhap!' I replied boldly, as we led our children away. 'Lessen that is, of course, that it is not instead the rottenness of the barrel that is doing the spoiling!'

I may have had the last word then, but even as I came away I had the feeling that Ezra might still make me pay for it...

Chapter Nine

January 1649

There was a great commotion in the village as an official Parliament messenger, having made great pain to get through upon our freezing, rutted roads stopped on his way through to Louth with the latest word from London. The news was stunning! The 'traitor' was dead, he had proclaimed before swiftly passing on to Rasen. Our sovereign, King Charles Stuart, was dead. It was over. After a thousand years of Kings, we were no longer anyone's kingdom other than God's and under the protection the Parliamentarians.

Then a few days later another determined traveller passed by, though this one tarried overnight at the village inn for food and to rest his horse. He was a nobleman and on his way back home to the North. Word spread like mites among chickens as those of us who could, gathered at the tavern to hear his shocking account.

'I never was for the King,' he had explained in trembling tones as he sat at his supper of roast beef and bread with a host of curious onlookers hanging upon his every morsel of news. 'Yet never was I truly agin[20] him either! And that which I have witnessed in London these weeks past hath been a sorry affair that doth truly put all English men to shame! For those that signed for his execution were no better than murderers themselves in taking away the King's life. No matter whether he be guilty or not of the crimes they set before him. Was murder done by Parliament? It was murder because it was carried out by hands that, under the law of our land, had no authority to do it!'

This gentleman then went on to relate, in unflinching detail, the final days of the King. Charles Stuart had been brought to trial before a chosen jury made up of Parliamentarians, army officers, and major landowners. They numbered some one hundred and thirty or more in all, though most, like General Fairfax, did not turn up for the trial.

'Indeed,' the gentleman explained, 'when Fairfax's name was called out in court he was nowhere to be seen. A masked lady stepped forward in his stead and spake[21] out loudly saying that he had more wit than to be there and that perhaps those that were would have done better not to have been there either. Aye! There was such dissent from amongst even their own that it was wickedness itself for Parliament to proceed, and indeed with such a reckless haste.'

Apparently, this predominantly Roundhead court had then charged the King with 'waging war upon Parliament', a representation of the people – and so the people of England themselves. Indeed, the full responsibility for all of the murders, burnings, damages and mischiefs to the nation in the Civil War was laid clearly upon His Majesty's head.

In his defence, the King steadfastly refused to make answer against these indictments, saying instead that, as God's representative on earth, this court had no authority to try him. When Parliament refused to be swayed by this argument, the King then went on to point out that as the Army had expelled several Members of Parliament from the House only weeks before, which even by Parliaments own yardstick, it had then not the legal authority to arrange his trial. As a result of this, Charles refused, steadfastly, to put forward any defence for himself. He also vehemently restated the King's own belief that he was God's chosen and divine representative on earth and that, being so, declared that no earthly court of law had *any* right to pass judgement upon him.

Arguments went back and forth for days afterwards as to the legality of Parliament's court to try the King. But unsurprisingly Parliament ultimately ruled itself to be legal. And then, on the twenty-seventh day of January, granted Charles one final opportunity to defend himself against the charges. When he again refused, he was found guilty by the remnant jury of fifty-nine men. They duly sentenced him to death.

Just three days later and with no chance of

appeal, King Charles was taken to a tall, black-cloth draped scaffold that had been especially built outside Whitehall Palace for his very public execution.

Mounted Roundheads were judiciously employed to keep the crowd some distance back from the execution, and so the public was mostly out of hearing when the King delivered his final and poignant address to his people. All most onlookers saw was a calm and composed monarch being led through a window and out upon the high platform. Once there, he was seen to reach inside his pocket for a scrap of paper before his mouth began to move with mostly inaudible words drifting into the frosty morning air. Then, turning to an officer in attendance, the King took off his cloak, stooped, and laid his head upon the wooden block. After a few moments of pause, the King then threw wide his arms. The axe fell almost immediately, severing his head with one blow.

'Here!' the traveller at the inn said, reaching inside his pocket and withdrawing a much crumpled pamphlet. 'Those of you that can read, look! Here are the King's last words, printed here plain for all to see.'

'...I never did begin the war with the two Houses of Parliament... They began war upon me... if anybody will look at the dates of what happened... they will see clearly that they [Parliament] began these unhappy troubles, not I... therefore I tell you I am the martyr of the people.'

So, King Charles Stuart was dead. He had gone to his execution that morning at White Hall, no doubt believing himself set to be considered a martyr as great as any of the saints. A martyr for Christ and a martyr for Kingship. No doubt, as he climbed upon the scaffold above the rabble, his comparison with Christ would not have been lost upon him. For here was a divinely anointed King handing his mortal body over to the mob for execution. I am certain that he died with unshakable conviction that, as the axe struck, he would be immediately translated into heaven, so far removed from the spectacle of his bloody head being held high by the executioner like any other common criminal. I thought him a fool for doing so.

Now told in full, the villagers dispersed, like dead leaves scattered on a chill winter wind, back to their homes. Yes, a few were elated and revelling in the King's demise, yet most were in deep shock after hearing the news of the execution. Many, as I did, wondered what would happen next. Would it be as Thomas had predicted? Five hundred little kings instead of one? Or were we to be presented with one new king, albeit in a different guise? A stinking rose by any other name?

I thought again about what Thomas had said. I had not then fully appreciated his words or even, I freely admit, understood them. Now, with the King dead and Puritan Parliamentarians at the helm of our newfound Commonwealth, I began to see...

'So that is that!' Hope sighed in bitter resignation. 'With the King dead, we have lost all chances of having our lands returned to us.'

'Then instead, we shall have to make the most of the lives we have here,' I told her. 'For we are now better off than most folks and have our God-given talents to put to good use.'

As for young Tom? While Hope and I had been reduced to living like peasants, I had grander plans for him. For while his mother had laboured on the land, I had taken every opportunity to school the boy. He could read and write and although we had no books for formal learning, I imparted to him, every scrap of knowledge of the world that I could summon into my mind. And he? From the all-new Shakespeare to the well-known Socrates, he devoured it all like a hungry animal, and was fast becoming a scholar with learning far beyond his years. I may not have known what the future might hold for Hope and me but I knew that an educated young man, no matter how humble his home, would have higher expectations than others as he made his way out into the world beyond.

For certain, talk persisted for many months

about 'what if Prince Charles returns to the country and raises an army?' Or, 'when monarchy is restored...'

The moment his father had met his death, the Prince of Wales had indeed been declared King Charles II by the surviving Royalists. And he had tried to regain his kingdom by force. But defeated, the young King Charles was forced to flee to Europe and self-exile along with his staunchest, die-hardest followers.

Thereafter, as the months turned into years under the awful Puritan yoke, any prospect of future England with a King once more at its head, soon faded away. How could 'restoration' happen? Things had surely gone too far... Many people like me had to come to accept this. After all, how can the egg be put back together once the shell is cracked and the yolk has spilled out?

*　　　*　　　*

That woman came to me like a familiar. She stopped me dead at the churchyard gate, and even as she started to speak I remember thinking that I could scarcely recall her passing but a clutch of words with me afore that day. Most of those were only lip-served greetings as we passed each other, going in or out of church on a Lord's Day. Yet that day she greeted me as if I were her life-long friend.

'Dear Bessie. Please won't you stop by and see my daughter, Katherine?' A crack of smile pleaded from her limestone white face and the palm of her outstretched hand lay subconsciously open as if in readiness to receive. I sensed at once that she must be desperately in need of something from me, and therefore at pains to make her overture as appealing as possible to my sensibilities.

Megan was her name, and she was not born of our village. Some say that she was the daughter of a drunken Welsh tinker and that her equally drunk soon-to-be-husband was intoxicated by her burnished coppery tumble of hair and cat green eyes the moment he met her in a Rasen alehouse on market day. So it was that ten years before she had 'married in' to the village. Yet, even wed that long, she was still treated by the others about as a 'stranger'. Even more so, since her husband had so recently died.

'Why, Mistress Megan?' I asked.

'She ails[22] so! She was not even fit for church this morning. Please, canst you stop by and see her?'

From the cursory discourse that followed, I gathered that Katherine had first fallen ill more than a month before. Yet as she had got no worse until today, so Megan had not troubled to get help for her, thinking that she would be better for biding some time.

'It has been a bad season for farmers' lung,' I noted 'Ne'er a household I know has not been affected by it this year.'

It had been an usually mild winter, yet damp, just like the autumn before.

'You know what they say?' another woman passing by who had overheard my remark, chipped in. 'Wam[23] winter, full churchyard.'

'Yes. And is that not ever so?' added another.

'Take no heed, Megan,' I said after they had passed on.'Tis probably nought more serious than a lingering cough. Of course I will come.'

Young Tom was impatiently tugging at his mother's skirts to be out of the chill, and so I bade Hope to go on home with him, and said that I would follow on presently after I had walk back from Megan's.

When we got there, Katherine was resting on a mattress by the door of the squalid cottage. Beside her sat a wizened old crone in a chair, holding a scarlet-cheeked infant upon her lap. The child was busily mouthing a smooth, round stone. One of Megan's neighbours, I assumed.

Megan beckoned her daughter to rise for me to inspect. Within moments I had noted that Katherine coughed almost incessantly with every move she made. I approached the child and gently placed my palm upon her forehead. She felt hot and clammy to the touch.

'So, young Katherine, 'tis a troublesome cough

you have there,' I said. 'How long have you been like this?'

The girl made to answer me but her mother cut in quickly with something in her natural tongue which I did not comprehend. She swiftly continued in English.

'A few weeks, Mistress Bessie... It comes and goes,' she said. 'Worse at some times... yet seldom better at others.'

'And her spittle? Is it clear?'

'No. 'Tis mostly greenish in hue and thick, when she can get it up that is!'

'Perhaps that is the problem,' I surmised. 'It is settled in her chest and needs to be shifting.'

I asked if I might listen at the child's back a moment, and so her mother quickly unlaced her bodice and lifted it aside. I crouched down beside Katherine and pressed my ear against her hot skin. In between coughs, I could hear her heart pounding away like a horse at the gallop, and the girl wheezed as she breathed out. 'Twas then that I had the first inkling that the cause might be a more serious ailment in her lungs than suggested, but dismissed that thought because it did not tally with what the mother was telling me. Then I tapped Katherine's back soundly with two fingers as if I were picking up a hot loaf from baking and testing to see if it were risen well. It should have sounded hollow inside, with lots of pockets of air just as properly cooked bread should be. Instead, Katherine's chest sounded doughy, and I thought I knew the root of her problem.

'She is definitely congested in there. No wonder she is coughing so much. She is probably full of phlegm. Are you absolutely certain that there is no blood coming up?' I asked.

'No. None... You can cure her then, can't you?' Megan asked pointedly.

'I can certainly give you something to ease the cough and her discomfort. But as for a cure? With most things in this life, that is up to the good Lord Himself. All I can do is make up a preparation to help ease her symptoms. But yes , with all you have told me of her history, I am very hopeful that Katherine will be well enough again with time. I will go home now and in the morning return with a goodly supply of medicine and will show you how you must give it.'

'I have no siller[24] to give you...' she said with a sigh.

From the state of her house, I would have been surprised if she had.

'No, mind Megan,' I said. 'I do want reward for what I can do.'

With that, I left.

Many weeks went by, and because Megan had said no more, I assumed her child was better. Spring, which had burst in upon us with a glory of lentern lilies, was already passing into summer with fading drifts of bluebells carpeting the woodland floor as far as the eye could see. Cow-parsley sprang up, and elderflower had clothed the hedgerows when I heard that still Megan's child had not recovered. And then I was called to the cottage again. I was perplexed and werrittin[25]' over the child's diminished condition, and wondering if what I had already administered had caused an adverse effect how. I no longer knew how best I could treat her. So I thought to try with stronger potions. All of a piece[26], as I sat downstairs by Katherine's bed, I noticed a heavily soiled rag tucked in by the edge of the mattress showing me that the child had been coughing up blood, despite her mother's assurance still that she was not. It was then that my suspicions were truly roused. The child had been ill for a lot longer and far worse than her mother would admit. However, to my added surprise, when I pressed Megan hard again on this subject, she steadfastly denied it was so.

I realised that the girl had consumption – a disease that does not usually play out as quickly as this supposedly had, and which even the most eminent physicians are both ineffectual to treat and even warier lest they too become infected.

'If you cannot be relied upon to give me the truth,' I warned Megan sternly, 'then how can I be expected to treat your daughter wisely?'

Megan barely blinked an eye.

I took Megan by the arm and put her aside, away from the poor child's hearing.

'I am sorry,' I said firmly,' but I do not think that this is now a simple case of congestion in the lungs. I fear that if Katherine does not improve soon, then this is a case of consumption and then... but a matter of time before she dies. You should pray for the Lord's mercy and hope for the best but prepare yourself for the worst.'

Megan turned waxy[27], said nothing with words but pulled sharply way from my grip.

Shortly afterwards, I left. But not without feeling the wrath in Megan's green eyes searing into my back as I walked back up along the lane towards my home...

Chapter Ten

Hope sneezed aloud, almost toppling the stool on which she was perching so precariously. Working together that day had so put me in mind of such cleaning days I had spent with my own late mother.

'These old beams seem to fair breed cobwebs,' I remember her moaning. 'Where are the spiders that made all of these webs?' Hope complained, sweeping them clear off the beams with a small swish of birch twigs. 'There must be a hundred webs up here but I still have yet to see a single spider!'

She was right. We rarely saw the culprits, for they were mostly the painfully thin type of spider with almost translucent long, spindly legs and tiny round pinhead bodies. They span an enormous amount of dust clinging silks in no less time than a back's turn and seemed capable of huddling themselves into almost invisible. They were not at all like the large, webless wolf spiders that, come autumn, would boldly scuttle across the cottage floor in plain sight of the flickering hearth. Either that, or they had to be tipped out of empty beakers standing on the mantle, or ejected from vacant shoes come morning. How Hope and Tom both hated those little creatures! Not necessarily out of fear, but more for the wretched surprise when they sprang out from nowhere upon the unwary.

'If I were to grow rich once more, then I would build my cottage with beams made of chestnut wood,' I told my daughter. 'For spiders never weave their webs in chestnut wood.'

Hope laughed, and was then just wiping her hand across her mouth as a knock came upon our already open door. I looked around to find Megan's old crone standing there. I welcomed her in, but she declined, preferring instead to conduct her visit with barely a toe set across my threshold. Yet her nervous eyes were already well inside my house, busily surveying every nook of our cottage until they fell upon Mister Lollop and he suddenly let out a loud squawk. After that, she looked only in my direction.

'Mistress Megan sent me,' she blurted with some hesitation 'She says how she needs your help again, Mistress Bessie.'

'In what way?' I asked.

''Tis her daughter. She is now so dreadfully ill and Megan says that she do know that only you have the power to heal her, if only she could afford to give you siller!'

'What nonsense! I have no such power!' I replied soundly with a tone of rebuke.' I have told Mistress Megan before that all I have is a humble knowledge of the workings of certain herbs. Those herbs may be of some comfort, but 'cures' are in the hands of the good Lord. Not in mine!'

'Please!' the crone pleaded.' Will you not go to her home and see to the daughter? She says that this time she will pay you anything! Anything you ask!'

'As well she knows,' I argued, 'I do not ask for *any* payment. But yes, of course I will come to the child.'

I was shocked and saddened to see young Katherine again. Her face was milky pale and her body so consumed and lethargic that she barely had wits about her to know that I was even there. I knew at once that there was little left that I could do for her, for even then death's rattle was upon the child's blue-edged lips.

I asked Megan for hot water and took out from my pocket some herbs I had brought with me, and then I steeped them into an infusion to ease Katherine's breathing. This I slowly spooned down her throat, sip by tentative sip, until she had taken the most part. Then I sat beside the girl, gently holding her hand and imparting what comfort I might.

'There!' Megan suddenly exclaimed as the rattle in Katherine's throat began to subside. 'She is getting better! Her breathing is easing!'

'No Megan,' I gently whispered.' Her breathing is easing because her effort is ceasing. Katherine is dying... Do you not understand? The end is at hand.'

Megan would not hear of it.

Within an hour or maybe less, the life slipped out of the child and she was gone. Gently, I closed her eyes amidst screams of abuse from her now distraught mother.

'Murderer!' she wailed and hissed like a she-cat.

Her neighbour came a-running as Megan continued to yowl out that I had murdered her child. That I had willfully let her Katherine die.

I left that house beneath a veil of tears of my own. I was deeply distressed for not being able to have done more for either of them. For I was a mother too and knew about loss...

*   *   *

I was not expecting Hope to come home so early. As soon as I saw her tear-streaked face and swollen eyes I knew that something was very wrong with my daughter.

'What ever is the matter, Hope?'

'I do not know!' she sobbed. 'For the breath in my body, I do not know what is the wrong that I am supposed to have done!'

'Why? What has happened'

'There I was, working away with the others when I suddenly noticed them passing some whisper along and amongst themseln. At first, I paid it no mind, but then I saw the looks they were all giving me. Yet, when I caught their eyes, they looked away again, really quickly. Then it happened... They rise up as one, like a gang of robbers! They made gads out of sticks and shooed me down the far corner of the field and into the patch of elders there. I was so frit[28] that I lited out[29] an ran here, all the way home!'

'They herded you into the holt[30]? ' Didn't they say why?'

'No! All they said was that I was to play there with my 'master' – the 'Old One'. 'Is that bad?'

'Yes! It is bad? Those trees are left at the corner

of fields out of silly superstition. They are there for the devil to play amongst, else he would go play in the fields and spoil the crops!'

'The devil?' Hope did not understand what she had done to be pushed into the devil's holt. Nor did I. Then, I quickly suspected that she had done nothing at all...

Not long after, Minister Ezra came. Though I sensed that a good many others had come with him, he alone kicked open the door and strode boldly into my cottage unbidden[31] .Then, almost immediately, he set about trying to kill Mister Lollop with a stout staff he had carried in with him for that sole purpose. Tom screamed in terror and before I could stop him, he had already run into the vile man's path to try to protect his pet. Ezra pushed the boy aside with a sweep of contempt as he continued to rain blow after blow upon the stricken bird. Tom continued to scream, and his mother too, for the minister to stop. But he would not. The crow scuttled along the floor towards the table and took shelter under it. Ezra followed, hurling aside the chairs in anger in his effort to get to the bird to kill it. Everything upon the table went a tip-tupping[32] in his wake, sending our pots and beakers over to smash on the floor and be troddled[33] under the minister's feet as his frenzied onslaught continued.

Somehow, Mister Lollop miraculously managed to eschew his would be murderer and, although injured, loped[34] and fluttered in panic towards the still open door and flew off past the mob gathered beyond.

Without further ado or even a word, Ezra turned his wrath against me instead. Grabbing my arm spitefully, he began to drag me outside.

'Leave her be!' Hope screeched, 'Leave her be!'

With that, Ezra turned as to menace Hope with such words as to say that she had best hold her tongue lessen her child soon became wanting for a mother too. Utterly bewildered, my daughter and grandson could not comprehend the reason or the wherefore of why I was being taken. I knew though. I knew, yet there was nothing in my power that I could do to put a halt to this madness. This was my repayment for trying to help a sickening child. I was about to be charged with witchcraft.

The minister handed me over to his men and had them take me up to the church, where I was chained inside the open porch like some unclaimed animal in the penfold[35]. There I was to be left to my own devices, with neither food nor water until my especially appointed Puritan inquisitor arrived the following morning from Boston. Until then, I crouched at the innermost corner to shelter against the cold, pitiless walls. I could do nothing but gaze across the churchyard, watching daylight fade beyond the horizon. Then darkness, in its stead, crept with long fingers across the half-toppled grave stones.

My sole comfort that night was knowing that my father lay close by. My mother and Judd somewhere also. Yet I was taunted too, the whole night through, by the knowledge that buried in unconsecrated ground somewhere beyond the grey, grim wall lay the wicked bones of my evil step-father, Nathan. Even after all of those years, as I sat alone in that moonless night, in amongst the shroud of shadows creeping along through the hours, I fancied that I could see him coming for me. But it was not Nathan I should have feared of coming. It should have been the witch-finder, Rech. For witches are fit for hanging...

*   *   *

'Next day, Minister Ezra called for 'order' after someone in court shouted: 'A witch is not the same as an ill-wisher! I know Megan, and she is the kind of woman that has a way to make folk wish her ill. I for one but that don't make me a witch!'

'Aye!' shouted back Megan's crone,' But Mistress Bessie has a winkersome[36] eye!'

Rech sat quietly by, with his hands together as if joined in prayer and tucked under his wizening chin. He looked on benignly as Minister Ezra went about setting out the case for him – as if he were preaching but another of his customary hell and damnation sermons. It must have been a rare joy for Rech to have found one as loathsome as he was and as eager to carry out his filthy 'duties' for him. However, Ezra was not to have it all his own way...

'Tis nonsense! Hope's employer protested loudly. 'My wife and my child owe their lives to Mistress Bessie!'

'And how can you be certain that their recovery was not owed to witchcraft?' Ezra prodded. 'Or that their illness was not inflicted deliberately so as to reap a ripe reward from you after?'

The farmer fell silent in contemplation. Who could blame him for having the seeds of doubt now cast into his mind by such an eloquently practiced tongue?

Ezra, sensing that one such doubt might begat[37] more, turned about and pierced the swine man with his needling glance.

'And what about you, Jack Bilber?' He pricked his memory. 'Did you not once tell me how you thought that Mistress Bessie had bewitched your pigs?'

Jack lowered his eyes, seemingly not wanting to be drawn.

'Well, I cannot say now as I did, or didn't,' he replied. 'Yet I can say how it pains me to see all of this defending and proving betwixt common folk.'

'Then perhaps we best hear the evidence from one that does know?' Ezra quickly sought out Megan with his eyes. 'Tell the court, pray Mistress Megan. What led you to believe that Mistress Bessie here had bewitched your child?'

Megan stood up somberly and began to spin out her woe-spun yarn, aided and abetted by the crone at her side.

'I axed[38] for her to heal my daughter but instead she let her die,' Megan said quietly.

Then the old woman cackled: 'I can vouch for that! I 'eard her myseln saying at first how the child had but a troublesome cough and how it could be righted – for a price!

'That is untrue!' I protested loudly. 'I never asked you for payment! And the daughter died of consumption!' Then I turned and caught her mother straight in the eye. 'I asked you all along for her symptoms, and from the outset you lied to me, making little of them and misleading me into the bargain! Then, when I at last realised what truly ailed her, I told you outright that there was no cure I knew for that. No doctor can cure consumption, so why should I be held to account for her death?'

Rech suddenly sprang to his feet.

'A prisoner accused of witchcraft may not talk until all of the evidence is put forward!' he ordered. 'Speak once more out of turn Mistress Bessie and I shall have you placed in a scold[39]!'

So it was, that this evil blackening continued, and yet I was unable to defend myself. But Rech had not reckoned on my daughter filling that breech.

Then Megan shrilled back: 'Twasn't consumption that killed her! You put a spell upon my daughter!' As she screeched, she withdrew something from inside her secrets[40]. 'For when my Katherine lay dead, and when I was sewing her into her sheet for a shroud, I found these dried bones of a toad hidden in the straw of her mattress.'

Megan opened her hand to show the court a small collection of fine whitened bones. If true, then by popular superstition it indicated a powerful spell indeed.

'Not only that,' she continued, 'but three times Mistress Bessie came to my cottage, and each time she had left after my saying that I could not pay her. And then I saw that the fresh milk in the jug for my childer[41] had curdled!'

'I seen her!' The crone was crowing again. 'I seen her run around the outside of the church three times to call up the devil!'

'Blatherskate[42]! ' Hope scolded. 'That is but a spiteful lie! My mother can no more run once around the church than a chicken could fly up to perch on its steeple! Look at her! She is close on sixty years of age

147

and near to needing a stick for support!'

Undaunted, the old woman continued to sew mischief.

'And I seen you too, Mistress Hope! With me own two eyes I seen yer eating spiders in yer cottage!'

'This is madness!' Hope retorted. 'I have never done any such thing!'

'Then deny you this!' Megan found her shout 'When you first came up to my cottage as you left, I saw that there were seven magpies perched upon the thatch! 'Twas a sign that you had brought the 'Owld One[43]' in with you, if ever there was!'

At this mention of 'the devil', a loud murmur began to arise from the onlookers. For fear of the devil is the taproot that anchors simple peasants fast to superstition, so much so that they fear even to mention his name. My being accused of being in league with the devil gave cause enough for serious consideration by those, who up until that point, may have been swayed to give judgement in my favour.

'And I seen Mistress Bessie a-burning Elder-wood in her fire to let 'im out!' the old goat butted in. 'And what about her familiar? That wicked black crow that your mother keeps in her confidence?'

This provoked a new sense of unease that swelled among the rest of the villagers, who suddenly seemed convinced by the false testimony. Almost everyone in our village had either seen or heard of our bird, and many country folk, be they simple or schooled, harboured grave misgivings about such a superstitious creature residing in a house.

'Tis not a familiar nor any such thing to do with the evil!' Hope again responded. 'It was but an injured fledgling my young son fetched home and then tended with love and care into adulthood. If anything it be a sign that, with love and kindness, even the most black-hearted creature can be tamed by a pure heart. 'Tis a lesson of which you should take heed, Mister Rech!'

Some none too cautious souls laughed, for first impressions of Rech had already left a sorry mark upon many. Rech, who found himself being made a fool of, rose sharply in venomous retaliation.

'Yet on the subject of the black-hearted,' he spewed, 'tell the people here! Are you not born a wicked heathen of the New World, Mistress Hope?'

'Yes!' Hope answered defiantly. 'That is true. I am! And I cannot deny it, for look upon me... Am I not brown of skin? And look at my hair! 'Tis as black as the bird you hate!' As she said this, she cast off her cap to reveal her raven black hair. 'I too was a foundling, taken up from my dead mother's corpse and rescued by my Father during a raid upon my natural people...'

'You mean by your *adoptive* father? Rech cut in. He laboured the point of correcting her, no doubt hoping to show that as Hope shared no common birthright with those now standing in judgement, she therefore deserved no empathy. He badly preempted my daughter's reply.

'No sir! I mean Our most sacred Lord God, my Father in Heaven!' Again, this young woman had made Rech look the fool he was. 'For, with love and kindness, I too have thrived to stand before you now to bear witness of my mother's goodness in raising me to be a God-fearing Christian. Yet what of you, Rech. Do you not fear God for bearing false witness against an innocent woman?'

'Enough!' Rech shrieked, suddenly losing his facade of self-control and turning livid. 'Seize her! And cast her with the mother! I shall not listen to God's name being taken in vain with her lies!'
With that, I broke my silence.

'Wait!' I shouted. 'All I have ever done is try to ease the ills suffered by my neighbours! By my remedies? Yes! Yet always with prayer to my Lord God on high. That, through His grace and mercy, those I tended would recover.'

Ezra tried to have me gagged, but a number of people in the crowd called out persistently, 'Let her speak!' Their voices would not be stilled by threats. And then, to my continued surprise, Rech, perhaps fearing 'the mob', reluctantly gestured for Ezra to let me be and to continue – for the moment at least.

So I spoke what I was preparing as my last words.

'If this be deemed an evil thing, then go on!' I shouted defiantly. 'Hang me! Hang me, Rech! Or burn me! Or do what ever it is that will quench that thirsting hatred you have of me! Only do it now! Do it now, Rech! Because I am not afraid to die! For I know that when I die I will stand before my Lord God innocent of your charges of witchcraft!

'Yet what of you?' I said, turning to the crowd ' What will be your reply when He calls you to account if you stand by and condone my murder? For 'tis you who will be held to account also! Do you want to be regarded as this man's accomplice and made also to pay the price for his evil deeds?'

'My evil deeds?' Rech squawked. 'You have spoken before these people today as if you are unblemished! But you are not, are you Mistress? Tell me, how many of these fine upright folk here have been fooled into bearing witness to your goodliness? How many of them realise that you are but a wicked adulteress and bear the brand of a harlot upon your breast?'

Their shock was audible. For on hearing these words, I so swear that such a silence fell upon my support that you could have heard a leaf fall off a tree. Once more, I feared, Rech had succeeded in laying me low in the sight of everyone, and with his spite, in an instant had ruined my hard-salvaged reputation. How many times must I struggle to overcome outrageous misfortune, only to be cast straight down again? I was on the brink of wishing myself dead. My fight was gone.

''Tis true!' a man's voice somewhere shouted out. The lady bears the brand of a harlot , sure enough, burnt upon her after standing trial at Stowe.'

Rech smiled broadly, having seemingly found an ally to help clinch his case.

I heard those words too, yet my heart suddenly leapt up to rally me on.

'Yet,' the voice continued, 'what is past is past.

Surely? The lady was tried and made to pay the severest penalty. Besides, I have stood by today and listened to all that has been said, and 'tis clear to me that there is a might of spite in the air just now. I see no case to be answered here other than petty vindictive tittle-tattle from ones that ought to know better. Yet, in all of this, I am curious to know more of the motive of this here magistrate, Rech. I hear tell that he claims to be a true man of God and a seeker of truth. Yet the truth is before him clear as day in this matter, but he seems content not to see it!'

Rech squirmed. A man who had grown accustomed to having his own way was suddenly uneasy, and obviously uncertain to what end this stranger had put him to the hook.

'Could it be,' my gallant Captain Quick continued, 'that Mister Rech knows this woman from some time before? That he had perhaps held some past grievance with her late Royalist husband and so has hounded her, even here, merely to serve out his own revenge against her instead?'

Rech had managed to retain his mask of a confident grin, yet his eyes were fixed in shock, or perhaps even in terror. And that slash of a smile that had been set in a gloating countenance was about to prove itself fleeting. My poacher friend was abouts reveal all.

'Aye!' he continued. 'This Mistress Bessie, as you all know her, was brought to trial for passing herself off as the wife of Sir Thomas of Stowe, a Royalist gentleman, and for bearing him a bastard son. Mister Rech here, oversaw the case himself. Only it was not true! Was it Rech?'

Quick turned on him like a terrier on a rat. 'Only I had the privilege to serve alongside Sir Thomas, and I oftimes heard him speak warm and lovingly of his wife, Lady Elizabeth. And of how they were married in the Separatist convention that surely you, Rech, as a Puritan, should have commended.

'Good people,' Quick said, looking about him, to

emphasise that he was addressing everyone present except Rech, 'that fine upstanding Lady Elizabeth is that same woman you see standing before you now. The charges brought against her at Stowe were false. They were unjustly brought against her by Rech, with the sole intention of depriving Sir Thomas' lawful heirs of their rightful inheritance. He blackmailed Lady Elizabeth into pleading guilty by guile and by threatening to deport her beloved adoptive daughter back to the natives of Virginia, and to a fate worse than death! Lady Elizabeth was forced to sacrifice herself and lay down her honour in order to save Mistress Hope's life!'

'Is this true?' Angry protests burst from the crowd like puss from a lanced boil.

Rech squirmed again, and then shuddered. He attempted to bleat out an answer but could no longer make himself heard above the villagers' growling howls of dissent.

Then, as suddenly as these people had turned against me, they arose as one into the angry mob that Rech feared and ran him and his chief cohort, Ezra, out of the village. I heard later that these two men were too afraid to stop until night pressed in, forcing them to take shelter at a tavern on the top road to Rasen.

For what happened next to Rech, I can not say even now that I am sorry. For even in this world, a man may reap what he has sewn – and so can expect to receive in accordance with what he hath given. Rech's one true passion in life had been to hate.

During the evening, while venturing out into the fresh air to relieve himself after a dubious meal of cold shoulder and bread, magistrate Rech was shot dead. His assassin was believed to have fired from the cover of trees, some two-hundred yards distance. They said whoever it was could only have been an expert with a musket. For the ball had hit home clean between Rech's beady eyes and obliterated the mole on his forehead. His killer was never found.

Chapter Eleven

Suddenly, after years of establishing himself as our Lord Protector, Oliver Cromwell was dead. The Commonwealth, like his shroud, still hung on grimly to the man. Yet it too was fast succumbing to decay. Cromwell's successor and son, Richard, was no match for the hard-liners in the Army. This younger Cromwell was not cut from the same tough cloth as his father, and so within months he stepped back from his inherited responsibility of national stewardship. And then for time society and order came dangerously close to unravelling at its seams.

Speculation spread, followed on by rumour, that the exiled King Charles Stuart II might be about to be invited back to England to reclaim his rightful throne. If the monarchy could be restored, then there would also be hope that lands seized from loyal Royalist supporters – as a consequence of their loyalty during the Civil War – might be returned to former owners.

*   *   *

The breeze slowly billowed out of the rustling green strands of willow edged on to my cottage. The scene was as tranquil as a meadow in summer. The warm current of air about my face and neck gently stirred tired grey whips of hair out from under my sullied cap as I worked on, alone, in my garden. I loved days like these – spent with my hands buried in the earth and with my mind free to wander. Often, on such days, with the swirl of leaves and the swish of branches above my head, the sounds rushed into my mind to take me back to Plimouth. I could close my eyes and be there, walking along the glistening sea shore on an unhurried afternoon. The deep reflection of my thought mirrored in the rock pools betwixt the sea strands, as I picked my way along the shore. I would be harvesting shells from the still wet sand with Francis Eaton at my side. The sea had brought us together and fixed us, like tangles of drifted seaweed upon life's battered shore. Not by design but by accident. Two lost souls, cast upon the winter breakers who, by summer's smile lay entwined upon the sand together until the wretched tide turned in upon us and, hapless[44], we were rent apart.

I often thought of him and the child. I was the second lost mother in that poor mite's life. How had Francis explained me away? And what of Francis, himself? Had he handed me on easily, back to the man I had wed before? Or had he fought for me, clasping tightly to the very last moment – to keep me with him? Or did he let slip of me gently, to be teased apart by the waves as we continued on our separate ways. Was it as easy as we had been put together? Had he missed me? Does he still live now? Does he wonder where I am or how I fared?

In my later years I often wondered, 'What if?' What if I had stayed on in Plimouth and lived out my life as Dorothy Eaton? What would I be doing there now? What if I had been allowed to live on in perfect ignorance of the fact that Thomas was still alive? What if he had never come after me at all? Would I ever have had children of my own? Might not the budding friendship betwixt my new husband and me have blossomed into the full flowering of a fully consummated union? Mayhap, given but a little more time, we might have mutually consented to remove the wooden board that held us separate in our bed at night.

I had a stepson of whom I was warmly fond, though I never fully bonded with him as I had later with Hope. I had cared for his daily needs as a mother would and gave him every comfort that I could. Yet looking back I realised that I never allowed myself to grow too fond of him, and at the time I could not understand why. Maybe then it had been too soon after the *others*. Perhaps it had been too soon after all of those other poor mites entrusted to my care upon the Mayflower had died so wretchedly. There seemed to have been too many little lives that I had nursed away into the darkness and still needed time to grieve over.

Then, when I opened my eyes and surveyed

my little patch of earth, I would suddenly feel such a deep sense of wellbeing. I felt as if I was standing beside God in His Garden of Eden, at the creation of the world. Such wonders with but my two bare hands had I achieved! And so well pleased was I at the fruit of my labours! If only I could have held onto that moment, the very essence of that moment forever, then I would have found my earthly paradise.

I had crops a plenty and food to store well into the following spring. I had my Indian corn, squash and beans as our staple with eggs, fowl, milk and cheese. And it was all so plentiful in surplus that we could barter for all the flour and other provisions for which we could wish. Above all this, I had built a solid reputation for my herbal remedies which, although I never charged people for my help, brought in bountiful rewards from grateful souls whom I, with the Lord's blessing, had cured.

That is why in that autumn of the year of our Lord sixteen-hundred-and-fifty-nine, I had found the decision then facing me so difficult to make. For I was almost decided that, should the King be restored, I would give up my tiny Lincolnshire homestead and go to London, where I would attempt to reclaim back my family's lost lands. 'Twas never simply for matters of profit and property. And this decision was certainly not born out a desire motivated by greed. It was a matter of honour and justice.

Yet to finance such a journey and to stay on in that city for, only the good Lord knew how long, and to see a petition through to completion, would mean my selling everything we owned, including the livestock. If at the end I failed, then my family and I would be back to having nothing.

I talked the possibilities over with Hope. She was at once adamant that if Restoration came, then we should do everything in our power to regain our titles and our lands. However, when Tom came to visit us, he was soundly opposed to our plan.

'I shall not go with you, Mother!' Tom had

steadfastly refused to accompany us , and with good reason. He had secured himself a position as clerk to a wealthy Lincoln merchant. He was paid more than a fair wage from his kindly master and had been provided with basic lodgings above his office. Moreover, unlike most other commoner lads, he had excellent prospects for self advancement and understood and valued these well.

'If I go with you I shall lose my position,' he argued 'And my master has promised me that, as he has no son to follow him in his venture, he will mentor me for attending to all his business in his old age, just as if I were his own son. For my part, I must in return prove that I am honest and equally dependable. I cannot leave him now, Mother. For if I do, then I not only risk losing everything for which I have worked, but I would be proving my honour false. And all for what? A maybe? A chance? For a gamble in place of a certainty?'

'And you would choose ambition above your mother?' Hope scalded him with her hot words.

'Now then!' I interjected, as I tried to cool the air. 'Ambition is not a sin, Hope! On the contrary, honest ambition followed through by honest dealing 'tis pleasing to God's eyes. And Tom is being honest. He is looking to the future, and I dare say not only to his own wellbeing but even to a means of keeping his dear mother in her old age. So daughter, have a mind not to scold the lad so!'

But regardless of my remonstration, Hope continued trying to persuade Tom that, come the time, he should come away with us. When her arguments failed, she turned to me again.

'Make him see, Mother! Make him see that, as my son, he is honour-bound to do his duty for me before that of an employer, and so to come with us.'

'Oh that I could easily do,' I sighed. 'I could bully him with duty and burden him with guilt. But why should I? Can you not see that the lad is of an age and wit to have a duty to himself? Besides, he is safe here. Safer still, for he will not be having to make his irksome journey through the clagging[45] mud road from Lincoln to visit us here.'

Then Tom added, 'It is not only I who have much to lose, Grandmother. Look to yourselves also, and all you have here. Can you really afford the risk?

'Besides,' he continued, trying to calm his troubled mother, 'it is nought now but rumour... all this about the King returning from exile! We have been a commonwealth for as long as I have memories, and many at Lincoln say that shall not now end. Maybe we are fretting over rainbows!'

Yet it would end. And on the day the news that the monarchy was about to be restored arrived in our village, it was almost impossible for me to sleep that night. My mind and my stomach churned on and on. I found myself recalling events and places in my life and pondering upon what then the future might hold for us now that the Commonwealth was finally to be put away in its coffin.

I had witnessed so much. From maidservant to housekeeper at Gainsborough Hall, from wife to widow, then from wife to bigamist and all of the hardships I had endured in the two colonies of the New World. From being made a lady to being branded a harlot, from outcast to home-comer. Now I was an aging grandmother to a fatherless child and mother to a husbandless daughter. My life had been in constant shift, like the sands on Plimouth beach. And now, after more than thirteen years in this cottage with our settled country life, I was contemplating yet another radical change – whether to go to London or not.

Thoughts raced through my mind. Thoughts can be like bright lights sighted at sea when a vessel is caught in a storm. One cannot tell whether they are there to guide one safely into harbour or set but as mischief. Were my thoughts like a fire – that would not guide us but would instead wreck us upon the rocky shore? I knew that I had intelligence and logic, so surely I could reason this through. Intelligence is such a gift and such a burden, though at any given time I could never be certain of which. I could oftimes be too clever for my own good – thinking too closely about possible pitfalls instead of sometimes following through to where my heart and instinct led me.

Eventually, my exhausted mind began to slip away, with my thoughts still turning over and spinning through space, like Hope's bright silver shilling. Then all of a piece, they suddenly grounded, tails up. My head had lost. Instinct prevailed and I felt peace at last in what I should do. In the morning I would start making plans for Hope and me to go to London. It would be one last chance, even a gamble, to set things right. I would pray that I would not lose.

*   *   *

'Twas a crisp October day and but a week or two after our arrival in the capital. Having been caught up the crowd heaving towards Charing Cross, it was Hope's and my grave misfortune to witness an execution. They hung and drew a fellow there, and we were so tightly pressed by the throngs that we could not move away from the area. I learned afterwards that he was one of Cromwell's Major-Generals. He had been one of those Parliamentarians who had actively participated in the regicide of the late King.

To cheers and clapping, the slim, elegant, but hapless man, calmly ascended the wooden steps up to the gallows' platform. He seemed like an actor caught in the gaze of his adoring public – tripping out upon the boards to take one more but final curtain call. Silence fell as he took up his position centre stage and, after drawing out a piece of paper, stood for a few fleeting moments delivering a brief oration. Having finished speaking, this leading man was swiftly joined by two others, both dressed in black, who made their solemn entrance from the wings. Then, with faces shrouded by macabre masks, this pair bound the Major-General's hands behind his back, before one of the men escorted him across to the unmoved rope for the tragedy to play out. Once there, and without further performance, the noose was slipped about the bound gentleman's neck and he was hanged.

'Twas thunderous – the gasp that went up as he took the short drop without the easement of hangers-on[46]. How he struggled then! He kicked out his heels at the air for a breath-stopping age, as he dangled on the end of the rope. The gloating crowd fixed its gaze on his every twitch and jerk. The people seemed mesmerised.

Then, just when the victim had quietened, but was clearly still very much alive, the hangman took up a great metal hook. It flashed like a diamond in the sad sunlight before it dulled into flesh, slitting though the Major-General's fresh white shirt and into his belly – all of a one, from under his chest and down to his groin. Then all at once intestines and vital organs spewed out in one great grey pulsating rush. There was no squeal at the slaughter, save that from those queasy amongst the crowd. He was still alive, but with the noose still choking him there was no way for him to exude a scream.

The audience applauded wildly. And then by way of an encore the victim was cut down and dragged by his executioners to what looked like a great butcher's block. There he was laid out upon it like a pig carcass for portioning. One of the men in black hacked off the head with a cleaver and held it aloft – to a rapturous cheer from the crowd. The other man, in tandem, cut out the heart and vaunted the bloody trophy in vile spectacle.

I wondered if he too died thinking himself a martyr to his cause. Had his dead eyes glazed over imprinted with the sight of loathing and derision as had the King, whom he had helped to dispatch before? It doth shame all England to see a Christian man's brutality towards his brother in Christ, no matter what his crime. As the sky then opened, God must have wept.

At last, mercifully, the Major-General's suffering was over and the show passed. Then the baying pack was dismissed. However, what we witnessed was but a start to the bloodshed in revenge for the death of the new King's father. Another ten executions followed on during the course of that week, none of which we chose to witness. I had my belly full of such revenge under the Parliamentarians and had hoped that the Royalists of this Restoration would have proved better than they.

Had it really been thirty five years since I had last been in London? It seemed too impossibly long to be true. The capital had changed but not, I fear for the better. Its theatres, bear pit and other pleasure centres had long gone dark, though there was optimistic talk abroad that even they would soon be restored. Mayhaps the time was ripe for cheer after so many years of enforced repression. I remembered the theatre and the shared love of Shakespeare betwixt Thomas and me.

I recognised too the rancid air, heady with the odours of stale urine, horse-dung and rotting meat, and the open sewers flowing down her streets. Sulphurous choking air would catch the back of the throat on smoky, foggy London nights. There were so many chimneys with so many fires, belching out smoke, come rain or fine, that they ever cast above the skyline a miserable yellowing shroud. And so many buildings... all stacked but a hair's breath apart along its endless narrow streets! Narrower too, the winding lanes and narrowest of all its starved-thin alleys, just wide enough to let pass a handcart to move a body. The chitter chatter of rats had usurped bird song, as had dampness and drabness the sunlight. This was where cats and dogs roamed freely and fleas and lice rejoiced.

This was where the poor lived in such dire squalor as I have never witnessed in any Lincolnshire parish. They crowded together, dying together through poverty or common neglect just yards from where the rich merchants' shops stood, where there was every luxury that could be afforded – though only to those with the means to pay. While overlooked across the ensuing years, the poor had silently multiplied, uncounted and

160

unheeded. Festering like a pustule[47] that must soon be excised to heal.

London, it seemed, was now awash with others like us, people who had been dispossessed under Oliver Cromwell. Each day the narrow streets about the Palace of White Hall were clogged by hoards of people – all of a push to get close forward should the royal carriage chance to appear. Then they might hand over their petitions to the King's equerry. Every time the carriage *did* appear, clattering along the narrow breach of cobbles, a sea of white papers surged forward in waves of outstretched arms. Each with a wrong to be righted. All through every luckless day we waited there. I noted with growing gloom that in its every passing but a handful would be plucked out of the clamour by the lace-cuffed hand reaching out from the rear of the coach as it hurried on its way. And it eventually dawned hopeless on me that we would ever succeed in getting our papers before the King's attention.

'How are we to get this petition into the King's hands?' I had sighed. 'For I never had supposed that it would be this difficult – even impossible!'

'No,' Hope said, 'it is not impossible, Mother!'

Then she turned to me with a glint in her eyes and said, 'I have been thinking. All that we need to do is to somehow draw His Majesty's attention towards *us* the next time he passes by.'

'But how are we going to do that?'

'I have a plan,' she said with a smile as broad as a barn. 'For all of my life I have been put at pains to blend in with every one else. Tomorrow I shall dare to be different!'

At first I was not certain as to what plan Hope had in mind. However, as the day progressed and she went eagerly about a string of unusual errands, my curiosity strengthened. Then, all at once, it fell plain into my sight...

The next morning we returned to our usual spot in the street by the palace gates. Only this time, as the Royal carriage drew into sight, Hope suddenly threw off her long, hooded cape and stepped out into the drab, chill morning like a radiant shaft of exotic sun. Beneath her dress was but a home-dyed brown shift with hand-fringed cuffs and hem, caught about her voluptuous hips by a bright red, tasseled shawl. Her neck was adorned with countless strands of brightly coloured beans painstakingly threaded by flickering candlelight late into the night before. Her long, sleek raven hair was greased into two, waist length braids and dressed with a fan of turkey feathers begged from an admiring butcher near Ludgate.

Excited cries rose from onlookers of, 'Stand back!' and 'Make way for Princess Pocahontas!' Although her attire was far from authentic in detail, who was there to say it was not? For she certainly had the appearance to impoverished and unschooled London eyes of being every inch the Native American princess of old.

Boldly, Hope strode forward. Immediately the surprised host parted for her like The Red Sea being before Moses, allowing her to walk straight to the very front of the crush. And then just as the King's carriage reached her, Hope thrust out her arm with the ribbon tied parchment waving vigorously above her head amid her cries of 'A petition Sire, from a loyal Virginian subject!'

She told me later that she had more than caught a glimpse of the face within smile broadly before he turned to pass rapid words to a gentleman at his side. This second fine sir then immediately jumped up to signal to the aide standing to rear of the carriage, who was frantically harvesting in as many such petitions as he could, and with his arms already fit to drop with them. Realising this, the handsome gentleman then himself leaned across and out towards Hope and deftly plucked her petition from her fingers. He smiled, and his efforts evoked some approval from the crowd that sent up a rousing cheer.

'Ye know ooh tha' woz, don' ye Doockie?' a toothless hag beside me cackled.

She seemed astonished that I had replied that I did

not.

'Tha' be 'e Duke o' York wiv 'e King hiself!' she exclaimed. 'Well in I says, wiv 'at dar' beau'y o' yours!'

As the carriage hurried away, Hope turned and made her way back towards me with a clear passage through admiring men bowing low before her with caps in hands and good humoured remarks passed in her wake.

'Well, that is done!' she said with a sigh of relief. 'All that we can do now is to wait and pray.'

Chapter Twelve

I should never have let her out in that cold in a dress so scant. For the fever that she went down with would not break. Hope lay on her bed, deathly pale for all of her exotic colour. Fever in its self is not dangerous, but the dreadful cough and the congestion that Hope had in her lungs made me fear the worst. And then after all of the years of bringing her up as an English woman, I was forced to come to terms with the stark truth that she was not. Hope was a natural from Virginia, and such natural ne'er did well upon relocating to our capital.

Captain John Smith had warned Thomas and me about this not long after we first arrived in London from the New World.

'Do not tarry in London too long,' he warned. 'And do not grow too attached to the child!'

He had not meant to be cruel, or to bring hurt or malice in those words. Instead it had been said by way of kind warning.

'They do not live long in this wretched country,' Smith added. 'It is their lungs. They do not seem fit as ours to cope with these bad miasmas[48] of this crowded dung-pit!'

He was referring to the natives of Virginia. Naturals like Hope. Naturals like his beloved friend, Rebecca Rolfe, or Pocahontas as she was more famously known. She had not been the first or last native of North America to come to this capital. Many naturals had come across and indeed returned home unscathed. Though it was those, like Pocahontas, who had tarried for just a little too long here who never returned to their own land alive. She had been in London with her husband John Rolfe and young son, Thomas, on a whirlwind visit just as the tobacco boom hit the Virgina-London trade. Smith had seen her briefly and renewed their acquaintance only to be troubled by her waning[49]. Within weeks, and already aboard ship for her return home, she was taken ill with breathing trouble. And then after being taken ashore at Gravesend, there was no saving her.

She slipped away as her husband sat helpless at her side. After her hurried funeral and now hard pressed to return to the colonies, a grief-stricken John Rolfe set off once more – only to realise to his misery that his only son was now also desperately ill with the same vicious complaint. Fearing that the child would die too if he continued the voyage at sea, Rolfe again had the ship put in and the boy taken off to be nursed ashore. With the greatest misgivings and still deeply shocked at the death of his wife, Rolfe reluctantly entrusted his young son's care to that of his relatives while he continued onward to Virginia. Rolfe wrote afterwards in a letter back to England how despairing he had been at making that decision. Yet, at the time, he had feared more for his son's survival than of others in Virgina who might have well cast a finger of selfishness in his direction for deserting his poor motherless son so far away and amongst strangers. Rolfe had always intended sending for his son as soon as he was deemed fit and strong enough to make the arduous voyage to America. Sadly, this was never to be. John Rolf died in March of sixteen-hundred-and-twenty-two, either shortly before or during the dreadful massacre that year. It remained uncertain which. Thomas Rolfe had recovered, and I believe was last said to be alive and well and living not far from Jamestown. Thomas Rolfe had the advantage of being only half natural.

Meanwhile, my Hope lay sickening. I had scoured what open lands there are in this foul city but was unable to find the herbs I desperately needed, nor any who knew where I might procure some. No wonder so many get ill here! They have so removed themselves from their natural roots to plant themselves in London that they have excised all of their common senses. Instead, I was forced to fall back upon the penny apothecary for what ever dubious potions they had to recommend. None of them worked. None of their remedies seemed to be able to cure her and our money was fast running out. In fact, we had only recently moved into much poorer accommodation. And I feared that, following on from my own thoughtlessness and selfishness in bringing her here on this fool's pursuit, she might be about to lose her life. Why? Why? I asked myself. Why had I left the security of our little cottage and our pleasant enough country life only to see her die in some squalid, backstreet London hovel? And she lay so far from the last embrace of her son!

*　　　*　　　*

I put on my Sunday best and prepared for the most difficult appointment of my life. I felt so very old and tired that day, and not even certain that I had the heart to go on any longer.

Alone, I made my way along the heaving streets towards White Hall. When I reached the gates, the royal guards looked me up and down with such great suspicion that I thought, at first, that they were going to refuse me entry. I swear that if they had, I would have simply turned about and gone on my way again – never to return. However, after carefully inspecting the letter with its broken red-wax royal seal, they let me pass.

A young footman, dressed in grey silk and white stockings, politely led me along a maze of magnificently furnished corridors until we reached a towering door. He knocked once and it was smartly opened from within, before I was immediately ushered into the cavernous Great Chamber beyond.

The room was swarming with courtiers – including ladies dressed in the finest shimmering silks. They fluttered about me like a host of iridescent butterflies caught up in a sudden wave of excitement. But I, clothed in my humble and relatively shabby best, in comparison felt like an ugly common house fly.

In complete naivety with regard to the affairs of court, I had imagined that my petition would have been heard in camera[50]. Instead, my audience was to be held in open hearing, in what I suspected would be some casual afternoon entertainment. I was distraught by this prospect of having intimate details of my private life publicly paraded before some of the most notable people in the land. In my past, I had suffered trial and retribution at the hands of far less beautiful people than they were. For all of their finery, why should I now expect a better justice metered out here?

My mouth dried and I was on the very cusp of turning about to leave as quickly as I could. But I could not. For the King, seated on a dais in a fabulous gilded chair had already espied me.

While uncertain as to the expected protocol, I curtseyed low and respectfully before him – just as my Lady Rose had taught me so many years before. The King smiled in my direction then rose to his feet and extended his long slender hand towards me. I noticed then how so very tall he was. Head and shoulder well above any other man there.

'Ah, our Jamestown Woman!' he exclaimed cheerily. 'We have been expecting you. Pray, draw closer!'

Excited chattering hushed into intent silence in anticipation of the discourse betwixt the King and me. It was as if, suddenly, all else present had simply melted away into nothing leaving him and me completely alone.

Of course, I did as my sovereign bade and nervously walked towards him. On nearing, I was shocked when he all at once cusp my lowly hand in his and kissed it. The King of England has just kissed my hand! All I could feel was deeply uncomfortable and embarrassed by his compliment.

Then the King sat once more and, reaching across to a small ebony side table, picked up my petition from the top of a large heap of papers. I could see that the seal Hope had so carefully applied was broken, but it was still adorned with the ribbon she had waxed to it. Then at once I took comfort as I pictured her beautiful smiling face in my mind.

'Hmn!' His Majesty said, with the look of a grave-digger upon his face. 'Tis an interesting petition that you have placed before me. One in which you plead for us to overturn a judgement made against you in

Parliament's rule.'

'Yes, Your Majesty,' I replied, still stooped with apprehension.

'We have studied the records of your case very carefully indeed. The crux of the matter seeming hanging upon charge that you were not, in fact, married to Sir Thomas of Stowe?'

'Yes, Sire. That was the charge.'

'And yet we see that you, in fact, pleaded guilty to the charges at that time. If that is so, then we cannot see what it is you would have me do? If you were not legally wed, then you have no legal claim to either the estate or the title. Whether judged then or now – the law is the law.'

'Your Majesty!' I pleaded. 'Sir Thomas and I *were* legally wed.'

The King looked bemused by my outburst, and as if it was what he wanted to hear. So stern was his gaze, straight into my eyes, that it was like that of the most hardened inquisitor. And yet he had such a coaxing smile upon his lips that I felt safe to tell him all, even that which might sound shameful. I got the distinct impression from that moment that I was being played.

'Then why did you tell the court differently?' he asked bluntly.

'I lied, your Majesty,' I admitted. 'To my lasting shame I lied, and in so doing denounced the very man I loved... in order to save our daughter.'

'Your daughter? Arh!' he sighed loudly, shuffling through the papers spread out before him. 'This 'daughter' of which you speak... Is she not in fact a native Virginian foundling you and your husband took in?'

That was the truth, I stated.

'Was your guardianship of this newborn child widely known in the colony?'

'No, Sire. It was not.'

'And pray, why not?'

'Sire, the colony was in a state of war with the

Powhatans. Had we been discovered harbouring an orphaned Powhatan infant, then my husband feared that the Company men would have taken her from us and...'

'And what had you to fear of the Company men?'

'That they would kill her, Sire. My husband feared that they would take her out from the town and smash her head against the nearest tree.'

The thought of a baby – even that of an enemy – being so brutally murdered drew gasps of horror from the genteel women of court, who were listening intently as my audience drew out.

'So, you believed that this innocent child's life would be forfeit should the Virgina Company find out?'

'Yes, Sire.'

'And so both you and your husband took extraordinary lengths not only to disguise this child and to smuggle her out of the country, but also to love and nurture her and bring her up as if she were your own?'

'Yes, Sire. We did.'

'Very admirable, we must say.' The King turned to address his courtiers as if in search of approval. 'For does not our Heavenly Lord beseech us to "love thine enemy as thine self"?'

He was honoured by a loud murmur of agreement.

'Yet, going back to your trial... you say that you denied your marriage to your husband in order to save this same child? Will you please tell us how so?'

I explained the King all about how Rech had threatened to send Hope back to Virginia – to be 'repatriated' to her Powhatan people and how she could have expected to be treated. I then told him how Rech had promised to 'spare' her if I in returned pleaded guilty to charges he had laid out against me.'

'So, dear lady? This man, Rech? 'Tis strange for this fellow to take such an exception towards you for the sake of a foundling child that must have meant very little to him. If you had not slighted him in any personal way, which we assume you had not, then why this malice? Or are we to take it that this had nothing to do with you but rather that he held some sort of personal grudge against your late husband?'

'Yes, Sire. I believe that he did.'

'And do you know the reason for this animosity?'

'For certain, no, Sire. I do not.'

'Tell me then, Mistress. Is it true that your husband was a spy?'

'Yes, Sire. I believe that he was.'

'Do you have an understanding of the depths of your late husband's covert activities?'

'No, Sire, I do not.'

'Well!' The King exclaimed with mischievous laughter. 'We are glad to hear it! Only a bad spy would confide in his wife about his duties!'

The court burst into laughter, at my expense I began to fear, and wishing that I had never come to court to make my appeal to the King.

'Your husband was a good spy, my good lady!' continued the King, but this time with a more serious tone. 'For a good spy would not disclose anything of the nature of his work to his wife for fear that knowledge, no matter how slight, might put his own life and the lives of others at risk. A spy has worry enough for his own outcome, without bearing the burden of knowing that one unguarded remark might have put at risk those of his loved ones too.'

Those words struck great discord within my heart. I had been so blind not to have seen that Thomas, far from excluding me from his life out of any selfish motive, had instead kept his own counsel as a precaution to protect me.

'In fact,' the King added, 'Your late husband was the very best spy our late father had. So good was his intelligence, that he must have been responsible for saving many hundreds of his fellow Royalists' lives at one time or another. He also served our grandfather, King James well too, we recall. In the colonies, was it not? Oh! Of course, we presume you did not know that either? Well, needless to say, spies make enemies and no worse enemies than the enemy himself. This man, Rech? Did he know you and your husband from your time in Jamestown?'

'He did, Sire. Mister Rech arrived in Virginia not long after my husband had fetched me there.

'From England?'

'No, Sire, from Plimouth.'

'Hmmm! So your husband may have inadvertently done something to harm this Mister Rech's personal interests, of which you know not and of which your husband did not speak. Then mayhap it was by way of his espionage in the service of his country. In any case, after the untimely death of your husband, not being able to act out his revenge on Sir Thomas, Rech therefore vented his anger against you, a defenceless widow of a notable Royalist gentleman. Knowing full well that if he could blackmail you into denying your marriage to Sir Thomas, Rech could legally deprive Sir Thomas' rightful heirs of all his lawful possessions. More than this, are we correct in believing that this man Rech then had you branded as a common whore and whipped out of your own village?'

I nodded my head instead of answering the King's question directly, for I was on the brink of tears and barely able to speak.

'Quite remarkable villainy, even for a Parliamentarian!' the King exclaimed. 'The man truly was deserving of his name.'

Then His Majesty tempered his tone and, with a voice now like the sweetest honey, he continued: 'Dear lady. I have *personally* sifted through all of the evidence you see set before me. I have done so not only in the name of justice but also out of recognition of the high regard in which our own father held the late Sir Thomas. And we must tell you now that we can see no dishonour in any of your late husband's dealings regarding this man Rech.'

These words gave me great comfort.

'To the contrary,' His Majesty added, 'it appears that this Rech later made a petition of his own to Parliament to have your estates in Lincolnshire signed over to him – but this was dismissed, no doubt causing the man to harbour an even deeper resentment towards your remaining family. It might also surprise you to know that your trial at Stowe was meticulously documented by Rech, and supported with much documentary evidence used to secure your conviction. I have it all here. However...' he paused with some deliberation, 'there was one submission that the prosecution mysteriously omitted to produce. It is this letter...'

As the King spoke, he proffered a slim parchment. 'In this is a sworn statement made from one Mister Winslow, late of our Plimouth Colony, who testified to the fact that he was a witness in Dartmouth to a Separatist marriage between you and your late husband, Sir Thomas of Stowe. We are now convinced that you were the victim of spiteful conspiracy and entirely innocent of any breach of the law. In short, our dear Lady, we judge in favour of your petition!'

I was astounded further as the King took me by the hand and gently presented me before the assembly. All the proceedings leading to that moment had unfolded like some play at the theatre, where His Majesty was the playwright. Only then I realised what he had so obviously planned all along. At no point, no matter his demeanor, had it ever been his intention to shame me. The King had instead stage-managed my audience in order to reveal my innocence in public, and of course to my greatest future advantage. This was his way of making certain that all gathered there knew that I had his full approval, and thereby should also automatically receive theirs without question.

'Regard this woman!' His Majesty King beseeched the court. 'And look to her well! For she is the very spirit of my kingdom incarnate. She has innocently suffered such atrocity by the hand of Cromwell's criminals. Her land, her title, and her very reputation had all

173

been stolen by those black-hearted thieves, just as it was so from our own beloved father. Yet she has come through it all now, with her spirit unbroken and ripe for restoration!'

Having spoken these words, the King took a backward step to stand behind me. Slipping his hands upon my shoulders he then let slip his fingers downwards across my chest, like a lover's caress, and fumbled for the edges of my closely wrapped shawl. Then, he drew his warm lips close to my ear and whispered, enticingly, for me to let him have his way.

How could I resist him? With my nod of consent he clasped the edges of the cloth and pulled my shawl open, like a stage curtain, to reveal to everyone assembled the top of my cleavage. A collective sigh rose throughout the chamber as the angry brand set deep within my flesh was exposed to their open gaze.

'Well you may gasp!' The King exclaimed dramatically. 'Yet this 'H' you see burned into this innocent woman's breast shall no longer be seen as a mark of shame. By our Royal Decree, this woman shall have her rightful title of 'Lady' restored to her. And this cruel branding, from this day forward, shall mark Lady Elizabeth out for what she truly is... This letter 'H' shall stand for 'Heroine'! For this is what she is – heroine of this kingdom!'

Then the King moved to stand in front of me and bowed – to me! And then he took up my hand once more and kissed it.

'Now,' he whispered, 'take your bow, our lady, and then forever after hold your head high. Your audience awaits you, and you deserve their admiration!'

And so that is what I did, and to rapturous applause and cries of approval so loud and so long that it felt as if it would never cease. And all the while the King stood by my side and encouraged this accolade. Then, when eventually it died down, he again took me by the hand and led me to a seat, hastily summoned, to the right side of his dais.

I was indeed greatly honoured, yet also troubled,

because the King had no mention of the return of my lands. And for this reason I began to worry that the audience was perhaps little more than a fine though empty gesture – like that the King's grandfather had bestowed on my late husband after our life in Jamestown. My title, after all, had cost him nothing... but what about the return of my family's lands? The lands would not come free.

When court was at last dismissed, His Majesty turned towards me and, taking up my hand again, led me from my chair and across the room to a side chamber.

'Lady Elizabeth,' he said, standing before its closed door, 'We have up to now omitted to inform you that we had previously received a petition regarding your family's lands at Stowe. And we have already ruled in favour of this other party's submission. You must understand the vexing nature of these times, and the magnitude of the task in unravelling the truth to remake the wrongs done to our people in the past. So, under the circumstances, we do think that you might meet this fellow yourself and tell him of your grievance. Maybe the two of you will be able to settle on some sort of mutually agreeable arrangement as to rightful ownership. Yet we stress to you now; we hold this man most dear to our heart and we pray that you shall too!'

With that, His Majesty placed my hand upon the chamber handle, looked me straight in the eyes, and then smiled mysteriously as he turned and abruptly took his leave.

I was dumbfounded. In one moment he told me that some usurper had staked claim to my family's property and that he will not intervene on my behalf, and in the next he is entreating me to negotiate a settlement with this mysterious scoundrel. I had no choice. My angry curiosity led me through the door, determined that I would have it out with this wicked usurper...

Chapter Thirteen

I mistook the room for empty. For when I entered I saw neither hide nor hair of another living being. Though I could still see in my mind's eye the knavish look upon the King's face as he had parted from me and hurried along the great corridor. So I wondered as to what mischief he had set to play.

Then, just as I was turning to leave, my eye caught the cast of flickering shadow upon the muted gold walls, emanating from within the hidden bay of a far widow. Someone, I thought, must be standing and looking out upon the London din beyond, while oblivious to my presence.

Then, as stealthy as a cat, I stepped quietly along the richly woven runner to better see my competition. I wanted to weigh him up, this rascal who would steal my grand son's inheritance from him... For me, it was like seeing a ghost from the grave of my past. The likeness of him I had long thought buried and devoured by the churchyard maggots. That oh so familiar stance! That cavalier demeanour! That same rugged profile!

I was about to call out, but he turned before I could do so. He looked at me and smiled simultaneously. And that smile made my heart shudder... Suddenly I felt sick. I felt faint. I felt elated. As I returned his gaze I felt cheated. I felt robbed, and yet in the very same instant – blessed. Blessed with the greatest gift of all. There stood my Thomas! This man was every inch my husband. My Thomas, come back to me once more from across the void of endless, heart-broken years.

As I stood, totally bewitched in the man's presence, I felt my heart pounding inside my chest and nearly called out his name. Then reality hit me like a slap in the face. Fool! How could this be? Had I not seen Thomas die? Had I not cried the night long at the side of his corpse and then watched numbly as it was lowered into its gaping grave and swallowed up by the earth? My brain screamed, this man could not be my Thomas! Yet still my heart leapt with boundless joy. For *it* had recognised the stranger long before my senses or my eyes.

'Mother!'

The man raced to me, clasped me, and then held me so tightly in his arms that I feared I would break. The shock! The shock stopped me from uttering a word. I could not talk. It was all I could do to stand without fainting. Here was James! My son!

'Oh Mother!' he cried, with his arms locked about me like a great bear. 'I thought you were dead! I thought that I would never see you again!' is all he could say as he hugged me tightly.

'I thought you were dead...' is all I could whisper through my tears of joy. 'I though you were dead too...'

'And Hope?' he sighed after a moment.

'She never gave up.' I sobbed. 'Hope always believed that you would come back one day...'

James loosed his grip and sought out my face. I could see the light draining from out of his eyes as he then asked all a-tremble, 'Is she dead?'

'No! No!' I assured him quickly. 'Hope is not dead. But she has been most poorly[51] up until yesterday morning.'

I saw relief sweep across his face as I continued to speak. 'When the summons arrived from the King, she suddenly began to rally. By the time I left her this morning, she was sitting up in bed and sipping a few spoonfuls of broth. I did not want to leave her but she begged me to come.'

'And Tom?'

'He is in Lincoln. Oh, James, he has grown into such a fine young man! You will be so proud of him!'
He smiled at this news of the son he had only before seen as a babe in Hope's arms.

'But what of you James? Where have you been all of this time?'

'With the King!' he said. 'And before that, with the King's late father and Prince Rupert...'

James explained how he had arrived at Naseby field late in the day – and to find the Royalist

Army in defeat and the King in retreat. He rode north with the King and the rag-bag remnant of his shattered army, in the hope that survivors from the battle would shortly follow and regroup to fight another day. But the king's hopes were soon cruelly dashed as he realised that he had lost most of his best fighting men. Later, James learned that his still absent father had been seen struck down by the enemy and lying lifeless on the ground beneath his dead, grey horse.

On learning that James was Thomas' son, the King immediately insisted that he remain at His Majesty's side. After all, who better to replace the father than the son? And there was the added advantage that James' face was unknown to the enemy.

Later still, James followed the King's command to go into exile with Prince Rupert. The King had also entrusted James with important papers to take to the Queen and commanded him to protect his precious successor, his son Charles – the Prince of Wales, with his life. This James did, betwixt missions to England to smuggle across messages to the King, who was under arrest. And then afterwards he fought again with him and his second army until the King's recapture and ultimate execution.

'I did come back to Stowe,' James explained, 'but by then it had been more than two years since I had last seen you all. Ned told me that Father was dead, and then I found out that you had gone and all about the wretched circumstances under which you had left. I felt such anger towards myself then… that I had not returned before to take care of you. I had however entrusted a letter to a fellow officer to get through to you after Naseby, to tell you that I was alive and well. Though now I see that it did not reach you.

After leaving Stowe I didst come looking for you! For more than a month I scoured the county, yet all to no avail. At Gainsborough Hall I found that Sir Willoughby had died and that his bitter widow, Lady Bridget, was most quiet upon the matter. 'Twas as if all three of you had vanished off the face of the earth!' he sighed deeply.

'I retuned to the Prince and his mother the Queen, to be at their service. But whenever again in England I did make enquiries after you, and I did urge those in the Midlands to do likewise. Yet time and again I held myself in great disappointment when no news could be had and so I began to fear the worst – that I was now alone in this world, without family. All this only served to strengthen my daring in my missions for the Stuarts. For I felt that I only had my life left to lose and so avowed that I would willingly give it up for my sovereign King.

I took part in slim missions. I was amongst those who helped the late King escape from Hampton Court, though I now earnestly wished I had not. We praised God at the time for our good fortune and the Parliament's laxity in making his escape so easy. Yet now? Now I fear that all along it was Cromwell's intention that we should do so. That instead of helping the King to eschew Parliament, we instead helped to deliver His Majesty into the waiting hands of his executioners.

While merely incarcerated at their pleasure, the King had been safe and set upon playing the long game. He was still the country's sovereign King, and although held in check, refused to surrender the board to Cromwell's mate. Instead, he continued to alter his position, square by square, until his avoidance tactics wore the Parliamentarians' patience murderously thin. The danger for them was that the common people would tire of living in this limbo-land, where Parliament could not properly govern nor pass new laws amid uncertainty of their ultimate legitimacy – for as long as the King was suppressed but alive.

Yet the greatest fear was that this prolonged state of stalemate could create disillusionment and be used to rally support back to the King. So, with hindsight, it seems that we played into Cromwell's hands. So certain was he that he could crush any further support for the King and vanquish a second Royalist Army, that Cromwell let Charles Stuart escape to do just that. Only this time, he knew that he could make the recaptured King out to be a criminal. Cromwell could then claim that the King had absconded during genuine negotiation and had wantonly and needlessly sacrificed more innocent lives in the process. Cromwell knew that he could then make the King stand trial for his life – which of course, Cromwell made certain he would forfeit. It was all part of Parliaments' plan from the start. 'Twas never intended to fall short of anything other than regicide!'

'And so you have been with the new King ever since?' I asked.

'Yes,' James replied in solemn tones. 'I was at the late King's side right up until his final defeat. At last seeing how the field was set, His Majesty ordered me back from the lines and instead to go to the Prince of Wales. King Charles made me swear an oath that I would fight to restore his son back onto the English throne, or that I would give up my life in the trying. I gave it gladly and have been at the new King's service ever since.

'So,' James smiled radiantly, 'you can imagine His Majesty's delight in receiving your petition, and at once realising that it could have only come from my mother!'

'So, you knew all along that I was here?'

'No! Not until a few moments ago. I was specifically ordered by His Majesty, first thing after breakfast, to bide my time here in this room until summoned. But I know the King as a man knows a friend. To be able to restore to me my lost parent would have given him the greatest of satisfaction. I know!' He exclaimed.

All I was told was to expect to meet a relative of my father's family, petitioning to lay claim to our estates at Stowe. I presumed it might be some distant cousin or some sort. But never you, Mother! I had never dared hoped to hold you again.' And then having said that, he drew me up tightly into his arms once more and cried – like my baby.

I cannot explain in mere words the rapture of Hope and James' reunion later that day. As I led James up the dingy stairwell and into our humble abode, his eyes met hers and they instantly fell into each others' arms. It was as if heaven had opened and all of its joy had tumbled down to earth at once and into that tiny room. Their tears of joy and the crying out of so much past anguish was something that I shall never forget until my dying hour.

I stayed and celebrated with them but briefly – before taking up my shawl and hat once more and stepping out into the mean, cold streets. For a while, at least, I wanted to afford them a little privacy so they might properly be re-acquainted.

I was so happy for them both, and yet I felt great pangs of sadness too. Sadness that they had to be parted for so many long years, and also with more than a little of my self-pity. For as I stepped away into that London gloom, I could not help but regret that my Thomas and I could not have shared such a happy reunion as theirs, when he came from the dead to me at Plimouth. Although, for us, time did win out and we eventually fell in love anew, it could never be as joyous as this re-meeting of a true love that had never faltered. To be honest, I envied them that.

*   *   *

'This will never do!' James exclaimed on my return. 'Pack up your belongings, Mother, while I fetch a carriage to take us away.'

'Away to where?'

'To his apartments!' Hope said excitedly. 'James has rooms at the Palace and he is taking us there to be with him now!'

Within the hour, we were indeed back at the Palace of White Hall and installed into the most sumptuous of surroundings. In the days that followed, as Hope quickly gathered strength, she and I were spoiled beyond description. We sampled the finest foods and the most luxurious of indulgences, including new silk dresses from the Queen's own dressmaker, shoes, jewels, feathered hats, and all of the trimmings of nobility. Every time I protested at the cost of this frippery[52], James simply laughed it away. Yet worry was growing inside me at how my son was going to pay for all of this extravagance. Surely no Stuart King e'er paid a man so handsomely?

Over the coming weeks, I came to grow to know this re-found son of my mine, and marvelled of the changes in him. Not only in his manly physique, but how spiritually he had grown also. During our long conversations, I also grew to know more about this new monarch of ours.

'The King? You must know him and the Royal family intimately by now?' I dared to enquire one day. 'Is he secretly a Catholic by faith?'

'His mother has always been so,' James replied. ''Tis common knowledge! As is his brother, James. As for His Majesty... Well...'Twas ever made clear to him that he could never hope to redeem his kingdom if he were anything but a Protestant. And in truth, in all of these years that I have known him, I have never seen him take Mass. Though I do know that he is often to be found at prayer with his mother and brother.

'Yet, what if he were a Catholic? What does it matter, Mother?' James unexpectedly asked of me. 'If a man believes in the one true God and in His Son, Jesus Christ and in the Resurrection, does it matter if he calls himself Catholic? Or Anglican, Puritan or Separatist, come to that? Why is there conflict in faith if we are all brothers in the sight of God and through our love of Christ? Therefore, should not our morals be similarly shaped if we all follow Him as our example?'

I was pleased by the clarity of his argument, yet I countered it as devil's advocate.

'A father rarely favours all of his sons equally. And not all sons do honour to their fathers,' I replied.

'On earth, perhaps,' James immediately responded, 'but a Heavenly Father would, I am certain, look upon all of His children with equity. 'Tis divisions temporal[53] that divide us by faith and maybe not matters of faith at all! A Church needs a figurehead. A shepherd to lead the flock, just as Christ once did. Yet we all know that the Church of Rome and the Church in England are riddled by the same haughty flaws leeched into it over a millennium of separation from its humble beginnings. Yet also that this seam of corruption may not be hacked out and repaired in an instant, lest our churches fall about our heads and religion in our realms be completely destabilized along with all Christian society.

'This is where our past Puritan zealots went so badly awry[54]. They demanded too much and too soon. Now this King hints at tolerance so that all men might follow their faith. And for that I find him a more enlightened soul than any that might at present oppose him in Parliament.

'Before the Civil War, Parliament begged for a King of such persuasion! Yet, now that we are blessed with one, still they seem determined to set themselves against him for the sake of past petty grievances from his father's time. Just as we as a nation are, in turn, still aggrieved by France and Spain and the Lowlanders for theirs. If only we were wise enough to accept tolerance come matters of faith, then would not all mankind benefit?'

'Fine sentiments,' I said, 'yet what when all else fails and it comes to war?'

'Then as when facing any difficult choice, you do that which you hope doth offend the Lord least. And that with which after your conscience will allow you to live. Or, equally, to die.'

'Yet what of the Catholics?' I continued. 'Hath they not contrived in the past to regain the souls of Protestant Englishmen under duress or by the threat of burning? They despise us all as heretics! So how can they and we ever be reconciled?'

'Tis true. Just as it is true also that a dog, on sighting a cat, will naturally chase it down and, if caught, may indeed savage it unto death. Yet, is it not

184

also witnessed that if the two are gradually introduced to each other, that same dog and cat might grow accustomed to one another and in time, made fit to lie down together in front of the same hearth.'

'Oh James!' I conceded at last. 'What wise thoughts you have marshalled in that mind of yours!'

'These are not mine own, Mother,' he said, 'but those of my father.'

James proceeded to tell me how, at Oxford, he last met with my Thomas. He had told his son all about that time when he and his congregation had made a stand for tolerance in religion for Separatists. James explained how, on that eve of his leaving Oxford, his father believed then that he was making a stand for tolerance in religion for all. For he had said to James that if the radical Parliamentarians were not stopped then, there would be no tolerance for any dissenting under their brand of Puritanism. As it turned out, James surmised, his father had not been wrong.

'Yes, James,' I replied. 'I now see that he was not.'

*   *   *

My son's outrageous spending went on unabated. I feared that he was running up some great unmanageable debt in order to somehow make up for all of our hardships suffered during our separation. James had by then sent to Lincoln for his son, and after little debate, engaged a ludicrously expensive tutor to instruct Tom upon the finer qualities of the courtier class.

At length, my worry caused me to ask my son outright where all this money was coming from. 'Tis one thing to live with a King but quite another to spend like one!' I said. 'I fear that you are becoming too indebted to your creditors?'

'My creditors?' he replied.

'Then... the King?' I enquired further.

'I have purchased nothing that I have not paid for, Mother!' He rebuked me gently. 'As for the

King? It is oftimes him or the Duke of York who owes me money!'

I could not comprehend what my son was saying.

'Mother,' he expanded upon my probing, 'did you not appreciate the extent of your husband's lands in the colonies?'

I was puzzled.

'A few plots,' I said. 'He had told me so. "A few plots for future investment." But that is all, James.'

'A few plots? Huh!' James laughed loudly. 'Ahead of the King's decision to return to England, I was sent out to the colonies to gauge the support that he might expect from the assemblies there. While in Virgina, I was privy[55] to the Governor's land records there and discovered the full extent of my father's holdings. Long after returning to England, he had continued to accrue countless plots of virgin land over the years. Thousands of acres of what many at the time must have deemed 'valueless'. Mostly it was land on the very cusp of the colony, and then still dangerously subject to Powhatan incursion. Only now, with the subjugation of the naturals and the rapid expansion of the colony, they are in prime locations and aching for cultivation. In short, they are worth a incredible fortune, Mother!'

'And if this is so,' I asked tentatively, although I knew in my heart the answer already, 'do you not wish to return to Virginia to oversee them?'

'Yes, Mother. Of course I do. Even the King has asked me to return. He has said that he would have me be his most trusted eyes and ears there, yet he pressures me not. He understands my present situation and leaves the decision to me. Though I think that I shall not go yet. Not now that I have found you again. I shall wait...'

'Wait for me to die, James? But this fine prospect in Virginia will not wait for forever. Look at yourself! You are no longer a young man.'

'I know. But you could never contemplate making such a journey as that and hope to survive. So,

I choose to stay.'

'And what if I were not here? Or if I were to die tomorrow? What then, James? Would you not take your family to Virginia then?'

'Yes, Mother. Of course I would and without hesitation.'

'Then do it James. You must do it now. I am of an age when I might well expect to die tomorrow, or the next day, or the day after that. There are no warnings, no certainties about when our lives might end. Though for me, at least, that certainly grows apace with each new sunrise.'

'Then I shall wait until then.'

'And what if I were to live another ten years? What if you were to die first with all this dream unfulfilled? You should go James. Take your family to the New World with you. Look forward to your new lives and never look back to the old with regret. Take Hope to Virginia and show her the land of her birth. Go reap your father's inheritance and sow an even better one for your son while you still may. I have had *my* life, James.

'Now that I know that you are alive and well and reunited with Hope and Tom, there is nothing more for me to desire. I can die happy, whether you be here at my side, or three thousand miles away. I want you to go to Virgina, James, for I do believe that this is your destiny.'

'But how could we leave you behind, Mother, after all that you have been through?'

'Fear not for me. I have lived my life and I have nothing to fear from death. I have witnessed little children close their eyes and die, so if they can go quietly away what have I to fear? For I also now know that the dead never really die, and that they never leave the living either. We may not always feel the presence of our loved ones at our side but I am certain now that does not mean that they are not there. I shall always live on in you and you in me, for all time, until we meet again some day. Wherever you go, James, I shall always be with you. You must go to Virginia James,' I pleaded. 'You all three must go and leave me behind...'

Chapter Fourteen

I fumbled with the gold ring between my fingers, holding it up to the candlelight, trying to make out the shape of the letters inside the band. It was no good. My eyes were too old to make out the inscription. Yet I knew full full what it read – 'To my beloved wife. 1620.'

It was good fortune that James had been able to retrieve the chest that we had buried at Stowe. It held all our valued possessions. These included the deeds to the farm and valuables such as silver candlesticks, though all had paled in importance by now. But the string of pearls and the ring, especially, were priceless to me. The ring had been given to me by Thomas. Despite the passage of years, it glinted as brightly as ever it did, and willingly slipped onto my bony old finger.

I never did return to Blackthorn Farm. What would I do with an estate anyway, now that my children had gone to Virginia? I had no friends there, and there was no other connection. So, in possession of an outrageously large amount of capital, far in excess of my humble needs, I took up residence in West London and soon found myself living a new life in a new age. The age of restoration. Restoration of the monarchy but not of the era gone by. That is dead, I am afraid, and lost for ever. For this is an age of jollity. One of the return to playhouses, entertainments, music and laughter. And these return with vengeance! This does not surprise me, considering that the pendulum, having been swung so violently in the one direction of repression, should then return with equal force to the opposite direction.

This is also the age of modernity, an age of great promise, an age of science and new ways of thinking. Even at my great age, not a day goes by without my discovering something new or some new avenue in science or knowledge opening up to mankind. We are at 'the pinnacle of science, knowledge and innovation,' and 'we stand at the dawning of an age of reason,' I am told constantly. Yet, this oft seems to me, at times, to be a topsy-turvy sort of reasoning, a kind that has lately spawned a world in which a life of impropriety and infamy are mostly held in greater esteem than one of chastity or virtue.

So it is that, since my family's departure to the New World, I have lately come into my own. The tale of my trials and suffering at the hand of the Commonwealth has become common currency to be exchanged between every market-day gaggle. The brand that was burnt into my breast no longer sets me apart as a 'harlot' and a thing to be despised. Instead, the letter 'H' emblazoned upon my skin has indeed marked me out as a 'heroine' – a survivor of 'the dreadful scourge' and a figurehead of the Restoration. That is why the crowds flocked to my side whenever I arrived at White Hall. They were always there, hoping to spy me, this ageing 'star' of the new King's court.

His Majesty is such a rake! Inside the Great Chamber, it was always his custom to greet me by taking my hand in his and raising it tenderly to his lips. Then he would smile wryly and fix my gaze to his with such a seductive glint in his eye that it could have unpicked a virgin's bedroom lock in an instant! Then again, I am no virgin, and in truth I have noticed that he always looked at every woman that way. As if undressing them with his eyes and caressing their bodies with his senses, while in reality he would simply be planting a kiss on the back of a hand. Even at my great age, and with the knowledge that it was but a play that he put on for all his female subjects, my heart still fluttered like a foolish young girl's.

Afterwards, he always led me to a small gilded, red-cushioned chair set at the edge of the dais and bade me to sit in his presence, while all other courtiers, the high and mighty, were required to stand. Openly, he referred to me as his 'treasure'. I had heard a jealous tongue or two amongst titled ladies, who agreed among themselves that, as with all the best treasure, I should soon be buried. I pretended not to hear, though I did not care. Why should I have done so? The wind was behind me and I was no longer forced to walk face into it.

It is in this age that I finally found my voice. I spake out and others walked the clouds that hung on my words. I was perceived to be wise, yet I saw my wisdom as little more than the wealth of experience that had come as a result of great age. Naturally, I had made many a mistake over the course of my life, yet I had the advantage of having survived long enough to have learned from my mistakes. And more importantly, to have outlived anyone who might have remembered them.

Great age though, had also brought with it my greater self confidence. For what cared I now? The worst that I could ever be made to forfeit for speaking my mind was my life, and there was surely precious little enough of that left of which I could be deprived. No, I spake out, and still do so when I wish. I say what I think or see and hang the consequence! And for that, or more likely out of gratitude for many heroic deeds done in the past by my Royalist son and husband, the King revelled in me and kept me close to his side. From time to time he had even been known to turn to me during some mighty discussion and ask aloud, 'Pray, we wonder what Lady Elizabeth's opinion on this might be?' assured that some witty remark or observation on my part might be relied upon to break any difficult moment that *he* might have need of escape from.

Court life could be both exhilarating and exasperating. It was a strange company in which I found myself – this elite of minds, this den of rogues! Born gentleman were often pressed into close company and held equal to those risen from the trading class. Duchesses and ladies made to huddle in genteel gossip with former whores and actresses, raised by the King's own hand and expected to be accepted as their peers.

Indeed, in the name of equality, the King himself makes no distinction between them. He will sleep with a lady of hereditary title as eagerly as one who has none. Married or nay, he collects women like brood mares and has, I am most reliably informed, a string of bastards to show for it. Not only that, he seems to then hand out these same mounts as favours, like sweetmeats from a gilded tray to his most favoured cohorts. And while this continues to be his custom, who can condemn his closest subjects from following his lead?

Take Sam Pepys[56], for example. To me, he is the epitome of a Restoration man. For some time I cared not much for this fellow, though others flocked about him like bees to honeysuckle. I found nothing attractive in either his personality or his suit. It is not that he is but the son of a tailor and his uncle a common White Chapel butcher, for who am I to talk – being of but humble peasant birth? No, it was not he who bothered me, but the man he contrived to be. He bore himself like a gentleman, and I daresay much of his grooming and good manners came from his time at school alongside 'genuine' young gentlemen in Huntingdon. Not that his parents could well have afforded it. Rather, it being by benefit of his Aunt Paulina, having married extremely well into the Montague family, marrying a brother of the first Earl of Manchester. Being already distraught by the loss of several brothers to plague that oftimes hath afflicted London, and moved by his parent's fears of a further outbreak in the city, well-to-do relatives had plucked the sickly nine-year-old Sam out of London and sent him into the relative health of the countryside. Albeit then, to a Parliamentarian lair.

He is such a favorite of the King, this Pepys, and the epitome of a loyal subject. Yet I had heard it told, and straight from one who heard it from is own lips, that he had actually rejoiced in the execution of the late King. There again, there are many I know who wear a satin Royalist coat on the outside while hiding a plain Puritan lining within. It seems that there is so very little about which I do not get to hear.

Nowadays, after obtaining a degree from Cambridge, and advancement in the employ of Edward Montegu, Earl of Sandwich and First Lord of the Admiralty, Pepys enjoys considerable power and moderate wealth. Yet like many of these modern men in this wretched city, his morals do not match those I have known to be natural gentlemen and of far meaner positions in life than his.

Then there is his wife, whom I believe is wasted upon him. Mistress Pepys is a pretty young thing with a pleasant disposition. A Huguenot, as I understand, and her French accent, which renders her speech almost childlike, only serves to mark her out even more so as an innocent abroad in a den of reprobates.

I cannot help think that if only she had a child to occupy her days and upon whom to lavish attention, and in return to receive love, she would be so much happier. I hear that she longs for a child, and that her husband sulks because none is forthcoming. 'Tis a sorry state of affairs! Yet, I also hear numerous accounts of his dalliances. The man seems unable to help himself! Or rather that he does, far too easily and far too often, to the charms of other women.

Pepys cannot love this poor wife of his, not as a man should. Then again, perhaps Pepys has not enough love to lavish upon his wife after lavishing so great a portion of his share upon himself. For this is indeed a man who loves himself. He spends so much on silk finery, velvet jackets, shirts and cravats, that other men visit him regularly – simply to look upon the latest clothes in his wardrobe. And he certainly seems to have more silk suits than his wife has dresses.

Then, second to this infamous love of himself, must be his unbridled passion for books. For I hear that he coddles them like mistresses, all lined upon his shelf and fondled daily, in a way of which I am certain must cause some jealously on the part of Mistress Pepys.

I know, when it comes to breaking our Lord's commandments, I cannot be one to pass judgement. For who am I to be casting stones? I too have sinned, and deeply. I have fornicated before marriage by deliberate act and even, by error, committed bigamy. And I have even prostituted my body in return for food for my family. Often, when I sinned intentionally, 'twas done so out of dire 'necessity'. Yet, sin is sin, and so I have since cast myself upon my knees in repentance over all my sins, great and small, and then received the Lord Jesus Christ's grace – His undeserved love and forgiveness.

Oh, how it is my desire that my King and fellow courtiers would experience the peace and following joy of doing likewise! For them, fornication appears to have become elevated to the level of some sort of 'sport' – a pastime whereby casual couplings mean little more than immediate self-gratification, and where God's order for our long-term wellbeing is disregarded. In truth, fornication is an almost *acceptable* sin that is carried out throughout the week and then repented of upon a Lord's Day, but then only to be repeated ere[57] Monday has fully broken!

Perhaps this current preoccupation with sex and revelry and laxity of good morals is really but a diversion from the real problems at court, and from this Restoration of our monarch. For the sins of the father now lie with the son. The same sins, the same problems of religion, now dog this third Stuart Kingdom.

This time it is our second King Charles who appeals for religious tolerance towards Puritans, non-conformists and Catholics alike, as Parliament is now awash with Anglican Church zealots. They rise from their seats to openly shout the King down, saying that opening the way to dissenters is tantamount to opening the door once more to anarchy. 'Tis as plain as the nose on Sam Pepys face to see why the King would wish otherwise. 'Tis ever the thorny issue of succession. For this King has yet no legitimate heir, despite his unquestionable virility, and yet would stand steadfastly by his wife, the Queen, during a succession of miscarriages.

What if the King were to remain without a lawfully begotten child from his marriage? What then, if at the last, the King cannot be persuaded to legitimise one of his Protestant bastard sons? Surely his brother, James, the Duke of York, could not be legally impeded from ascending the throne as King himself? James Stuart is, always has been, and looks steadfastly to remain so, a fully practicing member of the Catholic faith. Protestant England would then have a Catholic at the head of its Church. Yet the country and the court freewheels on as if none of this has even been considered. The fox is seated boldly at the door of the hen-house. Yet none of the chickens can see him! The bloody history of the Tudors of Lady Rose's youth is in danger of repeating itself, and so this is why I fear that our Restoration may yet prove very short lived.

Thus so it is that the court laughs on and dangerously makes merry while cavorting ever closer to an inevitable abyss. 'Tis like a masked ball in a fool's paradise. Yet what is beyond my understanding is how so many intelligent men have been seduced into it, and then blinded by the imminent dangers?

*   *   *

Death had stalked the Mayflower without one shred of compassion. It had struck at us with such an incomprehensible ferocity that the the sheer horror and wantonness of it shall never be put away from my mind. The stench of death, daily in my nostrils, and the taste of it upon my lips still haunts my darkest dreams, even some forty years on. Oftimes I would wake up gagging as I relived trying my best to revive those stricken by their unrelenting suffering. The stench of living rotting flesh had been almost more than I could bear. A newly delivered mother, a devoted husband, a loving child – death showed neither mercy nor preference as to whom it would next consume.

If our modern and most learned physicians are right, then the miasmas confined below the decks of that ship should have taken its toll upon all of us who were shut in with it. Mary Brewster and I touched and were touched by dozens of our company, and we washed and bathed the unable, in both life and in death. Those who had died we made presentable to our Lord before they were sewn into sail cloth and slipped into the sea. Yet she and I did not succumb to the terrible visitation that killed half of our number during those first few months anchored off Plimouth, New England.

Were we lucky? Were we spared by the Lord for His further works? We knew not. Indeed, each snatched moment of respite, be it waking or at sleep, we passed in dread that we would be next to succumb. We lived from moment to moment, in constant vigil looking inwards to ourselves for the beginnings of this evil disease, believing that we too were bound to die. Such fears, such horrors become so ingrained within our memories that no passage of time can ever erase them. Sometimes, though, a far greater horror draws beside me, to make them pale in comparison...

Chapter Fifteen

One summer, when I was a girl, it was so hot that the parched earth yawned open into great gaping cracks, and the wheat stands were so dry that they crackled loudly as Humility and I ran through them in play. I can scarcely remember another such dry, hot summer like it, not in all the years that I have lived on this earth. Not, that is, until last year. It was suddenly so hot that most of London's fine ladies, instead of swarming like moths around a lamp, openly resisted the invitation to attend court. Especially after a clutch of them swooned, all at once, to the ground like ale house skittles during an audience with the King. It was too hot to move, other than to fetch up a cooling drink to one's parched lips or to mop the damp glow from one's brow with a kerchief.

Then, on the tenth day of June and with no break from the weather in prospect, we heard that it had arrived. The plague!

When at first they said that plague was abroad in London, my acquaintances from court scarce raised a plucked and dewy eyebrow. Plague was a familiar part of English life, especially in the sumer months, the length and breath of the realm. I recalled outbreaks at Gainsborough. They usually started down near the river with the squalid ale houses that the poor and sailors frequented. Plague was brought in from abroad and never home-grown, or so the physicians assured us.

Therefore, once that there was an outbreak, strangers were treated with great suspicion by the townsfolk, who would keep their distance as if their very lives depended upon it. Merchants refused to trade face-to-face with outsiders, and tolls and payments from the ferries and the port were never pressed from one flesh to another. Instead, they were collected in a large plague bowl full of a disarming potion of vinegar steeped with herbs. If it could bring metal coins back to their original brilliance then surely it could clean away the 'venomous atoms' which clung about all like smoke or perfume and infected salubrious[58] air, and thus rendering it 'miasmatic'.

'One can never be too careful,' the apothecary had then warned Lady Rose. 'For the unseen and mysterious miasmas of the plague and every conceivable ill invisibly fill the air. So, mayhap they have fallen upon coins. Or may even to be transmitted by a simple touch. No matter! Any outbreak must surely run its course in claiming a sorry quota of lives before it is bound to suddenly disappear again, to who knows where?'

Plague is not like consumption, which lingeringly saps the life out of a body inch by inch. Nor is it like scurvy, that creeps on by stealth and when much advanced may yet, with good fortune, be still overcome. No, plague is not like that. Plague is the soldier that takes no prisoners. It kills almost every one that it attacks. It will call you out and knock you straight down. And once you are down, you will ne'er rise once it has you bloodied.

I am told that it starts with a ring o'roses[59], and such a blinding headache to make one feel as if a blacksmith's red-hot nail had been driven through your skull. Then fever comes with such terrible shivers as to make a body quake all over. Some then start with retching and yet still might put this sickness down to rank meat or bad ale, and so bide their time for the symptoms to pass. But they do not pass, for fever continues to shake you until you are prostrate with exhaustion. Downed and incapable of standing because of the soreness that creeps into the very marrow of the long bones and the spine. By this point, few recover.

For within the next day or so *they* appear – *buboes.* They are great burning lumps under arms, bulging upon necks or sore hidden in the loins. Some are as big and as hard as an onion. They turn black and split open like over ripe plums, oozing foul-smelling puss and blood. Blood then exudes from every orifice, in the piss-water, in the stools – all of which smells as much of putrefaction as does the victim's dying breath. If you live long enough to sneeze, then at least you know that the mercy of death is close at hand to put an end to your agony.

My friend Comfort's family died of the plague. Her mother, her widower husband, and her innocent, motherless baby – all died of plague in Gainsborough town. All buried in a pit in the corner of the churchyard. They were shunned in death as they were in the last days of their lives. May God bless their bones, for I loved them all so!

Plague was no different here in London. Past outbreaks had struck hard at the poor, because trapped within the filth in which they were compelled to live, they bore the brunt of such visitations of suffering. Rarely did the well-to-do have occasion to frequent those lowly neighbourhoods nor deal with the poor in person. And so when plague came it rarely affected the rich and influential at the heart of the city. Instead, plague had come to be regarded as an annual and relatively 'minor' occurrence, regardless of the fact that it was almost always fatal for so many people. Besides, in the height of summer and the season when such outbreaks tended to peak, it was also customary for those with means to remove themselves from the heavily built up mercantile parts of the city and away into the fresher greener districts of the countryside, far from the stink of the great open sewers that are part of the streets of London and the Thames itself.

Should I go away, I wondered. It was still only early June and far yet from the height of summer. Also, the prospect of spending so long away from my home seemed an over reaction. I decided instead to stay put, as had most of my acquaintances, who were much longer inhabitants of London and seemingly much at ease, though the King had taken leave to Oxford.

However, by that second week of June the total of dead from plague was forty-one. By the third, that had risen to one-hundred-and-fourteen. It was clear that far from staying at bay, plague had dared to breach its usual city bounds. Yet still, in this year of our Lord, sixteen-hundred-and-sixty-five, none realised that this was not set to be any common, sporadic, short-lived outbreak of summertime disease. Instead, it turned into a deadly, all consuming pandemic.

In the space of a few short weeks we found ourselves surrounded by such a magnitude of death as to make us stop in our arrogant tracks and wonder if we might not be bearing witness to the extinction of mankind. In the coming weeks, death stalked ever more freely abroad – unchallenged in his quest for more souls. For we had no cure for this dreadful ill, and it soon became clear that all who were struck down with it died. They died a wretched death in terrible torment.

The City Fathers, in an effort to stay the ravages of this vile pestilence hastily drew up a host of numerous regulations for curtailing its spread. They decreed that from that time forth, and for the remaining time of this visitation, the dead should be buried either before sunrise or before its setting. And then only in the presence of the church wardens or constable. They further ordered that no neighbour or friend be allowed to accompany the corpse to church, nor should they be permitted to enter the house where one has died of the plague. Anyone doing so would risk having his own house shut up, with himself and his household imprisoned there until proven not to be also infected.

No corpse suspected of having died from the Plague was allowed to rest inside any church building during times of service, sermon or common prayer. No children were permitted to attend any funeral, nor were they allowed to go near corpses, coffins or graves. All graves had to be dug at least six feet deep, and public gatherings or assemblies at any burial were prohibited, at least until the outbreak was over.

Since none were allowed to follow the bodies of their loved ones to the grave, corpses were bundled unceremoniously out of houses in whatever came to hand as a shroud. Soon the cry of, 'Bring out your dead!' and the low rumble of the dead carts broke into the warm summer nights, which proved all too short for the never ending task in hand. The vile stench that hung about those summer days was utterly indescribable.

Bodies, increasingly became consigned to great gaping pits with often but a cursory prayer, if indeed any at all, from those labouring under the trauma of witnessing up close the immensity of this unnatural culling of the human race.

Yet the most disturbing of all was the marking out of those houses where the plague had visited. The regulations had further decreed that those homes should be daubed with large red cross in the middle of the door along with the words, 'Lord have mercy on us'. Certainly, there was little anyone on earth could now do to help them. The rest of the household occupants were compelled to stay therein until such a time as all proved free of the disease or had succumbed to it. To overcome those unwilling to submit to this period of quarantine, the doors and the windows were often nailed shut from without and only prised open for the 'searchers' to call.

The city was divided into districts and each assigned nurses, watchers, dog and cat killers, and grave-diggers. Many endured, out of a sense of duty, to perform their allotted tasks. Others, with generous wages, were assisted by liberal libations of beer that they were able to buy. And there was tobacco too, which is widely chewed for its medicinal purpose of warding of disease. Oftimes these scant pleasures, and that of never having to go without food through lack of money, was all that saw them through till they too, became victims consigned to the earth.

Yet despite these measures, the death toll continued to rise unabated. The last week of July alone saw some seventeen or eighteen-hundred persons dead of the plague. During the same week, in the following month of August, it had risen to more than six-thousand.

*   *   *

'I thought that you would have removed yourselves to the country!' Pepys exclaimed as he called in on me unexpectedly.

'And I you, sir!' I replied, yet knowing that I could perceive of nothing that could force Pepys away from his office and from the hub of a crisis – whereby he might be seen to shine as indispensable to the King. For there was nothing quite like a good crisis for Pepys to display his invaluableness to society at large. Besides which, I could not see him being parted from his books or possessions.

'No, Not I!' he explained. 'I feel strongly that it is my duty to stay in the city and be as an instrument of intelligence and information gathering for the King. My wife, though, is safely removed to Woolwich.'

'Then you are still very much abroad in the city?'

'Plague or no, there is still much to do at my office. The Navy cannot be neglected, nor matters of our defence.'

'Then what news is there, Sam? How goes the plague?' I enquired cautiously.

'Very badly, my Lady Elizabeth. Worse than one could ever have imagined!'

Apparently most of the aristocracy and gentry had by then fled the city, as the plague continued to ravage all about us to the east. I had anguished from the start over whether or not my housekeeper, Hannah, and I should have done likewise. But moving out to the country held no guarantee that wherever we chose to go would be free of the plague. Pepys had also been sent word saying how it was now common to hear of such rural retreats refusing admittance from anyone from London, no matter how highborn or wealthy.

'How few people I now see out and about,' Pepys continued, 'and those I do are like people who have taken leave of the world! When I went to the exchange yesterday there were but fifty on it.'

'Are the numbers of dead as bad as the bill?' I dared.

'Worse, I would say. This week nearer to ten-thousand, I would think. Partly because the poor are dead in such great number that they cannot be properly noticed. Nor the Quakers or others, who refused to have any bell ring for them. Which is a small blessing, I suppose, as there are scarcely enough hours in the day in which to toll a bell for each death as it is! There are dead everywhere! The other night it was dark before I could get home from Woolwich, and on landing at the church yard stairs I came across a plague corpse lying in the narrow alley beyond. I saw it in time and was able to step over him, but I thank God that I was not much disturbed by it. However, I shall beware of being abroad late again. Even in broad daylight you cannot avoid them.

'Today, at noon, I came across a sick person covered in sores being carried close by me in a hackney-coach. Then, when in dire need of sustenance I went out of my way to walk down Tower Hill, only to find the Angel Tavern boarded shut. Worse still, so was the alehouse at the Tower stairs, where the landlord has died. I was only last in there a little while ago at night, in search of a table to write a short letter upon, you understand?'

I understood.

'I had overheard the landlord's wife saying that one of the guests was very ill but I did not think it was of the plague. Word came to me that Payne, my waterman who usually ferries me to and fro from Woolwich, had already lost a child and is now dying himself. So too another waterman who landed me there on Friday morning last.

Then that a labourer I had sent just the other day to Dagenhams to see how they fared is also dead. And both my men servants have lost their fathers, both in St Sepulchar's parish. In short, this past week doth make me greatly apprehensive and full of melancholy. And with good reason! I think I may take my leave of the streets altogether after today, but if only my duties were not so pressing! Still, today they are, and I must now take my leave of you.' He said this cheerily, as if he had just been discussing his butcher's bill. 'So God preserve us, all friends long and continue health among us!'

Pepys briskly went upon his way and I called Hannah in to me. As usual, I had given her leave to listen to our conversation at the door.

The King had several times offered a carriage to be put at our disposal but I had declined it. So, knowing my penchant for medicinal steepings, he had instead insisted on sending me a parcel of some newly discovered and extraordinarily expensive Chinese herbal leaves called 'tee', and some tobacco to ward off bad miasmas, along with a large supply of fancy provisions from his own household stocks. After Pepys' sorry report I was perhaps beginning to regret that we had not gone away while we could.

'If we stay, then I appreciate that we are in peril of catching this dreadful disease. Yet how can one escape the unseen? Where should we go for safety?' I confided in Hannah.

'I am sure I do not know, my lady,' she said. 'But I think that you may be right. We cannot avoid that which we can not see. Besides, if this visitation has been sent from on high by the Lord, as some say, as a punishment for this city's wicked and lewd ways, what have the likes of you and I to fear?'

'If so, then why have so many innocents died?' I reminded her.

'Then 'tis the end of the world and we will all die anyway! So 'tis best we die here in the familiar comfort of our own home than in some stranger's house in the country.'

That is what I love about Hannah. Her forthright, straight forward way. Here we were in a city where all about people were dying by the thousand, and yet she could still make sense of our grim situation. 'Twas as well that we could and that we were both of that same temperament, else we would have worried ourselves into our graves already.

'Then perhaps if we think about this logically, we might be able to work out a strategy to best afford us the greatest protection,' I suggested.

'And the basis for your plan, my lady? For I do not quite understand...'

'If it is deemed necessary, segregate the sick in

order to contain this grim visitation, then perhaps we would be best served to quarantine ourselves within this house to keep the plague out, Hannah.'

'I see! Then perhaps,' she surmised, 'we should also be looking towards curtailing Mister Pepys visits.'

'I am afraid that I think you are right. He is too much broad in the city and has already admitted how he has all but side-stepped death of late. The problem is that one might yet have the plague upon them without yet knowing of it. If only we knew for certain how it passed from one to another. If it is wholly through touch then we might well be able to avoid it. But if it is from the bad miasma in the air, then there may be no escaping it, for any of us.'

'In which case, we could all be doomed to fall prey of it!'

'Maybe so. Which means that there is nothing we can do to save ourselves. We shall die. Yet, if the first scenario be true, then we may weather this out. We have our own private well out back of the house, and so no one else can contaminate that. What stores do we have to hand, Hannah?'

'Plenty of flour, my lady. Four sacks left out of five delivered last month. Half a dozen round cheeses sent down from Hinchingbrooke. And our six black hens are still laying well. Other than that? A little meat, half a barrel of salt fish and few vegetables in the basket. Oh, and the King's 'fancies'. That is all.'

'Then those, at least cannot be affected, for they have been in the house this long and have not made us sick yet. But we cannot live long on bread, cheese and salt fish alone. Do the tradesmen in from the country still call at the door with their wares?'

'Yes, they have been so far. But not so many.'

'Good! Then use them Hannah, but only as long as they look in fine fettle[60]. Bid them to leave our provisions on the doorstep and then pass them payment in a dish at arms length from the window. That way you can avoid direct contact and the dish may be washed. I do not want you going to the market from now on,

Hannah. People still need to eat and so will continue to congregate there with too much interchange going on where this disease could be easily spread, if it does come by touch or by air. And no more milk! We shall buy only that which can be washed. Hopefully vinegar-water can wash away any touch. Oh! And I shall go now to my slope[61] and write a polite note that until further notice, I shall not be able to entertain personal callers. You may nail that to our door.'

So it was, that with all of these precautions duly in place and practised for some weeks that I was somewhat deeply perturbed when, in response to a loud rapping upon our front door late on one evening that I looked out from my upstairs window to see my Hannah, out in the street talking to an old drab carrying a tall white wand. The woman was clearly employed as a 'searcher', one who's job involved going into the houses of the dead to ascertain if the corpses inside had died of plague.

I watched a rather animated exchange pass between the two at some distance, then the woman turned and walked away again into the twilight. Then I immediately made shift to go downstairs and intercepted Hannah ascending the steps.

'Who was that at the door, Hannah?'
She looked at me furtively then, and I noticed the tears well in her eye.

''Twas my dead husband's sister, my lady,' her voice faltered. 'She came to tell me that apart from her, I am now all alone in the world. All of her family and mine are now dead of the plague. She, for her part, has been shut up in her house these past forty days and nights and, having survived, is now freed.'

'And she has become a searcher?'

'Yes. She came to tell me so. And to make her peace.'

'But why? After cheating death? Why submit herself to such danger?'

'She says that she must. Mayhap God has spared her for this purpose? If not, then she says that she no longer cares. If it pleases God to take her too, then so be it. I am all that she has left in the world now and so she came to say that she was sorry that she had not done more for her late brother's wife. That she believed also that the time of great reckoning was almost upon us, and so she wanted to come to see me for herself and to know that she and I were in good grace before she went upon her way...'

With that Hannah went to her room, and then we would never speak of that day again.

Like all previous outbreaks of plague, by Christmastide this wicked one did eventually feast itself out. Yet not before it had taken away with it some sixty-eight thousand souls, and leaving every city churchyard crammed tightly with pits full of festering bodies. In these pits the plague miasmas might live on and, if disturbed, so strike out at us once more...

Chapter Sixteen

Letters from Virgina continued to fill me with great excitement. My children already seemed settled there. They had quickly built a fine new house and had a flourishing plantation. Hope also informed me early on that my grandson was courting a very pretty young lady indeed. She was from an equally prestigious family and planned to marry in a year or so.

From James' accounts, the New World has changed beyond all recognition since my arrival there more than forty years ago. He tells me that settlement is increasing at break-neck speed, especially as war with the Powatans had long since ceased. Indeed, in many parts, the naturals there have quit altogether to seek out their living as far removed from the English planters as they are able.

Hope, she said, was well received by the blossoming circle of society there, as well she ought! Young Tom also fares well, despite being a half-cast in a prejudiced society, perhaps enjoying the precedent set by Thomas Rolfe's success.

Sad to me though, were James' reports of Plimoth which he had visited on business for the King. Bradford and the others are all now passed away. And that for the most part, their Separatist ideals have been overwhelmed by the deluge of Puritans that have flooded into New England during the past thirty years or so. The colony's principles of tolerance in matters spiritual, and towards the natural population there, have been mostly swept aside by the greater number and authority of those new-comers at Boston. In short, our Separatist dream seemed to be all but over. For with the failing of its leading lights, these Pilgrim Fathers, their vision too seems to have dimmed from the eyes of their successors. But still, to me at least, they live on!

*   *   *

September 2nd 1666

I awoke in the small hours as, having to endure
the afflictions of old age, I often do. Glancing across my
chamber towards the widow, I noticed a most unusually
crimson sunrise that compelled me to recall my father's
recitation of an old country proverb on such a dawning
as this – 'a red sky in morning bodes ill warning'. Yet, I
lay abed for quite some while before suddenly realising
that outside it was getting no lighter and that I could
distinctly smell something other than the usual tang of
woodsmoke in the air.

Throwing back my fine linen sheets and
duck feather quilt, I must have caught my nightstand,
for I sent my extinguished candle and heavy silver holder
crashing to the floor. But unperturbed I continued
to ease myself out of bed and onto my feet and then
started to shuffle stiffly across the room to the half open
window. Looking out, I could not at first fathom that
which my eyes were seeing. This was not dawn! Yet the
whole sky was aglow from a great fiery red orb some
way off and low beyond the still silhouetted roof-line of
this respectable part of the city.

Just then a flush-faced, Hannah, rushed into
my chamber.

'My lady!' She was in a considerable state of
anxiety. 'Beg your pardon, but I heard a noise and
feared that you had fallen.'

'Thank you, Hannah. 'Twas but my own silly fault.
In my eagerness to get up I toppled my candlestick. But
never mind that! Have you seen this?' I said beckoning
her to the window.

She walked to my side there.

'It looks like a fire, my lady! A huge fire... though
quite some way off.'

Fire was no stranger to the city. I could recall at least
a dozen in the five or more years in which I had been
living there. 'Twas ever a consequence waiting to
occur, one that stemmed from living in such a closely
confined mishmash of timber-framed houses, and with

all those who were careless with its use. Such neglect of caution could be the un-snuffed candle, or a wine-induced stupor, or a housewife retiring while an ember still smouldered in her oven. In truth, we have all made such mistakes in our time. Usually, thankfully, without consequence. Yet, with the multiplicity of the tens of thousands of households that we had crammed into the confines of this ancient city that spilled ever outwards from its original walls, the marvel was that there had not been a great many more.

This fire indeed was yet some way off, I fathomed. Probably way down towards the river front.

'Could it be a ship, ablaze?' I remember thinking aloud? For there was such a ship on fire not so long before, when the watch was lax and a lamp toppled over, destroying the ship and its cargo of pitch and several lighters moored nearby. Yet, I did not recall seeing such a bright fury as I saw then.

Hannah and I stood watching for quite some while, but with the standing starting to sore vex my arthritic spine and what with the fire so far away, Hannah soon scolded me lightly.

''Tis doing your poor bones no good standing here like this in this draft,' she said closing the window and drawing the curtains, 'else you'll be as stiff as a board by morning, my lady – or worse! Besides, 'tis nothing to be troubling yourself with, and it will soon be put out, no doubt. Now, let me help you back to your bed.'

Dear Hannah! She was always so concerned for my health that I did not care to resist her, for fear of injuring her feelings. Instead, I meekly let her shepherd me back to my bed where I tried to settle down to sleep once more.

I did so, and quite soundly, for in my next moments of conciousness I was being shaken awake by Hannah. It was mid-morning.

'Oh, my lady!' she gushed. 'My lady, the city is on fire!'

'Are you certain?'

'Yes, Lady Elizabeth. As I bought milk from the maid at our doorstep, I overheard some gentleman in the street saying that more than three hundred houses have been burned down in the night!'

Hannah helped me up and into my robe, in order that I might look once more from the vantage of my high window. Yet, if anything, the fire now looked less than it did before and if appeared even further off.

'Did the man say whether the fire was was now under control?'

'No my lady, he did not,' Hannah replied. 'Though he did say that fire was burning all along Fish Street by London Bridge, and that St Magnus Church was completely burned to the ground.'

That was worrying indeed to hear. Yet, as we were unaffected and the calamity so far removed, Hannah and I got on with our day as much as usual, though I went, from time to time, back to my window to see if I could check upon the fire's movement. Every time I hoped that it was under control and being put out. It was hard to determine anything by now as a shroud of dense smoke hung heavily above the skyline.

However, come the dark of evening, the true and terrifying extent of the fire still rampaging through the city became terrifyingly clear. Previously, daylight had belittled its potency. The fire had not retreated at all. In fact, its hellish red hallo now arched above the city as far as my eyes could see.

Later, at nine of the clock, came a furious rapping at our door. Hannah answered to find Sam Pepys' servant with more reports of the fire. She soon rushed up to bring me his news.

'Mister Pepys conveys, my lady, how that there is as yet no immediate danger to us. But he advises that we hold ourselves in readiness should the worse come to the worst and we need to evacuate our home.'

'Leave our home?' I had not realised that our situation in this area of London was anywhere near that serious. 'But where does he expect to go?' I wondered aloud.

'He adds that you are not to fret, my lady. He says that he has today met with the King himself and the Duke of York at White Hall. And that although efforts to put out the fire by hooking down houses in its path hath failed, plans are even now in hand to use gunpowder to blow up an area that will create a breach that the fire cannot traverse. But Mister Pepys also says that, should all else fail, and the unhappy need to evacuate become manifest, then on the King's behalf, he will personally see to it that arrangements are put in hand for our removal to some suitable place of safety.'

'Despite my dislike of the fellow,' I remarked, 'I must admit that it appears that Sam Pepys is not as self-centred as I have always thought. It was kindness indeed for him to take trouble over us. Perhaps, under his fine silk suits, there beats a heart there after all!'

Hannah immediately set about bundling up the barest of necessities for our leaving, should that become a reality. I bade her to be rational in her choosing and that no frivolous items were to be taken on my behalf, pointing out that I needed but one 'sensible' day dress besides the one I would be wearing. Of course I would need my nightgown, slippers and a change of shoes. Only after much debate would Hannah comply, for fear that I, her mistress and a titled lady, lay my standards too low.

Meanwhile, I pondered upon the situation quite stoically. After all, I told myself, this would not be the first time I had been forced out of my house and away from all of my belongings. This time though, I had been granted that luxury of being forewarned and able to take up what personal items there were long in my possession. These were items I could not bear to lose, and committed myself to take those and only those. All else could be replaced easily with money.

There was my journal, of course, and my almost completed autobiography. My entire life lay imprinted along with the very substance of my being upon those leaves. I needed to be certain that it would 'live on' after my death, for my children's sake.

My father died when I was still quite young, and although I remember some parts of my life with him with frightening vividness, I knew nothing about him as a person other than his being my 'father'. Then there was my mother. In my later years I grew to deeply regret not making time and effort to really get to know her, when I had ample opportunity to do so. No, this was to be no great work for public scrutiny. Rather, it would bear testimony to my life so that, through it, my children and grandson might get to know me better when I am gone away. So I avowed to, if necessary, move heaven itself to keep my writing safe!

Then there were my pearls. Those held such deep personal value, and I felt sure that Hope would one day treasure those as well. It seemed only yesterday that she and I were burying them in our garden at Stowe lest the Roundheads came and looted them.

Meanwhile, Hannah went out every so often into the street to see what word she might pick up about the fire. Each time she returned to give me a report the situation seemed grimmer than before.

'They are saying that if only this strong easterly breeze would desist then there might be a chance of putting it out. Or at least containing it by fire breaks. But so long as it blows the fire is raging so fiercely and jumping back and forth upon itself, and into all directions that it is difficult predicting its pathway and letting off the explosives in the right place to make a void.'

It was soon ten of the clock. For even in the midst of disaster the bellman still came to call out the hour, and with it now the latest progress of the fire towards our direction. Exhausted by the unexpected effort and the lateness of the hour, Hannah and I, content that we had made ready as much as we could be expected, decided it best to try to get some rest. And so still fully clothed, I retired to my bed whilst she slept down in the parlour, ready to answer the door to callers. Outside, all about us, was urgent activity and commotion. There were people arriving by cart, dressed in their nightclothes, bringing goods from now ruined homes into those of my neighbours for safety. But at the very same time, others were trying to carry their possessions away from our street and out of the city altogether. It was utter chaos.

And so it was we that slept a while in spits and spurts as we could, above the great noise of all that was at shift outside in the street.

But at midnight came news that the fire had reached the first house at the bottom of our street. We knew then that it could only be a matter of time before we would have to leave our own home. 'Twas only then that Hannah took a shovel out into the back garden, dug a pit, and buried our dinner service and silver-ware, all bundled up in a sack cloth. At least there, it would probably be spared the ravages of the fire.

Shortly after a royal carriage came to the house, bearing the Kings arms and with liveried men for all to see. Pepys had proved true to his word!

'And where pray, are we to be conveyed?' I asked of its driver.

'To Merton, Lady Elizabeth,' the King's man replied. 'We are instructed to take you across the river to Merton and to the respectable home of Mister William Rutlish.'

So it was that dear Hannah and I were quickly helped aboard and, with our few chattels carefully stowed, were transported as swiftly as possible out of the city.

Surprisingly, for quite some distance we travelled unhindered, though every now and then we herd a voice booming, 'Make way for the King's carriage!' From its shelter we observed that much of what we surveyed was still blessed with surprising normality. But this proved false comfort – for our driver had come away from the heart of the fire only to drive through thoroughfares he knew still to be open, though congested with terrified crowds, before trying to make south for the river. For then we found ourselves cast close to the heart of the orange many-headed 'beast'.

Flames licked at the hapless buildings. I thought of bloodied tongues of serpents from hell as they mercilessly devoured their prey. With terrifying swiftness, houses were being completely engulfed by fire as we watched. Even before ravaging one victim, the flames were already moving on to raze the next. As buildings crackled and creaked in their death throes, the fire hissed and spewed out a great shower of red hot cinders that rained onto roof tops of neighbouring homes and onto the terrified bystanders below. Thus the fire spread at an alarming rate, speeded on by the willing wind.

The summer just past had been warm and dry. Especially so the weeks leading into September, barely breached by rain so as to leave everything still tinder dry. A strong breeze aided the fire by fanning the flames, letting them skip and dance from roof to roof with such ease – ever onwards to the next building. Fresh fire flared up sending smoke spiralling upwards and away, even as the frantic householders below were still trying to rescue their wretched possessions. These poor people were dashing back and forth from inside carrying out arms full of belongings, until eventually beaten away for good by the smoke and heat of the blaze.

Yet not all men were content to stand idly by and let the beast rampage through their livelihoods unchallenged. Great ranks of them tried desperately to quench its appetite. They scaled flimsy ladders to fight back the flames, armed only with leather buckets of water that they were passing hand over hand along a chain of courageous helpers. But it was impossible. 'Twas as if this fire was a living thing – a malicious creature too long caged up by man, and now freed and reeking its revenge upon its keepers.

The narrow streets had became so crowded that our progress almost ground to a halt. Panic-stricken crowds don't care about whose coachmen are demanding the rights of privilege. That is, if people even heard the commands.

In amongst the fallen debris, a burnt-bald

cat crouched mewing pathetically from beneath a half-toppled chimney stack. Two sooty faced women sat weeping with terrified children huddled at their sides, close to what little of their possessions they had managed to grab. Many sat amid the mayhem with nowhere else to go, and without any transport even if they had. And it seemed that where there had been something, horses had been panicked by the choking smoke, and roaring and scorching flames that devoured the buildings. They had bolted and left overturned carts with luggage spilled out across the road and obstructing passage. But our well-trained horses from the Royal Stables held their course.

Ｏne man stood sobbing a little way from his blazing shop. I heard him crying out for the fire to take him too, for he had nothing left in life for which to live. His business was gone, and with it his home and all he had worked for over a lifetime to achieve. He was screaming about having nothing left with which to start over and that he would be better off dead. It was heart-breaking to see!

Yet just a little further along, a genteel woman dressed in a green silk gown sat with her young house-maid – amid a trampled garden, eating her meal off a fine porcelain plate. And all at such an unhurried pace as to seem totally surreal. As we inched our way through the carnage, 'twas as if we were witnessing the final day of the end of the world.

As the fire spread, spent buildings collapsed into the street before us, sending our blinkered horses neighing onto their hind legs. Several times such destruction blocked our way, forcing our driver to double back upon ourselves and to find another route to the river.

Then, all of a piece, we came upon a church. I know not which one, for by now I had completely lost my bearings within this mayhem. Stained glass windows lay shattered beneath its great stone carved windows. Tear drops of molten lead wept from its burning vaulted roof and pooled, before slowly trickling down the cobbled street like a river of tarnished silver. Bare, blackened roof-beams arched upwards like the ribcage of some great dying creature being tormented in its throes of death by the demonic fire. Caught up amongst it all, the wretched pigeons, not knowing where else to go in their confusion, tried repeatedly to return to their fiery roost, until many with singed feathers fell exhausted and helpless to the ground.

Yet to this day, it is none of these dreadful sights that I remember most – but a smell. 'Twas the smell of this church burning, but not the acrid smoke that had compelled us to hold up our kerchiefs about our noses and mouths as before – when we had hurried through the endless ranks of burning houses. No, instead this church smelt like an offering of heady incense hanging heavily in the air, and permeating our clothing. It was like a final offering given up by its age-old timbers. Like myrrh for this now dead church, where a host of ancients had kept faith for so long down the uncertain centuries, but now given up to this Sodom and Gomorrah.

I shouted out to the driver to stop, feeling an overwhelming compulsion to step down from the carriage to witness the horror – as did Hannah and many others – of the demise of this house of God. She helped me down, then turned and cried out in anguish.

'Oh mercy on us, my lady! 'Tis the end of the world!'

'Mercy upon us indeed!' I agreed, reaching out and drawing her close like a terrified child.
Watching it burn felt something like betrayal. For I wondered, where was God now in all of this?

Amid our silent prayers, the great edifice succumbed. And then with a soul wrenching groan, its mighty tower heaved, and with a sigh akin to a death rattle, it fell. Crashing inwards upon itself, it sent a shower of a million crimson sparks flaring upwards – towards an even more fiery firmament above. It was, indeed, like the end of our world.

Suddenly this church lay as but one more heap of ruination amongst the embers of the numberless scores. Meanwhile, people in that street, seeking only to flee to safety, were being hampered by onlookers such as ourselves – compelled to witness this tragic spectacle. I felt that we ran the risk of straying just a little too near and staying a little too long. My companion by then could barely withstand the heat upon her face or the cobbles burning underfoot like hot coals. Naturally, Hannah wanted us back on our way. Yet I stood in awe of the fire's mesmerising but malicious beauty. Almost stunned, only with great reluctance would I allow her to eventually draw me away. For I was convinced that I had never seen such vivid flames before in any ordinary fire. Then again, I had never before seen a fire so great as to ark like a great crimson sunset clear across the cityscape, and one burning so brightly as to turn night into day.

Chapter Seventeen

Eventually we reached the River Thames, where we found the Royal Barge ready and waiting to take us south-side. As the conflagration bore down, all about us people pleaded and begged with the lighter men to help them escape. However, what few craft remained went to the highest bidders, who were loathe to take aboard any but their own and their belongings. No matter if that meant setting off to safety but half empty.

At that moment my fear was not as theirs – that of charring where we stood – but of having to step down into the boat while avoiding what for me was the real danger of falling and breaking a bone. 'Twas not an unreasonable fear, for the stairs were all swarmed and steep, and to descend them without mishap would prove no mean feat at my advanced age. I should not have worried though, for the burley royal boatmen ran to snatch me up and lift me aboard, as if I were but the weight of a bantam.

Once Hannah and I were safely seated and our possessions stowed, I ordered the men to take with us as many wretched souls as we could cram aboard, which they reluctantly agreed to do. Yet those we beckoned come hither, although greatly afraid and facing such peril, were loathe to prevail upon us for help when they realised that it would be to board His Majesty's vessel. So, reluctantly, we cast off alone.

Looking back was like watching a great eruption of showers of glowing orange rain, as fire consumed more ancient spires and brought them crashing to earth. I could just make out the lights from the squeeze of houses tightly packed across London Bridge. Although fire was everywhere, that structure looked intact, though it was quite impossible for anyone to cross it either way, because of fire on its approach from the city side.

I wondered, as we crossed the water, what those above were thinking as they huddled by their windows and doorways. Surly they were catching glimpses of hell as they looked out across the water betwixt the fire in the sky and the smoke lying thick upon the water. Did they look down upon us, cast upon the river, and at those still caught up in the teeth of the fire while praying earnestly for our safe deliverance? I like to believe that we were being watched over that night.

Navigating across the Thames proved almost as hazardous as our journey by road. For apart from the poor visibility, the river was crammed with an array of tiny craft -all desperately trying to cross or make their way up or down stream... or anywhere away from the raging inferno. Adding to this danger of collision and being sunk, were the countless pieces of bobbing flotsam being drawn by the incoming tide.

Safely at last upon the south side of the river, we reached the King's private mooring, where another fine carriage waited to speed us on our way to Merton, along the Dorking Road. Even here, standing at Bankside, the air was very much clearer, so that my lungs no longer felt fit to burst with every breath. And my eyes were no longer smarting from the acrid smoke. We rested in the coach awhile, until dawn began to break and we could see the road to travel on to Merton. Ten miles on, the fire was still visible and the sight and smell of smoke was still very much in the sky.

I arrived at Merton exhausted, and then quickly settled into the kind hospitality I was grateful to find there. Although large, as befitting his station, Mister William Rutlish's home was tastefully and modestly furnished, and perhaps rather understated. However, one could not help to notice that all about it benefited from beautiful embellishment by way of exquisite examples of his own handiwork. Whoever it was who suggested that I be given sanctuary in this household above all others, I owe my eternal indebtedness. For I could not have asked for more congenial surrounding nor more gracious hosts as William and his wife, Mary.

Rutlish was such a sweet, unassuming man of above sixty years, with white hair and yet exceedingly dark eyebrows mantling the calmest of bright blue eyes. My enduring impression will always surely remain of that occasion, our first introduction. He was seated beside a large window, squinting against the early morning sunshine through a pair of silver eye-glasses, while clutching an embroidery hoop with one hand as the other drew through a needle with a long blue strand of silken thread. He busily working upon an exquisitely fashioned peacock. I had never seen a man embroider before. Sew, yes, for that is a basic functional skill imperative to everyone. But I had never observed what with later inspection proved to be such mastery of precision looping that went into forming the body of the bird. Nor had I witnessed such intricate and delicate feathering stitch-work used in the peacock's plumage. I was truly astounded by its sheer artistry. For no mean reason was William Rutlish 'Embroiderer to the King'. He was the man responsible for the creation of all the intricate hand-stitched decorations, often with real silver and gold thread, upon King Charles' sumptuous wardrobe of clothes.

Nowadays though, it was not all done personally by his own hand. Though he did still insist on executing the most intricate and prestigious pieces himself. Instead, he had trained up a clutch of hand-picked boy apprentices who copied exactly the stitching of his hand-drawn designs under his ever watchful supervision. He was a perfectionist. And he passed his skills on to his apprentices through patient example, a commodity of which he seemed have stores in abundance.

Though probably born at about the same time as I had started service as a maidservant at Gainsborough Hall, Rutlish was the nearest acquaintance – close to my own generation – I had the pleasure in coming to know in a long time. He understood the changes I had seen and lived through having witnessed most of them himself. He had lived cheek by jowl with royalty and no doubt knew the King intimately, and yet he was simple in his aspirations and godly by his nature, making light of the esteem in which he was held by the King. For one so honoured, he remained perfectly unaffected at home in this same pleasant country parish where he had been born and raised.

Though so removed from the city, Rutlish was kept remarkably well informed about the fire and its effect. Upon learning that I was well acquainted with Sam Pepys, he suggested that I might like to meet his cousin, Thomas Pepys, who was being put up at a nearby great house built at the remains of Merton Abbey. Having previously heard of this cousin being referred to as 'The Executor' by Sam, coupled with mention of his strong Puritan views, I at first resisted William's suggestion. I was not keen to spoil my time there by sharing my company with Thomas, should he share any latent family traits already exposed by his cousin.

However, one evening shortly afterwards, I was to be pleasantly surprised when making this Pepys' acquaintance over dinner. For he could not have been more different from his kinsman as lemon is to honey. From William Rutlish's smile across the candlelit table, I came to suspect that he had already anticipated my opinion to be so.

'Any news from London as to when it might be possibly safe to return?' I ventured to enquire of William's guest.

'Yesterday all seemed positive that the fire is mostly out. Though there are numerous cellars of oil and brimstone and the such still burning,' Thomas Pepys replied, 'I hear from my cousin that the latest London gossip is that this fire is no accident!' he laughed. 'Sam hath written to me to say that he has heard it widely put abroad that Catholic agents in the pay of the French set the fire and that the Dutch fleet might sail up the Thames at any moment to invade us!'

'Surely not!' William countered in disbelief.

'Surely not indeed, Sir! Yet there are those who would much prefer there to be a conspiracy when it comes to attributing blame. Especially in the case of such a catastrophe which, to be blunt, hath long since been a promise in the offing. However, as I say, there are those who would rather believe the dramatic above the plain truth. Take Sam, for example. For I know how my dear Coz does like a drama! And his eggs fluffed up with cream and a good pinch of spice instead of plain boiled. I suspect that he is in his element just now and inked in as the leading man upon those pages of his endless scribble. For as surely as the moon revolves around the earth, I am certain Sam truly believes that London revolves around him!'

Merton, even in autumn, seemed to me the most perfect of retreats from London, which could have lain a hundred miles away beyond the fields instead of barely an hour or two's ride distant.

I would have so liked to have had the opportunity to revisit it in summer. The parish's church of St Mary the Virgin was so calm and serene that, for the first time since coming to London, I could sense myself truly in God's presence as I sat there, in prayer, at the Sunday service. Though even in this idyll, I soon discovered from the still bare hump of a plague pit snug in the corner of the churchyard, that some of the horrors of the city could reach even here. Sadly, my stay there amongst such pleasing company was to prove all too brief.

The return to the city was for me, the most shocking sight I had ever seen. For in our flight by night, Hannah and I had witnessed such horrific scenes of destruction, yet never realised the true extent of the peril faced by London that night, when masked in vibrant scarlet and cloaked in billowing smoke. Only as we returned, and made approach from Lambeth and across the Thames by the bridge, did the full horror of the devastation make its impact upon us. There was now next to nothing left standing intact betwixt the river and the area all the way up to and beyond the now missing St Paul's Cathedral.

Wiped from the skyline were the great spires and towers of more than three quarters of the one-hundred-and-eighteen churches that had proudly stood before. Instead, it was as if there was one great glaring void where city landmarks had once proclaimed this blackened shell to be London, the capital of our country. It seemed impossible to imagine how all of this might ever be put to rights again. Then, of course, it probably never will.

The old London was gone to ash and dust. Like a body burnt, it could never be again. The fire, which had started at Pudding Lane, had burnt its way across four-fifths of the city as it was hurried on by the easterly wind. With the aid of gunpowder, houses that yet stood in its path untouched were blown up to make firebreaks. But by the grace of God, after almost a week and the loss of more than thirteen-thousand buildings, the flames were eventually vanquished just short of Pie Corner in the west. There, I was grieved to discover that all about Newgate, where Thomas and I had visited with Captain John Smith in his house, was near raised to the ground. And that St Sepulchre's Church, where the Captain lay buried, had been almost destroyed.

Yet, in all of this, I have not given an account of my own little house. After a painfully slow journey, picking our way through endless miles of derelict streets, Hannah and I eventually arrived back to find it relatively intact. It was the very last house still standing on my street. So from that time it forlornly rises up from its blackened surroundings like some lone relic amongst the ashes of the past. Having been licked by flames and with its windows put out, it should not be here at all. By rights, it should have been gone. Gone and done away with to make way for the new as, I fear, so should I. How I longed for that mournful September wind to shake this shrivelled apple down from the tree. To let me drop at last to lie amongst the other lost fruit in gentle rest, safe on the soft earth below. Instead I still hung on.

Until then, I was in good health. My housekeeper, Hannah, made certain of that. Unfortunately that state was already in shift. Little did Hannah realise that as she continued diligently about her daily chores, cleaning and dusting the rooms and caring for my every need, that one day this house would be hers. I had bequeathed it to her in my will, along with a sizeable annuity. I should have no use of it after my death. And if I had left it to James and Hope, I suspect it would only be boarded up and left to decay, for I cannot see them leaving their new lives in Virgina to return to this squalid little island. Besides, I would go upon my own journey home, much easier in the knowledge that I had at least left Hannah some comfort in return for that which she has given me.

Hannah is a widow too. Much younger than I am, but was just as alone in this world when I had first found her on the streets, begging for bread. Hannah had lost both her husband and their only child to that wicked war. Both had been infantry men on the Parliamentarian side and both died at Naseby, where my own husband was so badly injured. Our menfolk may have been deadly enemies, but she and I held so much in common – pain – as to be bonded by this war instead of cast apart.

My sincerest prayer is that Dear God will heal those dark schisms that, despite the Restoration, still fester on in others, lest the rift should open once more, and civil war return. Yet, from all that I have seen and continue to hear, I fear very much that our remaining young men may be set to march that wretched road again...

Chapter Eighteen

It is December and I have not left my house since my return from Merton. And I no longer go to court to watch the mad yarn spin out. Instead, I stay snug in my own little world. A world that is mostly populated by dead people. They crowd into my waking thoughts and inhabit my dreams. Then again, perhaps that it is not so surprising. For I have known and loved so very many people who are now long passed away. Far more than I know in life now. They bring comfort to me in these long drab winter days with snatchlets of conversation and memories from the past, replaying faithfully in my mind.

I have stirring sentiments from William Brewster to lift my soul when I feel spiritually low. And oftimes his gentle words lead me into quiet prayer. I have Lady Rose Hickman's life example to show me how to face the ever mounting difficulties of extreme old-age with fortitude and grace. So much time has gone by, so many years since I was first but a lowly serving girl at Gainsborough Hall with my Lady Rose. How I had marvelled at her great age then, little knowing that I would eventually encounter as much myself, lingering on in my seventy-ninth year.

My father comes also, and I soon smile as he sits with me in the soft dappled sunshine and talks to me like his little girl once more. Many others come bide with me too from across the void to reminisce of times slipped by. Yet, I also sense someone else at hand... Someone close by, like a visitor hovering beyond my closed bedroom door waiting for me to open it and let him step once more inside my world. I will not. Not now. I am not ready to face him just yet.

I have lain awake at night often these past years now vexed by the bone ache. Upon my darkened bed too oft I have listened in the shadows at the first chirrup of birdsong breaking through the night and into a new dawn. There is no bird song now. Too many trees and their perches, I suppose, were burnt away in the fire.

Maybe the birds will never sing again in London. Mayhap even the elusive cuckoos, in whichever undiscovered place they go to sleep away the winter cold, are all dead too? Perhaps our English summer may never come again either, without them to herald it?

So much uncertainty abounds! I feel that we are but teetering on the brink of such uncertainty as has never befallen our nation. I have lived through and survived such turbulence before now, yet this latest catastrophe? Our houses of God and sanctuaries are gone. Even the bells that marked out our hours upon this earth have been silenced. How can normality ever be restored? What if this city cannot be rebuilt? What then? Can this aged body of a realm carry on without its heart? Are our foreign enemies poised, even now as we writhe in our agonies, to invade us and rend all that remains asunder?

I have seen so much change! I do not think I have the stomach or the will to witness much more. I need desperately to hear that bird call, once more. For it to sing out to me from the darkness and to bring cheer that the light will soon come back again into our blackened world.

I often look back on my life and wonder what has it all been for? Why have I had to endure such pain, to re-find, in turn, both a lost husband and a son, only to then be deprived of their company again all too soon. Yes, Hannah is quick to remind me constantly that I still have my children. Yet they live on only in my thoughts and the paper of the all too infrequent letters that bridges the distance between us.

But perhaps I am beginning to see that my life has had its purpose after all, and in a way that I could never have foreseen. My children are to be the very seed of this New World, while I am destined to remain in this old one. I, a constant reminder of their past, and they the hope for a better and more tolerant future.

These past few months, my bones pain me so that I can no longer venture down my own stairs, let alone leave the house. Instead, I now receive what few visitors I have up here in my chamber. Else I idle away the day writing up my memoirs or looking out of the bare window upon the vast tract of ruined city beyond. Though when the day is bright, as much as I would like, I dare not open my window – not even a crack. For the air outside is so tainted still.

When the Great Fire raged at its height, at least it burned hot and cleanly with much of the clouds of smoke billowing swiftly upwards and away high on the winds. What foul air stooped below, was quickly sucked out of lungs by the force of the firestorm as it consumed everything about it. Now, there is an acrid pall of smoke that on still frosty days sulks about at street level from the smouldering contents of abandoned cellars, where so many buildings once stood. From oil, from coal, stores and lumber, small remnants of the fire burn on – like a reminder of Hades underfoot.

I hear that relatively few lives were actually lost to the Great Fire, considering the scale of the disaster. Yet no tally seems to have been made of those who have died since, and are still dying, from the effects of inhaling its deadly smoke, even now, some three months on. Nor for the newly impoverished who are without either homes or trades to go to. They now shiver and beg in the street. Or of those who starve through the still exorbitant prices being charged for our daily bread.

'We shall reap advantage from out of the seeds of adversity and use this opportunity to build London again!' Sam Pepys recently assured me, on one of his thankfully now rare visits. That recovery is in hand, and he should know. He seems to be in the hub of it all as usual, and with those planning the rebuilding of London. Never let it be said that where there was a profit waiting to be born, that midwife Pepys was not to be found loitering close at hand to mind its delivery into the world.

'The hooks are already out!' Sam had proclaimed enthusiastically. 'Men go about the city in gangs grappling down the charred skeletons of dead houses in readiness for redevelopment. Mind you, 'tis impossible for the likes of you, I fear, to get around in a sedan or a carriage for the debris strewn about the thoroughfares. Especially along Ludgate just now. It is such an impediment! 'Tis as well that these days you spend so much time at home,' he sighed whilst putting away at least half of the cloved ham that Hannah had freshly boiled that morning along with more than his share of a pitcher of ale. All this, even though he had arrived at my door professing to be a little 'out of sorts' and only able to partake of the lightest of suppers.

As usual, Pepys was accompanied on this visit by his ever attentive young wife, though I could not but help notice that she looked so gaunt and pale these days. She remained perched beside him like a little waxened doll. Her translucent features were closely matched by the sheen of her washed-out grey silk gown.

Meanwhile, Pepys prattled on about how he and Mistress Pepys had been married for ten years, though his wife was quick to correct by reminding him that she was but fifteen years old when made his bride. And so it was, in fact, eleven years.

Unperturbed, he went on in great detail about all that he ate and drank in celebration of that 'happy occasion', while I sat just wishing that I had enough strength and ill manners to rise from my chair and throttle the living breath out the self-centered swaggard of a man. Instead, I was forced to endure his verbal effluence and to smile sweetly back at Mistress Pepys.

As I read her eyes, I sensed such unspoken sadness. The eyes have it all, you know. They convey so much that words cannot. Hers were like mine, wide open yet inside longing to close upon the world... Now weary of looking out on the same set scene, they yearn to fall upon that peaceful vista promised beyond. I am old. In my instance it's understandable. But she? She was weary beyond her years to be as I am. It made me afraid for her. Afraid that she might be fretting her life away, and all seemly unnoticed by her undeserving buffoon of a husband. 'Twas so sad a sight to see.

From Pepys' exasperating account of his toing and froing about the city, and the fine meals he has sat down to along his way this past month, one would assume that all was well with others in London. Thankfully for him, his house and office were spared, yet he was at such pains to bemoan how he faced 'ruin' for the lack of money coming in. And then he changed tack completely, almost mid-sentence, to comment on the King and the Duke of York's latest fashion for waistcoats and how he must have one.

Not even in one breath did I hear him commenting on the fate of those burnt out by the fire. Those poor souls who in actuality were already ruined financially, and who had little hope of any immediate improvement to their plight. Over thirteen-thousand homes had been burnt down; five-sixths of the city destroyed. And yet unless it was the loss of one of Pepys' personal tradesman, or a well loved drinking hole, or some other favorite haunt, he made little compassionate comment.

'From out of those ruined and narrow prospects, wide fine avenues shall now radiate and inspire,' Pepys continued his monologue. 'And from the wretched ruins of eighty-seven ancient churches, along with the Cathedral of St Paul, a new edifice of God shall appear such as to marvel the rest of the world!'

Eighty-seven churches. Was there really the need for so many within the city? I asked myself, for the likes of Pepys to be seen attending or to be heard complaining that the sermon was 'not good' or 'so long last Lord's Day that the roast for my dinner was over done?' He freely admitted that he did not attend church even every week, or that he often leaves if he finds it too crowed or not well attended by society he knows.

Why not spend the money, instead, on immediate aid for the dispossessed? After all, the King, in October, and not a month since, had ordered a day of fasting on account of the fire and told the Lord Mayor to support collections for its victims. Yet I had not heard Pepys make mention of his contribution.

'And tell me, Sam,' I eventually dared venture. 'What if Christ were to come again this very day? Would He spend this kingly fortune on building more new churches? Would he not use it to build homes for those living on the street or to feed the city's hungry mouths?'

Pepys almost choked, as I had caught him on the swallow. For a moment his eyes bulged out from his rubric face as Mistress Pepys frantically patted him on the back as he struggled to regain his breath. 'Twas cruel, I know, but I continued all the same... 'Only then with a roof over every homeless man's head and a meal upon his table, do I think that Christ might consider building a house in honour of His Father. What mockery we mortal men make of His immortal word!'

Pepys did not have an answer. Instead he went on at length about how rebuilding the city is considered to be the only way out of its bankruptcy. Something about how embarking upon such a great undertaking, regardless of the inadequacies of its coffers to pay for it, would actually generate the income to sustain it all. An otherwise now idle workforce would be off the streets and in pay, which in turn will regenerate the tradesmen with whom they will spend their wages. And at the end of it all the exchequer will reap taxes to plough back into more rebuilding.

Pepys explained the theory behind it in great detail as he continued to pile his plate. But I must profess that the ins and outs of it were completely lost upon me. Such pearls of wisdom, however so eloquently strung, doth hang like mere baubles about the neck of this Philistine.

I did understand though, that among the great new cornerstones of government and commercial rebuilding that is planned, would indeed be dozens of new city churches and a new St Paul's Cathedral. They even intended to build a great monument at Pudding Lane to the fire itself. Can you imagine that? Monuments are usually erected to commemorate victors and not destroyers! Yet I suppose it is fitting in a way... For fire was the victor in the battle for this now heartless city. Fire had certainly cowered London to its knees and almost vanquished it. Now it seems that this ash-hearted phoenix is set to rise again.

*　　　*　　　*

For in truth I have done such a silly thing. I missed my footing on my bedroom rug and tripped, hitting the floor with such a crack that Hannah cried out with fright.

'My Lady!' she exclaimed. 'You must surely have broken a bone!'

I tried to shrug it off, and at first refused to allow her to send for a doctor. Yet it too soon became obvious that I must have done myself some dreadful injury, for the pain was incredible in my hip and my spine.

So, I have been in such unremitting agony these past few days since then that I scarce know where to start in finding the words to describe it. Hannah became so worried about my sorry state, that she defied my wishes and sent word to Mister Pepys. He in turn sent word to His Majesty, who immediately dispatched his own physician to call upon me.

'What cure do you have for carelessness in old age?' I asked him. But I do swear that he hath not even a modicum of humor lurking in some dull corner of his body. Instead he looked at me, smiled weakly, and then turned to Hannah, pressing into her hand a small blue bottle of some potent potion. And then he had the impertinence to whisper something to her behind his hand – as if I could not see – something that made her most upset. Then he gave her, loudly, instruction upon how to administer the bottle's contents at my need. He then smiled again in my direction, and spoke to me as if my mind was addled, when it is my hip that has failed and not my senses. He thinks that I do not know that the medicine that he hath prescribed is laudanum, or that it will not cure me, as he claims it will. But I know the truth. It cannot cure what ails me now but simply ease me away from here and into the next world. At last he mumbled some hollow words of comfort and farewell, then promptly left again on his way back to report to the King, no doubt.

I so fear the torture of having Hannah and the laundry girl helping me onto my comode. Even though they do handle me so gently as if I were but glass to shatter in their hands at the slightest mishap, I have abandoned its use. Instead, they have me like a helpless newborn, napkined and bedded upon a draw sheet lest I soil my feather mattress. I have lost so much dignity that I have resigned myself to eat no more, and to take but the tiniest sips of water so as to negate the necessity for any of this nuisance at all. By doing so, I do realise that it is now only a matter of time...

The time has come for me to soon put away my pens and my journal neatly in the drawer. Instead of idly looking out upon the endlessly mournful grey vista, by preference I dutifully sip my medicine from the silver spoon that Hannah so regularly brings me, so that I might slip away for a while to play at catching sticklebacks[62] in the beck as my father and the other men dip the sheep. Or I run in the meadow with Humility Brown, hand in hand, as we chase white butterflies through a host of blood-red poppies and burnished gold buttercups. The colours dazzling inside my head are so bright and so vivid, as are my memories! I have even dreamt of *him*, standing vigil at my bedside below decks on the Delver as we sailed on our way to Virginia. I could even swear that I have re-tasted the salt on his lips as he reached across to gently kiss me as I slept on.

Therefore in consequence and laudanum, I have found myself existing more and more in this half-world into which I float away from my pain, only to re-emerge all too soon... cringing back into the same miserable state as before. In reality, I can hardly move without inducing such exquisite agonies, whereas I am free and boundless in this beautiful other place. Though even there all is not constant bliss. For I sometimes fall foul of such wretched dreams that I truly believe that they are real. Dreams where I lift up my bed sheets to find rats running freely over my body. I look down and I find them dismembering my legs with their razor sharp teeth and chewing upon the ends of my long bones, and gnawing their way into the socket of my hip. I fear that my reason is fast giving way to delusion.

Then, just a short while ago on this wretched winter's night, I suddenly came to my senses. I was so weary by now with it all that I refused even to take the draft that Hannah brought and begged me to take so as to ease my pain. Strangely, I had moved on far beyond mere mortal pain. Instead, I asked her to help raise me a little upon my pillows and then to open the shutters so that I might see the moon bright in the sky outside.

'Tis so very cold tonight, my lady. And we need to keep the chill out!' she tried to reason with me yet I was not up for reason.

'But I want to see the sunrise,' I pleaded with her like a child.

Reluctantly, she did as I bade. Yet when I then told her that she looked weary and that she should take her leave of me and go to her room and look, for once, towards her own comfort, Hannah most adamantly refused. I tried my best to reassure her that I would be alright without her until daybreak, and vainly goaded her towards giving into my persuasion. But she would not. Instead she fetched a heavy blanket from her room, wrapped it about herself, and settled in the chair by the foot of my bed. Eventually, she fell asleep with her head rested upon the corner of my mattress.

While she lay peacefully, I sat propped upright up on my pillows, in lone vigil, watching wide-eyed as a hush of snowflakes whispered past my window, and while the candle at my side slowly burn down until almost nothing was left. Finally, the flame began to falter, spat in its pool of melted wax and snuffed out.

Then, in the darkness, I closed my eyes for a moment and fancied that I could smell the very essence of heaven itself. Of soft worn leather, musk rose, woodbine and lavender mingled with a handful of summer breeze. I felt the soft glance of a lover's lips upon my cheek and my heart lurched. Yet I opened my eyes to find nothing. The room was devoid of life and cast deep in the shroud of mournful shadow. Beyond that room the lucent rose of a December dawn was at that very moment prizing back the night to shaft its pale light in through the naked glass, and playing upon the polished window sill like droplets of quicksilver. Effortlessly, and to no small relief, I rose to my feet and scampered towards it trying to catch the light in my fingers like an excited child. Outside, all was hushed in timeless quiet until suddenly broken into by the lazy clip of hoof against cobble from somewhere along the tired street leading off towards the burnt out soul of the city.

It was then that he drifted into my sight. The lone figure of a man with a grey mare at his lead. He stopped, just yonder, and as the pale horse came to rest, he turned and glanced upwards just as I felt my heart stop. Smiling, he raised up his hand in welcome and beckoned to me to come join with him in the soft morning light. He had come for me, just as he had come for me once before – a long, long time ago.

With apprehension, I turned and glanced back across the still gloomy room towards Hannah slumped gently at the foot of my bed. I so wanted to give her one last farewell kiss, and yet as she slept on like a guardian angel, I was so loathe to break her restful state just on my account. Instead, I stood and watched. Then I heard the long low sigh as the old-woman frame, still coddled beneath my bed covers, fell still. Chill and any lingering fear suddenly took leave of me all at once to be replaced by an overwhelming warmth of joy and peace.

I turned back towards the light and called out to my man below, 'Wait, my darling Thomas... Wait! I am coming to you now...'

END

Author Notes

Sue says;

To my eternal shame I can admit now that, when I was a child, I deliberately played upon a plague pit.
When I lived in Merton, south London, during the darkest times of my troubled childhood, I often ran off to seek sanctuary in the nearby church of St. Mary the Virgin. With the death of my teenage brother, this church became somewhere I could run to in times of conflict. Some safe place where I could go to grieve in private. From the age of about eleven, this was the only place I knew where I could find some peace and welcome solitude in my painfully confused world. There I could take time out to reflect upon what was happening in my life and ponder upon what happiness the future might hold for me. I became such a regular sight at St. Mary's, especially during the school holidays, that none of the church wardens, the elderly lady organist or even the vicar took much mind of my being there and never attempted to turf me out. Instead they would go about their duties while, on rainy days especially, I might sit for ages, near Lord Nelson's bench, deep in thought or even occasional prayer. It was probably that sense of sanctuary and safety that I found inside the then always unlocked St. Mary's that gave me my life long passion and respect for old churches and other aged buildings.

Huddled amongst those ancient surrounding my thoughts could not help but linger upon the past and the fate of those interred beneath the stone floor of this beautiful Norman church. But on dry days I liked to browse amongst the tombstones outside, reading the inscriptions of those departed and wondering what their lives may have been like.

In this pleasant, almost country-like churchyard, I became so familiar with each lichen crusted stone or long forgotten obituary that I began to feel that I was 'amongst friends'

My imagination was drawn to one epitaph in particular which, if I recall correctly, is near to the south side of the outside church wall and dedicated to a man described as 'William Rutlish – Embroiderer to King Charles II'. As a girl I knew little about the man other than that my younger brother attended the local grammar school which also bore the name of Rutlish, as did the road in which my next school, Pelham Secondary School for Girls, stood. One day, I then promised myself, I would find out more.

Rounding the church and towards the corner of the graveyard, used to lay a distinct grassy mound quite bereft of any stones or markers close by. I clearly remember gazing hard at it one day just as an old lady was clearing away a bunch of brown, crisp flowers on a nearby grave. Sternly, she eyed me intently and warned me not to go near it.

'That's the plague-pit, Dearie' she scowled 'It's full of dead bodies! All killed by the Black Death, they were. And the germs down there might still be alive in the dirt ready to get you if you go playing on it!'

Of course, I did not dare go near it. Not, that is, until she had gone about her way and was long out of sight. Then I climbed on the mound in youthful defiance, daring death if it was still somewhere inside, to come and claim me too. When it did not, it was then I was persuaded that perhaps I was meant to live on after all, but to what purpose I could not imagine other than maybe becoming a poet- already my strongest talent at school. Never would I have dared to imagine then that now, in my middle age, that I would find myself weaving so many of the sights and sounds of my youth into my very own novels.

In researching the Restoration, no greater source of fascinating insights into the day to day life of that time can be had than by reading the diaries of Samuel Pepys. Again, growing up in Merton I had often wondered why there was a road named after him there. I now think that perhaps it was named after his cousin Thomas Pepys – the Executor- William Rutlish's dinner guest.

Personally I would prefer to think that. For, although Samuel Pepys' accounts are incredibly detailed and fascinating to read, I find that Pepys himself is not a nice man at all and as such have enjoyed the freedom of having Bessie being able to say for me, 'I care not much for this fellow'. Especially I disliked him for his boastfulness while setting down in his journal his sordid infidelities and dalliances with other women, many of which he describes in shameless detail, though sometimes through 'coded' entries so that should his poor wife happen upon them , then she would not understand.

As readers of Restoration Lady may have gathered, the dying years of the 1650's in England were very turbulent times indeed. With so much change going on to write about, it is no surprise that Pepys chose this time to start writing his diaries. By the time he gave up writing his almost daily accounts of Restoration life in the spring of 1669, Pepys was acknowledged as the 'right hand of the Navy' and his professional success was well established. He was also a man rich enough to retire and live 'with comfort, if not abundance' being the owner of a coach and a pair of black horses and master of an elegant household.

However, at this same time he was still also trying to recover from his wife's devastating discovery in the October of 1668, of his affair with her companion, Deborah Willett, of which he writes from the heart of his regret at his wife's great unhappiness over the matter, though he also notes his reluctance to give the other woman up

In the November of1669, Elizabeth Pepys died suddenly aged just twenty- nine. She is buried in St' Olaf's Church in London where there is a fine bust of her commissioned by her husband.

In researching all three novels I also found myself harbouring a growing and deep suspicion about the true religious intent of the Stuart monarchs. To understand more of this and their possible motives, I need first to explain a little about King James I and his formative years.

James Charles was the only child of Mary, Queen of Scots and her second husband, Henry Stuart, Lord Darnley. He was born on19th June 1566. Through his great-grandmother, Margaret Tudor, James was related by blood to Queen Elizabeth I of England.

As godmother *in absentia*, Elizabeth had sent a magnificent gold font as a christening gift for the baby prince. Unfortunately, his father Henry was murdered on February 10th 1567 and in the May his mother Mary soon married the man widely suspected of the crime. In June, Mary was arrested and imprisoned by Protestant rebels. She was forced to abdicate the throne of Scotland and to appoint James Stewart, Earl of Moray as regent to the young King. Mary was never to see her son again.

At thirteen months of age, James was formally crowned as King James VI of Scotland. The coronation sermon was preached by none other than the Geneva Calvinist, John Knox and James was strictly brought up as a Protestant in accordance with the prevailing belief of the then Scottish ruling class.

The infant James' day to day care was at first entrusted to the Earl and countess of Mar. The child was 'to be conserved, nursed, and up brought' in the security of Stirling Castle. His main educator, historian and poet George Buchanan, subjected the young king to regular beatings which can have done little to foster any lingering love James might felt for fellow puritans though he did gain a very good education.

A succession of regents came and went, felled by fair means or foul until Mar himself became regent, only to die at Stirling shortly after dining with the Earl of Morton, who then acquired the position himself.

However, Morton had made enemies and fell from grace with the arrival of Frenchman Esme Stewart, the future Earl of Lennox. It was then that Morton was rather belatedly charged with involvement in the murder of the King's father. He was duly executed, leaving the way clear for Esme to quickly become very powerful as the first of James's male 'favourites'. However, it was not long before the powerful Scottish Calvinists noticed the overtly physical displays of affection betwixt king and favourite, suspecting them of being marks of more than mere 'friendship'. In fact these outraged Calvinists went as far as to allege that Esme 'went about to draw the King to carnal lust' and in order to break this relationship had the King lured to Ruthven Castle and imprisoned while Esme was forced to leave Scotland. As a result, James had once again lost his only source of affection.

In short, James might have well grown up as an orphan for all of the stable 'parenting' he was to enjoy. And although he was King, for the duration of his early life it was in name only. He was but a helpless pawn in the power struggle going on all about him in which he was often physically abused and probably at times, feeling his own life threatened. Such a cold, chaotic upbringing, coupled with his mother's eventual execution, must surely have affected him greatly and perhaps mis-moulded his personality. Perhaps having grown up into a distrusting man, he became liable in later life to upholding an outward pretense to his court while inside keeping his own counsel as to his true intentions?

After he was eventually freed from his virtual imprisonment at Ruthven in 1583, James began to assert more and more power over his monarchy. In one or two instances, this 'dancing bear' was even able to turn about and bite his former 'keepers'.

However, in matters of religion, James often ran into trouble in asserting his royal authority over the strong Scottish Presbyterian Kirk which, unlike the Church of England, had in its own eyes already been successfully 'purified'.

There must have been many in England, as their great guiding star Queen Elizabeth began to dim and fail , hoping that her heir would allow changes too in matters of religion. The Puritans amongst them must surely have held high hopes that, as the monarch of an overwhelmingly Presbyterian country, with a Presbyterian national Kirk that James would look favourably upon their wishes for 'purification' of the

Anglican Church. Conversely, there must have been those amongst the long maligned Catholic population of England who were hoping for a degree of tolerance to be shown to them, especially as James' mother had been a Catholic. In all, a heady cocktail of hopes and aspirations that could so easily have led to civil unrest began to mix.

Queen Elizabeth died in 1603 and as James headed south to claim his throne in England, his new subjects flocked to see him. At the time, all parties involved must have been deeply relieved that the succession had gone so remarkably smoothly, triggering neither unrest nor invasion. For in times not so long since passed, the thought that a Scottish King would one day sit upon the throne of England, and the son of a Catholic to boot, would have been an anathema. Indeed Elizabeth's own father had once ruled it illegal that any Stuart ever should.

However, this honeymoon period would soon be over. Despite this early calm, James would survive two conspiracies in the first year of his reign which, among others, led to the arrest of Sir Walter Raleigh, one of the late queen's favourites.

In 1604, James made his stance against Puritans and Separatists public and started to take steps against all dissidents of all persuasions. James made it quite clear that he wanted the Church of England to remain as it was with its hierarchy of bishops intact and with himself at its head.

Meanwhile in foreign policy, James busied himself with being seen as devoted to his efforts in bringing the long Armada War with Spain to an end, having never been at war with them himself as King of Scotland. This he did, but the question of freedom of worship for Catholics in England continued to be a major objective of Spanish policy. This seemingly caused great dilemmas for James as he was distrusted abroad for repression of Catholics and yet at home would be equally distrusted for showing any tolerance of them. Presented with this almost impossible balancing act in order to keep his far from secure hold upon the English throne, the safest action for the King was to be seen to be trying to keep the status quo as bequeath to him by Queen Elizabeth – no matter which way he might have truly wished to go in open.

I personally suspect that James had more reason to keep the Church in England unreformed and intact other than his well–worn argument of 'no bishop- no king'. Indeed a more valid reason for keeping the status quo – the church in that current form- would be that, *had the King so wished*, it would remain all the much easier to return it to the Catholic faith *at some point* in the future whereas a splintered Church would prove impossible to herd back into the fold once more. As an author and a 'lay historian' if you wish, I cannot help but think that King James and his son heirs had a 'game plan'- its end perhaps to bring England back to Catholicism . Not at one foul stroke, as Bloody Queen Mary had tried, which would undoubtedly have resulted in a bloody uprising or even inviting assassination of the King. No, I believe that the Stuarts were initially content to play the long game and to subtly bring about the steps towards seeing a Catholic monarch being seated once more upon the throne of England over two or possibly even three generations. (Which, after all is exactly what eventually happened on the death of King Charles II, who died without a legitimate heir when he had plenty of opportunity previously to have legitimised one of his *Protestant* bastard children instead of knowingly leaving the accession to his throne to his blatantly Catholic brother- to which at that time, there was no legal impediment.)

Several points lead me towards this conclusion, not least being King James' part during the long drawn out failed brokering of a marriage between the Prince of Wales and the Spanish Infanta Maria, which dragged on for almost a decade. This action had been supported by the Howards and other Catholic-leaning ministers and diplomats—together known as the Spanish Party—and resulted in a policy deeply distrusted in Protestant

England.

Some historians argue that the delay had been deliberate because James had discovered it to be a good way of avoiding the additional costs of a war with Spain - that by protracting the negotiations while at the same time actively keeping them alive, he could maintain the peace benefits just as effectively as consummating the match but without actually doing so. I think it more likely that James was simply waiting for the 'right moment' to officially approve the match but that opportunity never presented itself fully in his lifetime.

If indeed this was the plan, then all of James' caution served for naught as marriage to a French Catholic was hastily untaken by the perhaps less patient and decidedly more head-strong Charles, within months of his father's death.

Perhaps some amongst the Parliamentarian stalwarts, who would later goad Charles into a bloody Civil War, also suspected the existence of this game plan and wanted to see it ended before it could pay itself out to fruition? As I freely admit, I am not a trained historian but merely an author fascinated by the history behind my stories. All I can suggest is for my readers to go away and read up on the times and events for themselves and to then come to their own conclusions.

Roger Says:

As an American, while helping Sue to research and co-write this New World trilogy, I have never ceased to be amazed by how many ancient buildings still survive in this wonderful country. Especially in this Midlands area of England.

Gainsborough Old Hall features in all three of our novels and is a beautiful and inspiring timber-framed 15th century Manor House, tucked away in a corner of Lincolnshire close to the River Trent and the boundary with Nottinghamshire. It was built between 1460 and 1490 by the first Lord Burgh. The manor later came into William Hickman's possession around 1596. Since then it had only been owned by these two families up until 1970, when it was eventually given to the nation and after much effort by the Friend's of Gainsborough Old Hall to save it from redevelopment into a parking lot!

Besides providing sanctuary to the Separatist congregation, as depicted in our novels, Gainsborough Hall has also played host to many famous visitors. These include Richard III in 1483 and Henry VIII, twice, in 1509 and 1541. On the later visit, King Henry stayed for four days with his fifth wife, Catherine Howard. It was during this period that she was accused of 'indiscretions' and executed the following February.

A chilling reminder of these turbulent days of uncertainty and the latent fear circulating amongst even the King's closest household members can be found scrawled upon a wall in the small antechamber to the hall's panelled dining room. Tudor graffiti written by one of the King's courtiers reads 'Trust truth only' – of course a tantalizing thread that eagle-eyed readers will realise we wove into *Mayflower Maid*.

Coincidently, King Henry's sixth wife, Katherine Parr, had once been married to one of the then Lord Burgh's sons, but widowed. It is uncertain whether she was also at the Hall at the time of this visit. The Hall also has several ghosts. One, dubbed the 'grey lady', was for a long period of time reported as being seen walking the long corridor upstairs before disappearing into a solid wall. Then, during restoration work to the property, a previously plastered over doorway was rediscovered just at the spot where the ghost was said to vanish. This doorway probably once fed into a now gone corridor and on towards the very bedchamber where Queen Catherine is believed to have slept.

Some two centuries later, John Wesley enjoyed the patronage of the Hickman family and preached at Gainsborough Hall- all of which goes to show how down the years Lady Rose's descendants were not faint-hearted either when it came to supporting new conventions in religion.

Stow Minster is another beautiful setting that features heavily in both *Jamestown Woman* and the opening chapters of *Restoration Lady*. The village of Stow is only around seven miles away, or a gentle fifteen minute drive from Gainsborough Old Hall and in our novels is thinly disguised as 'Stowe' - Thomas' home village.

Visitors to modern day Stow might well ask, as had I, why it should be so that such a large church is to be found in such a small village. Though Stow may have been a much larger settlement in the past than it is now, it has always been a rural place. Yet, it was also once the nerve-centre of a large block of estates, belonging to the Saxon bishops of Dorchester on Thames and here where Bishop Aelfnoth built a church around 975 AD to serve as head Minster for the Lincolnshire part of his large diocese.

The word minster or *mynster* is Old English and derived from the Latin *ministerium*, the 'office' or 'service, - the canonical hours which were sung at set times. So *minster* originally applied to the church of a monastery or a chapter and so there would have been an abbot who presided in the Minster rather than a bishop. In pre-reformation England, many cathedrals were also monastic. Part of the Bishop's household of priests lived in Stow and administered this part of the diocese - these later became the cathedral chapter at Lincoln. The memory of this period gave rise to the tradition that Stow was the Mother Church of Lincoln Cathedral.

Stow Minster probably can claim one of the tallest Saxon arches in Europe. It also boasts one of the earliest known examples of Viking graffiti in England in the form of a roughly etched outline of a Viking oared sailing ship from around the 10th century. It was most likely hurriedly executed prior to the church being set on fire.

The early baptismal font, as described during the passage about Bessie's interrogation by Mister Rech, is adorned with wonderful pagan symbols including a dragon, which for me makes it extremely interesting.

Later the Minster was enriched and endowed by Leofric, Earl of Mercia. We know his wife much better as the Lady Godiva of naked horse-riding fame. A charter of 1054 survives and describes what this couple did and how they furnished the church. Sadly by the middle of the nineteenth century the condition of this Minster was deplorable, and it was even suggested that it should be demolished and a 'convenient parish church' built in its place. Thankfully the then incumbent, the Reverend George Atkinson, raised money for repairs and the church was restored.

Back to Gainsborough and the bridge there, built in 1791, crosses the River Trent and leads into the Bassetlaw district of the county of Nottinghamshire – 'Robin Hood and Pilgrim Father Country'. It was this tidal river at Gainsborough that gave the author George Elliot inspiration for her novel *'The Mill on The Floss'*.

The nearest church on the Mayflower Trail is, Sturton-le- Steeple in Nottinghamshire. This is the birth place of John Robinson, later pastor to the Pilgrim Fathers during their self-imposed exile in Leyden, Holland. A permanent reminder of the Pilgrim Fathers hangs on the north wall of the nave of the Church of St. Peter and St. Paul in the form of a picture.

In the early springtime when the snowdrops are out, All Saints Church, Babworth is simply idyllic in its peaceful setting. However, do not let its 'back-water' location fool you. For just like the now quiet Scrooby, this church was once situated by the busy Great North Road before it was diverted. The origins of our Separatists are closely connected with this church as Richard Clifton was their preacher here between 1586 and 1605. The sterling silver chalice, that he once handled for communion, was later hidden among bones beneath the church floor – no doubt to save it from being melted down during the English Civil War as troops moved close by on the busy main highway. The chalice was only accidentally rediscovered in recent times.

St. Wilfrid's Scrooby is a pleasant village church which still contains a couple of ornately carved, dark oak bench pews dating back to William Brewster's time. A matching piece to one is housed in the Pilgrim Hall Museum in Plymouth, Massachusetts. I had the honour of raising the American flag the churchyard on the 4th of July 2007. This flag had been specially flown over the town hall of Plymouth Massachusetts and then donated to the village of Scooby by the Select Men (Councillors) of that town.

The remains of part of Scrooby Manor can be seen from across the fields by standing part way down in Station Road (near to the church). Sadly, at the time of writing Scrooby Manor is a private residence in private ownership and is therefore not open to the public.

Barely a ten minute drive from Scrooby, through Bawtry, is St Helena's, Austerfield and both mine and Sue's favourite out of the 'Mayflower Trail' churches. Second Governor of Plymouth Colony, William Bradford, was baptised in its ancient led-lined font. When the church had fallen into disuse, some renovations were financed by the Mayflower Society. But the famous font was missing. Later it was found in a pasture being used to water cattle. I am happy to say that the church with the font intact is back in use again.

Like Stow Minster, St. Helena's is a very ancient church and certainly Saxon in part. However, that is where the comparisons end. While the Minster is magnificently large in its proportion, St. Helena's is stunningly tiny but none the less beautiful and inspiring for all of that. I have often laughed to myself on hearing Sue say of it, when leading a tour party around the church, 'well... they don't make diamonds as big as bricks.'

Heading back towards Gainsborough on the A631, it is well worth turning off at Gringley-on-the-Hill, an historic village set on a high ridge offering splendid views over Pilgrim Country. From Beacon Hill it is possible to pick out Lincoln Cathedral on the horizon in one direction and the River Idle in the opposite. It was along this river that the Pilgrim Fathers made their second escape attempt up to the Humber.

Back across the River Trent and into Lincolnshire once

more, there are many more sites connected with our New World Trilogy of novels.

From *Mayflower Maid* is Boston in the south of the county and its guildhall of St.Mary's Guild. It was built around 1450 and during 2006/07 went through considerable restoration work which included a specially commissioned modern sculpture, in terracotta and glittering gold, depicting the Virgin Mary and child.

 After the Dissolution in King Henry VIII's reign, this building became Boston's town hall. It was to the lower level of this structure, in the autumn of 1607 that William Brewster and his company of Separatists were taken and locked in the goal following their betrayal while trying to escape the country. It was also the building where John Cotton, senior Puritan members of the town council and leading citizens of Boston would have met during the latter years of the 1620's before so many of them too, left Lincolnshire to set up a colony in the New World- Boston Massachusetts. In the nearby Boston parish church, more fondly known as 'the Stump' there are monuments to John Cotton and his colonist congregation.

 Not far from Boston, at the wild and often windy location of Fishtoft, there is a memorial marking the locality of the Pilgrim Father's failed attempt at escape. In a churchyard at Immingham, in the north of Lincolnshire and close by the Humber is another memorial. It was originally sited at Killingholme (latterly known as Immingham) Creek- the accepted point of the Pilgrim Fathers' final departure in the spring of 1608.

All of the Pilgrim Father's sites of interest in this part of England can easily be combined into one bespoke tour, tailored to suit individual time constraints, by an extremely good local Christian tour operator – Pilgrim Tours (UK) of Nottinghamshire.

Heading up county once more towards Alford, lies the tiny village of Willoughby. Its parish church of St. Helena boasts some beautiful stained glass windows depicting the life of my 16th great grand mother Pocahontas. Captain John Smith, one of the founders and second governor of the Virginia colony, was born in the village and baptised in this church. A copy of his baptismal record can be seen mounted upon the church wall. The second novel in our trilogy, *Jamestown Woman*, was launched inside St. Helena's and I shall never forget the thrill of sitting at a small table by the font with a shaft of beautifully coloured light falling upon the open pages of our books as we signed copies for our readers.

A five minute drive from Willoughby, nearby Alford has a wonderful thatched-roof early 1600's Manor House contemporary with *Jamestown Woman* and *Restoration Lady*. Sue and I often stop at the tea shop here for lunch when out and about in the neighbourhood.

Just a few hundred yards away from the Manor House is the parish church and inside quite the most evocative marble memorial I have seen. It marks a double interment and portrays two life-sized bodies laid out at rest, one a Royalist gentleman of the English Civil War and the other his dame – both complete with elaborately carved lace and flounced costume of that period.

Not mentioned in our novels but well worth a visit is Doddington Hall near the city of Lincoln. This pure Elizabethan house is approached through a gatehouse, which is believed to be a remnant of much an earlier residence built on the same site. The Hall was built between 1593 and 1600 by the great architect of his time, Robert Smythson and ranks as one of the best Elizabethan houses in England.

Although the Hussey family, who owned the house at the time of the Civil War, were staunch Royalists it survived retribution by the Parliamentarians, unlike many similar residences that were destroyed at the time on both sides of the divide and so can give valuable insight into life of the times to readers of *Restoration Lady*.

The city of Lincoln itself is a delightful place to spend a very full day's visit. Its magnificent cathedral was used as a 'double' for Westminster Abbey during the filming of *The Da Vinci Code*. Just opposite the Cathedral is Lincoln Castle, which houses one of the few remaining copies of

Magna Carta and boast amongst its other attractions an interesting example of a Victorian prison.

Of course, our New World Trilogy spans two continents and so we must mention the two English colonies in America where are our intrepid Thomas and Bessie both 'visit' during their adventures.

Jamestown, Virginia and Plymouth, New England have fabulous museum complexes that include excellent reconstructions of both of these early English settlements. The site of the original Jamestown fort was re-discovered only recently. Over a million artefacts have been found there so far. As I moved around this fort on a recent visit, I was suddenly struck by the fact that I was walking where my famous ancestor, Pocahontas, had trod. It was a humbling experience.

In the years between Bessie and Thomas' time there in *Jamestown Woman* and their son and adopted daughter, Hope's, emigration *in Restoration Lady*, Jamestown had rapidly changed out of all recognition.

By 1632, peace had been established between the English and the Powhatan naturals after a period of almost ten years of conflict. However, it was not to last. Within ten years a second war between the two cultures had broken out.

By the time of Cromwell's Commonwealth, the English appeared to have overcome the dreadful early death rate amongst the colonists as the estimated English population of Virginia had risen to fifteen – thousand with some additional three hundred or so African slaves- rising to some forty-eight thousand colonists by 1672 with some two thousand Africans.

As for the naturals, by as early as 1650 the Virginia Assembly had begun to establish reservations for the colony's native population which in 1669 (just as Pepys was ending his great diary) stood at around only three-thousand. In short, the English managed to eventually subdue the native Americans in their neighbourhood by simply multiplying successfully until the eventually outnumbered them.

In 1699 the fate of Jamestown as a settlement was sealed

when the government of Virginia was moved from there to a place formally known as Middle Plantation .This was by then renamed Williamsburg in honour of Queen Mary's consort, Prince William of Orange.

My time in England being involved in producing these three novels has proved an invaluable opportunity in reshaping and readjusting my attitude towards the relationship between Great Britain and the United States. Being an American, I have come to realize that, as I researched and wrote alongside a Brit about the history and culture of Britain, just how closely our two countries really are connected. From my experience in England it seems to me that the old adage still hold true, that our two countries are only separated by a common language and, of course, by a very big ocean.

Glossary of Terms

1 Fret = to worry

2 Rook = A crow like Old World bird, *Corvus frugilegus*

3 Gad = whip

4 Besom = a bundle of twigs attached to a handle and used as a broom (beez'um)

5 Seln = self

6 Haslet = the heart, liver and other edible vicera of a pig, compacted into a loaf, cooked and served cold.

7 Serpent = metal trigger designed to take a lighted piece of flax. The serpent would come down into the pan, light the gunpowder, producing a flame to enter the barrel, igniting the gunpowder there to fire the lead ball.

8 Flummox = to confuse, perplex

9 Watter = water

10 Durzent = does not

11 Clap post (of a gate) = the other post to the one with hinges on it

12 Poorly = ill

13 Frumenty = hulled wheat boiled in milk and flavoured with sugar and spices

14 Themseln = themselves

15 Rusk = a type of dry biscuit

16 The Anglican Church

17 The Puritan movement

18 God

19 Pig-cheer = sausages, pork-pies, Haslet, chine etc

20 Agin = against

21 Spake = spoke

22 Ails = to be ill or to be bothred by

23 Wam = warm

24 Siller = silver

25 Werrittin = worrying

26 All of a piece = all of a sudden

27 Waxy = angry

28 Frit = frightened

29 Lited out = got out

30 Holt = a triangular patch of trees or scrub left at the corner of a cultivated field.

31 Unbidden = uninvited

32 Tip-tupping = going up and down or back and forth.

33 Troddled = trodden

34 Lope = to move like a rabbit or a hare

35 Penfold, pinfold = A small pen for holding unclaimed livestock and strays

36 Winkersome eye = said of a witch with power in her stare.

37 Begat = to father, sire. to cause to exist.

38 Axed = asked

39 Scold = an instrument of punishment designed to inhibit speech.

40 Secrets = pockets tied on amongst a woman's under garments.

41 Childer = Children

42 Blatherskate = a babbling, foolish person.

43 'Owld One' = The Devil

44 Hapless = Luckless, unfortunate.

45 Clagging = sticky, clogging.

46 Hanger(s) on = (before the introduction of the trap and long drop method of hanging) a person of persons permitted, as a mercy, to cling onto a condemned persons legs to act as weight to hasten their death.

47 Pustule = a boil.

48 Miasma = a noxious atmosphere thought
to cause disease.

49 Waning = decline.

50 Camera = in private as in court with only
judge and litigants present.

51 Poorly = ill, unwell.

52 Frippery = pretentious elegance; ostentation.

53 Temporal = civil, secular or lay as opposed
to ecclesiastical

54 Awry = amiss, wrong, twisted to one side.

55 Privy = knowledge of something private or secret
shared between individuals.

56 Pronounced 'Peeps'

57 Ere = before, sooner than.

58 Salubrious = conducive or favourable to
health, wholesome.

59 Ring o'roses = a rash of red spots.

60 Fine fettle = good health.

61 Slope = writing slope.

62 Stickle-back = tiny, spined inedible fresh-water
fish popular with children pond dipping

Also by Sue Allan

The Mayflower Maid -

The first part of the New World Trilogy

400 years ago a group of like minded men and women fled England and religious persecution to start a new life on a new continent - America. One woman's story begins here....

In the infant colony of Plymouth in 1623 a woman lies consumed with fever. In her delirium she insists her name is not the one everyone has come to know and love her by.

The story of Dorothy's tragic journey amongst the Pilgrim Fathers is a vivid and moving account of a pivotal moment in history. The story of how she became the Mayflower Maid is an unforgettable tale of love and loss set amidst the strife and religious bigotry of Seventeenth Century England.

Jamestown Woman -

The second part of the New World Trilogy

Having weathered the perils of the Mayflower's voyage and the early days of the Plymouth colony; Dorothy neé Bessie and her husband Thomas are now cast adrift into even more stormy and dangerous waters. Seventeenth century politics are a violent and deadly business, as they are about to find out.

Sue Allan continues her spellbinding chronicles of the Mayflower Maid in 'Jamestown Woman', and once again fate casts her and Thomas into the paths of the great and not so good. The giant firgures of King James I, Captain John Smith and Oliver Cromwell cast their shadows over the lives of the Puritans as England is about to be engulfed by the horrors of The Civil war.